PERFECT TEN

JACQUELINE WARD

CORVUS

First published in Great Britain in 2018 by Corvus,
an imprint of Atlantic Books Ltd.

This edition published in 2019.

1 2 3 4 5 6 7 8 9

A CIP catalogue record for this book is available from the British Library.

Paperback: 978 178649 378 1
E-book: 978 178649 377 4

Printed and bound by CPI Group (UK) Ltd, Croydon, CR0 4YY

Corvus
An Imprint of Atlantic Books Ltd
Ormond House
26–27 Boswell Street
London
WC1N 3JZ

www.corvus-books.co.uk

For you, Mum.

' It is impossible to suffer without making someone pay for it; every complaint already contains revenge. '

Friedrich Nietzsche

Chapter One

I couldn't believe it when the delivery man rolled up to the door. As soon as I saw him standing there on our overgrown front pathway with your luggage, I knew that I would have my day after all.

'Mrs Atkinson?'

I nodded. It wasn't a lie. I'm still Mrs Atkinson. Even after a year. I never changed my name. For the sake of the kids, of course.

He fumbled for his signature machine and I counted the cases. Four large, matching Samsonites. My heart hurt as I realised that they were the luggage we took on our honeymoon. I signed – just a squiggle – never give your own signature in case there are damages. I learned that in the research lab at the university where I work. Yes, even after everything, I still have a chat at the coffee machine. I still have colleagues. You didn't destroy my life after all. Almost, but not quite.

I pulled the cases into the hallway as the driver walked away and I was just about to shut the front door when he hurried back.

'Oh, there's this one as well, Mrs Atkinson.'

I smiled. I liked the sound of it. It'd been a while. Then, as I looked down at his offering, I positively beamed. He handed me your black leather overnight bag and I already knew what was inside. I could feel the edges through the soft skin, the corners. The hairs on my arms stood up and my mouth went dry.

'Thank you. Thank you so much.'

I shut the door and stared at the cases. It was obvious what had happened. You hadn't changed the labels. When you left for Toronto a year ago you turned over the little pieces of paper so that our address was hidden. So that you could obliterate me. I can almost hear you saying it. *Blank slate.* But things have a funny way of turning back around, and you'll never forget me. I'll always be somewhere in the background.

You were back and waiting for your lost luggage. And it was in my hallway. I wanted to open it there and then, to smell your clothes and your cologne. To recapture the essence of you that's been gone so long from my life. But I didn't because, just in time, I remembered what a bastard you are. Instead, I grabbed my coat and bag and hurried off to work. It had been exactly a year and I figured that another eight hours wouldn't matter.

All day my mind alternated between fear and anticipation. What if someone found out that I'd pretended you still lived in the house we'd shared for eleven years? That I had accepted your things, knowing that you didn't live there? It would be like before. My hands shook as I poured my mid-morning coffee and checked my phone for missed calls. They never came. So I rationalised. The delivery man would have a record of the address. Sooner or later you would know what had happened and get the cases collected.

That moment, in my tiny office in the depths of the university, my life changed. I made a plan. After all the years of manipulation and lies at your hands, I took control. It was a long time coming, I knew. All the sadness and suffering, the uncertainty, everything that had rained down on me and caused me problems, all this would be resolved for me today. At two o'clock, when I couldn't wait a moment longer, I called the delivery company.

'This is Caroline Atkinson. Twenty-five Willow Avenue. There was a delivery today.'

The call-centre worker wasn't interested. She took the details. She wasn't suspicious at all. I didn't need to explain, but I did anyway – for the recording. Just in case. I didn't want any comebacks this time.

'I was so busy on my way to work that I didn't look properly. Not until the man had driven off. But the delivery was meant for my ex-husband and he doesn't live with me. Yes. There are four cases.'

I could sense her pity in the silence. Poor divorcee, not knowing her arse from her elbow, dithering around in the morning, dull eyes from crying over her lost love. Yet nothing could be further from the truth. I'm crying for my children.

Two things. One: you're a cheating bastard. Two: I'm well rid of you. But how could she know that? How could anyone? Because you muted everything that was bad about you. You were the one who ruined our marriage, yet you made me look as though I was howling at the moon. Like I was paranoid, jealous, almost infantile in my accusations. Because I could never prove it.

You made it look like I was mad. Worse, you made it look like I had no remorse for the things you lied about me doing. No conscience. And I suffered in unspeakable ways. I almost lost my job. You, with your Ph.D. in Environmental Science and your carefree, travel-the-world attitude; you told them that I was imagining it all. Your solicitor was good. Very good. Turning my profession around, my lifelong passion for psychology, until it was reduced to mere overthinking. Using my Ph.D. study into designing a psychopath test to suggest that I *was* a psychopath. It was never actually articulated, of course, simply alluded to. That I knew too much.

Worst of all, you took the children. You were clever. You knew you would never get custody because you were lying, so you manipulated the situation and you manipulated me. You thought it would break me and it almost did. But not quite.

All the while you smirked your way through life, shrugging and hinting that none of it was your fault. None of my complaining and ringing your hotel to make sure you were there, none of my checking your flights and calling work colleagues to understand your diary. None of it was your fault.

As the call-centre operative gave me a number to ring to get your bags collected and helpfully read out your destination address to me – thank you very much for that – I remembered that karma is rarely instant, no matter what John Lennon thought. No. It usually takes years for *what goes around comes around* and this is it.

This is it.

My hand's still shaking when I replace the receiver. Now, even though the delivery driver made a mistake and I signed, everyone will know that I did the right thing and got the cases picked up. Those four huge cases with all your belongings. I didn't try to keep them or even open them. I just left them in the hallway where I'm picturing them now.

Even my insides are shaking with anticipation. I watch the clock all day as I click, click, click away at the websites I'm collecting papers from. I'm lucky to have this job after what happened and I don't want to fuck it up. But as the day goes on I slip into the realisation that there, at home, in my hallway, is the key to everything that has nagged away at me for years. Even before you left. All the pain, all the sadness; the answer is waiting for me in that leather holdall.

No one would notice if I slipped away early. I sometimes wonder if anyone would notice if I didn't turn up at all. But I have my research deadlines. My job allows me to maintain the aura of respectability that I almost lost. That's what pisses you off, though.

My success. I've always excelled at my job, despite everything. It's an umbilical cord to keeping my lifestyle outside work, which, to be honest, wasn't that good recently, until today. But now I realise why. Everything was leading up to now, when I would finally have my answers. I'd been in limbo.

By four o'clock I can't bear it any longer. I see my reflection in the monitor, my pupils large, yet to all intents and purposes I look normal. Inside I'm anything but. My stomach is churning, a kind of turmoil that precedes a major discovery. When you know there's something big on the other side, but you don't know exactly what it is.

So I drive home and my fingers tap on the steering wheel at the traffic lights as I imagine you getting the call from the delivery people. I can pre-empt your reaction because I know you. Anger, because you wanted to come back here and start again. And straight away I'm somehow involved. Feigned worry that I will have your address, because you always do your best to keep up the pretence that I'm a psychopath. But the cases will arrive and you will breathe a sigh of relief until you know I've got your holdall.

You'll ring the delivery company and demand that they pick it up. I'll tell them that I never had it and it must have got lost, like your other luggage. Why did you check it in the hold, anyway? Then I remember you like to carry just a novel and a trendy messenger bag on – image is everything to you, isn't it?

You might even phone the police, but this time it's you who can't prove anything. I've been thinking about it all day. Turning it over in my mind. Everyone, even the police, work on the most likely explanation. Like when you painted yourself as a picture of glowing innocence and me as the screaming harpy? So, in the end, who did everyone believe? The calm, collected, secretly serial-cheating fucker or the manic, on her last nerve, desperately-in-love wife?

Horrible, isn't it, Jack? Knowing someone is lying but unable to prove it because there's another perfectly reasonable explanation for what's happened?

Of course, if it had been a clean divorce and you'd admitted what you had done there would be no need for all this unpleasantness now. If we could have shared the care of our children. If I could have retained at least a fraction of the life we built together I could have let it go.

As I turn the key in the front door, the delivery van pulls up behind my car. I push the oversized leather holdall behind the lounge door and stand by the huge suitcases. I exhale as I see it's not the same guy, it's an older, greyer version of him in the same brown uniform. I smile.

'Here they are. Sorry. Sorry. I was in a rush this morning and I didn't read the labels.'

He smiles back and scans the hallway, which is piled high with a year's worth of takeaway menus, then the cases.

'Wouldn't have mattered. Labels are blank. Driver must have turned one over instead of looking at the docket.'

He tuts and shows it to me. I can see the spider shadows of the black ink I used to write our address on those cases for our honeymoon, almost invisible on the other side. Turned inwards.

'Thank you, I did ring as soon as I realised what must have happened. These belong to my ex-husband and ...'

He's nodding diplomatically. No one wants you to mention a divorce. He reverently removes the cases and, apologetic, asks me to sign again. I replicate the scribble that means nothing and go inside.

My hands are itching. I'm half blind with giddiness and retribution and the knowledge that, in about half an hour, you'll know exactly what I'll be doing. For the first time since you closed that door behind you, our minds will be back in sync.

You know me, Jack. You know what I'm like. You know that I can't wait for anything. I must open things immediately, ripping off the wrappers and devouring instructions – with surgical gloves that I keep under the sink for unblocking the drains, of course, because you can't be too careful. You'll know that the first thing I do when the delivery van has left is to break the lock on the leather holdall and pull out your papers. The visas and the photograph of you and the kids. The business cards with a thick rubber band around them – you're still old school – and the Manila file that holds the record of your life. I flick through, even though I've seen it all before: birth certificate, our marriage certificate and our decree absolute. You're the petitioner, of course. Family arrangement documents. Various embassy documents and the address of your cheating fucking solicitor. You like to keep them all together when you travel, I remember that only too well. A whole year, you've been away, and nothing's changed. You still bundle everything together and lock it away.

I reach deeper into the bag and pull out a black leather briefcase. I've seen it lots of times, even touched it once or twice. But I've never actually been alone with it. You made sure of that. I don't know what's in here, but I know it's something you didn't want me to see. Something important that you carry everywhere with you. Something that disappeared when I needed to prove what a piece of shit you were.

I linger a little, reading the section of our divorce papers where you turned on me. After everything you did, you crucified me.

The petitioner feels that the respondent has
imagined or manufactured a set of baseless
accusations and has persecuted the petitioner
unreasonably. The petitioner would like to
stress that there is no basis to the claim of
adultery and that a divorce be granted on the
grounds of unreasonable behaviour.

No basis? We'll see if there's no basis. I'm waiting, checking the clock for the twenty-five minutes until your cases are delivered to you. I imagine your face when you realise that I have your precious possessions. I hope you panic and ring the delivery company, trying to explain how important it is that I don't get my hands on whatever is in this briefcase.

Finally, time's up and I find a sharp knife amidst the five-plus days of dirty pots and wipe it on a filthy tea towel. Things haven't been going well lately and I have a sudden insight into the fucking disaster area our beautiful home has turned into. I glimpse the piles of clothes and newspapers, and all the unopened boxes I bought during vodka nights alone in front of the shopping channel and from Amazon Prime. It's a mess. A crowded, built-up mess. No one comes here except Fiona Mast because you stole my friends, so why should I give a screw about the state of it?

I should, I know, because I want my children back. You made them think I was mad and you took them from me. It's spiralled from there, the way hopelessness does. But I knew you had a secret, something you didn't want me or anyone else to know about, and suddenly there is a spark of hope. Is it a dodgy business deal, something that will discredit you? Is it porn? Have you stolen something – apart from my children? Whatever it is, it's a way to show you for what you really are and it's about time.

I hack away at the lock, like you hacked at my heart, and it takes me a while to prise it away from the thick casing. Good. You'll know I'm doing this because you know me. You'll know that I'll lift out the two journals, both with locks. You'll know that I select the older one – you probably started a new one when you left and I want to know the whole story, from the beginning. You'll know that I open it and read it and you'll know exactly how my expression changes when the awful realisation of what this is hits.

Chapter Two

Alanis is playing on the radio now and she's telling you that *you oughta know*, and I can't find the radio or the plug socket in all this stuff to end it. It's brought my world into focus. The journal. I'm sitting in my kitchen – our kitchen – and I can hardly move for the shit I only bought to try to ease the pain of being alone. Of being wrong when, really, I'm right. It didn't work. Because I always knew that the thing I was searching for was in that case.

The first pages of the first journal make me think that I was wrong. Completely wrong. There's an early picture of you and me at nineteen, when we first met. My blondness, your jet-black crew cut – opposites attract. But we weren't opposites at all, really. We were both fiercely competitive and the darlings of our university year. We married a year later. I sometimes wonder if that's why things went wrong, because we were too young. Then I remember that things went wrong because you were sleeping with other people.

The phone rings and startles me. Five rings then I let it go to answerphone. Naturally it's you, Jack. Your voice, calm and controlled, booms around the kitchen.

'Caroline. I know you have my bag. I'm warning you. You need to give it back. All my papers ...'

But I'm not listening to you. I can't hear the words. I'm listening to the background of the call, ears desperately pricked for children's voices. Charlie and Laura. Are they there with you? You took them away and not a single moment has gone by in the last year when I didn't miss them. My babies. Every time I shut my eyes I see my son's face, terrified, as he realised I wasn't coming with you. Laura crying as you bundled her into the car. You prevented me from seeing them at every turn and forced fear into my soul.

The call ends and I sink back into the journal. I might pretend to myself that I care about your other women, and I did back then. But what I really care about is getting my children back. And this is a means to an end.

I force myself to turn the pages and see myself age slightly: us in front of the Christmas tree right here in this house, and your handwriting at the side of the picture. *Perfect ten*. The warm reminiscence turns a little cool. Perfect ten? That's what you said to me when we first slept together. You said it like I should be pleased, but all it made me do was think of who you were comparing me to.

'Oh, I bet you say that to all the girls.'

It was a statement, not a question. A warning shot. But you answered.

'No. I've never had a ten before. Eight. Nine. Yeah. But not a ten.'

You said it with a smile, but it niggled and I didn't know why. I suppose that I was still heavily invested in romance and love back then, and I just didn't expect you to mark me on my performance. I let it go. I shouldn't have. Because it led directly to this moment, when I turn the next page and see a picture of a blonde woman.

Younger than I was then. Around nineteen. Arms linked with yours. That would be around fourteen years ago, just after we married. You're at The Cabin, a nightclub you worked at as a part-time barman. It's stuck in with glue and I pull it from the page and turn it over. *Christine Dearden*. There were more photos, all dated, spanning two years. Then, overleaf, in the bottom right-hand corner of the page, I see it. You marked her too. *Eight out of ten.* You stuck hotel receipts and even a condom packet between the pages.

I turn the pages quickly. There are nine more women, all marked out of ten.

Julie Carson. Seven out of ten (possessive).

Frances Burrows. Six out of ten. (No BJ).

Pam Harding. Nine out of ten (would have been a ten but couldn't keep her mouth shut).

Alicia Turnbull. Seven out of ten (expensive tastes).

Lorna Kershaw. Three out of ten (great company but frigid).

Katy Squires. Eight out of ten (drinks too much).

Louise Shaw. Nine out of ten (would have been a ten if she hadn't wanted a kid).

Paula Lord. Nine and a half out of ten (nearly as good).

And the last one: Emma Parsons. Eight out of ten.

Each of these women had long-term affairs with my husband. Not one-night stands – those were at the end of the journal with a puny line each. Thirty-seven one-night stands, all marked out of ten. I try to tell myself that none of them knew that you were married to me, that we had two beautiful babies. I read the detailed descriptions of your mistresses, months and months of receipts tucked away, I stare at the picture of Paula. If I was in any doubt at all about these women being innocent, this killed it dead. Paula knew I was married to you. Paula was my bridesmaid. Paula is my sister.

My phone is in my hand and, fuming, I speed-dial the last number I had for her. Out of all of the women, this is the worst by far. It doesn't even ring out. Out of service. I start to dial my parents to see if they know where she is, but stop. They would ask how I am and right now I'm not sure.

I sit for a while on the kitchen floor, my back against our expensive units, my morbid curiosity driving me on to know everything. Somehow it feels like relief, because I knew this all along. I knew. All the times you were on late-night dives, working in far-off quarries, hiking the Scottish countryside, I knew. People would tell me they'd seen you around, and at first I was sure that they were mistaken. Then I saw you myself. I was driving through Manchester and you came out of the dry cleaner's. I pulled over and watched you walk towards the car park and drive your car away.

When I asked you why you were in Manchester, you didn't even try to make an excuse that you'd been delayed or had missed your flight. You'd straight-out lied. You told me that you weren't in town; you were in Milan at an environmental conference. You made me doubt my own sanity. It turns out that I was right all along.

I'm reading and rereading. It's as addictive as it is painful. There's a knock on the door. I look around at your possessions scattered all over the part of the kitchen floor that isn't occupied by unopened kitchen appliances. I peer around the door frame and see the outline of a brown uniform with a yellow lapel badge. Pushing the papers and the briefcase back into the holdall, I throw it out of the back door and close the door quietly.

'Coming. Just coming.'

I wrap a towel around my head and pull on my dressing gown over my clothes. I catch a glimpse of myself in the hallway mirror as I open the front door and realise I am crying.

'Oh. Hello again. Just in the shower.'

The delivery man looks past me into the hallway.

'Did I leave anything?'

I follow his gaze.

'No. I don't think so. There were the cases I gave you earlier.

That's all.'

He stands there, looking into the garden now.

'Could you check? Only there was another item.'

'Oh. Right. I don't think so. I don't remember anything else. But I'll have a look.'

I shut the door and back into the lounge. There's only a tiny floor space left that isn't filled with piled-up newspapers, academic papers and Amazon boxes, but I flick the light on and pretend to look for the bag. I count to fifty then go into the kitchen. Then I go back and open the door again.

'No sorry. Look, I don't know what I'm looking for so would you like to have a peep, just to see if it's here. I mean, the other man might have popped it inside ...'

He steps into the hallway and peers around the lounge door, then the kitchen door. His eyes meet mine and the shared acknowledgement that I'm not exactly coping flashes between us.

'Right. No. I can see it's not here. Must've been left in the van. I'll check tomorrow. Thanks, love. And this lot,' he points into the house, 'you can get help, you know.'

I nod and shut the door.

He's right. I could get help. But, unfortunately, I am the help. That's what everyone says. *Physician, heal thyself.* I only do it because it makes me feel better, but I do admit that it's got out of hand. You handed the house over to me as part of the divorce settlement. Why would you need it? Besides, it made you look ever more snow-white. With no mortgage to pay and a subsidised restaurant at the uni, I had minimum bills and a lot of salary.

Naturally, conversations in the staffroom revolved around unit trusts and high-power pensions. ISAs. Although I joined in and faked concern about my future, my need was more urgent. Every day, I'd leave my office and plan to watch a film or go to yoga, or something everyone else was planning for the evening ahead. Most days ended with me completely pissed in front of the shopping channel.

From the little I can remember, I would order anything that promised to make my life easier. It seemed to be a running theme on the labels of the items that appeared over the subsequent days. 'Save time with a combination microwave and oven.' 'Improve your kitchen experience with this food processor.'

I've been doing it most nights since you left with Charlie and Laura. My regular delivery people came every morning first call, leaving the items on the overgrown path if I was too hungover to surface. I'd heave them in and pile them up. They were almost ceiling high in the lounge, and the kitchen was catching up fast. The hallway was lined with smaller items, mostly costume jewellery. Opened once and then returned to the box.

I'd ordered toys. Lots of toys. There's a special section at the bottom of the stairs piled high with unopened boxes of toys that I started to buy for Christmas. Surely I'd get to see them at Christmas? Surely you weren't so cruel that you'd keep them from me then? The boxes never even made it upstairs. They're still there, a testament to my love.

It made me feel better and I was torn between seeing it as a disorder due to the suffering I had gone through and treating it as part of the healing process. Either way, my home was packed almost to the doors with boxed goods. There were little pathways here and there to allow me to, say, get upstairs, but, on the whole, the house looked nothing like it did when you were here. Maybe that was the point.

I retrieve the holdall and pack it back up, leaving only the briefcase on the kitchen side. The journal is still open on the floor, the pages fat with the evidence of your secret life. I bust open the second journal, which is much thinner. The pages are crammed with your neat handwriting, your thoughts sprawling over the buff. Men are supposed to compartmentalise, but this is ridiculous. It's almost as if there are two versions of Jack in front of me, and both of them are different to the Jack I knew.

The second journal has lists of books you've read, music you've bought, galleries you've visited on your travels. No surprises with the music. You love American rock and Madchester. I scan the galleries and wonder why on earth you kept your love of modern art to yourself. You've read hundreds of books and, right at the back, you've ranked your top ten.

You love biographies. Alec Ferguson. Robbie Williams. Roy Keane. Beckham. Obviously. Tom Jones. *Lord of the Rings. The Hobbit.* Terry Pratchett. Martin Amis. And Nick Hornby, *High Fidelity.* Really? And you've written a review. I can feel my blood pressure rise, the familiar redness sweep over my chest and neck as I read your words.

> *'... what a sucker. I'd never do that for Caroline. Apologising to exes? That'd be a long job. Work in progress. LOL. Anyway, she's too dense to know what it's all about. Clever academically, but ... well ...* ☺

I close the journal. That's enough for tonight. The words are shut between the pages with the receipts and the photographs and the condom wrappers. Sordid souvenirs of your life outside our life. It all seems like an anticlimax now as I reach for the blackcurrant-flavoured Absolut vodka.

Too dense to know what it's all about. I'm momentarily defensive, of course, but you're completely right. I was too stupid to know what you were up to and, when I did have an inkling, too clumsy. That's when it started, really. I'd been at your office, waiting outside to surprise you, take you out to dinner.

It was the early days of our marriage, just after our first anniversary. That first year had flown by in a mist of romantic lunches and late dinners. Then, just after we'd returned from a weekend in Paris to celebrate our first year, it tailed off. I'd mentioned it to my friend Anita.

'It's as if, well, as if he's ... losing interest.'

It was all I could do not to let the brimming tears out. She'd patted my arm gently over our cappuccinos.

'Well, I'm surprised it's lasted this long. Most people just settle back into their lives. But you two are strong. He's not losing interest. But if you feel like he is, up the stakes. Surprise him.'

I'd trawled the internet advice columns for hints and tips on 'surprising your husband'. Underwear and cooking seemed popular, but I settled on a surprise date. After all, you always decided what we did. You always paid. So I booked a table at The Ivy, where we'd joked about celeb-spotting. There'd been a cancellation and I snapped up a six-thirty table. You were working in your London office, so I took the train down and waited outside after work.

You weren't expecting me. That was clear. I saw you through the smoky glass, slightly swarthy with your five-o'clock shadow, and felt the familiar glow. Then I saw her. She followed you out and you were laughing and joking. My hackles rose but I reminded myself that you had female friends. Of course you did. That was normal. So why did I feel so angry?

Maybe I already knew deep down. Looking back, it was classic denial. You were always looking at other women and if I made a fuss you'd make a big deal about my 'green-eyed monster'. This time it was more. You were touching her, your arm around her shoulder. She was laughing into your face.

I hurried around the corner and watched as you stood on the pavement, hailing a taxi. I bit the bullet and walked around the corner as if I had just arrived. Suddenly you were colleagues. I remember thinking that it felt rehearsed, as if you'd been caught together in a lift or something. She knew who I was immediately.

You'd windmilled your arms towards me.

'Caro. My God. What a surprise.'

I was still shaken.

'Clearly.'

You looked at the woman.

'Sorry, how rude. This is Christine Dearden. She's in from our German office. I'm tasked with looking after her while she's here.'

I squared up.

'Well, that shouldn't be much of a trauma, should it? Going anywhere nice?'

I was arms folded, rigid with temper. But you continued.

'Caro. Don't be like that.' She was smiling. You shrugged. 'I was dropping her off at the Ibis before I got the train home. On my way. Anyway. What're you doing here?'

The doubt had crept in. Had I got it wrong? Had I?

'I booked a table at The Ivy. For us.'

I glanced territorially at Christine. She just smiled at me. Maybe I had been imagining it, I thought.

We went to The Ivy, but the next day, on my way back from dropping you off at your office in a taxi, I dropped by the Ibis. I asked the concierge to call Christine Dearden's room to tell her Lisa Phillips was waiting in reception for her. I watched his fingers carefully as he keyed in the room number. 252. I waited until he was busy with an elderly American couple asking directions to the British Museum and hurried to the lifts, doubling back to reception and feigning confusion.

'Oh, I've left my card in my room. 252. Christine Dearden. Energy Logistics.'

The receptionist checked the room and the booking and gave me a new key card. I clearly remember the feeling that descended. It appeared from nowhere, some kind of madness that drove me on. This didn't feel wrong, it felt like retribution.

I calmly took the lift to level two and opened the door. Christine Dearden's room was a mess. I packed her cases and swept all her make-up and toiletries into a plastic bag. I emptied the room, all except for a small bottle of Chanel No. 5, which I put into my own bag.

Then I wheeled the luggage to the lift and pressed the -1 button. It halted and the doors opened into a long corridor with a gym on one side and a fire exit at the end. I left her luggage by the fire exit. Serves her right, I thought, as I took the lift back up and exited the hotel. The mist lifted and I sprayed a little bit of the Chanel No. 5 on my wrist.

On the train home I felt slightly sick. What if they found out it was me? What if there were cameras? But as the days went by and you didn't mention it, I just forgot about it. But I kept a close eye on you. I felt like I'd redressed the balance over Christine, but I was uneasy and a spark in me had ignited.

Two weeks later we went out to dinner and I sprayed myself with Christine's perfume. I walked through a thick mist of it and, as the tiny droplets clung to me, I felt warm inside. Warm in the knowledge that you'd smell it and think of Christine. Maybe your brain would make the connection and you'd wonder, just for a moment, if I had anything to do with her missing belongings.

If you did, I never noticed. You never mentioned it and I never found out what happened. We went out to dinner and you were my Jack again. And yes, it did occur to me to just ask you. I'm a psychologist. I know all about Pavlov's dog. How you offer the reward and ring the bell. Well, I was Jack's bitch. You'd conditioned me not to ask awkward questions by completely switching off when I did. Then, when I stopped, you'd be the best husband in the world. Good girl, Caro. Good girl.

I swig the blackcurrant vodka and suddenly realise that I can find out all the things I desperately wanted to ask. Right now. I open the journal again and turn back, right to the beginning. There she is. More than a page. Christine Dearden. Eight out of ten. A couple of hotel receipts. I run my fingers over the Ibis receipt. Room 252. Then she'd moved to the Hilton just around the corner. Paid for by Jack.

Panic. She didn't work for Energy Logistics at all. She didn't work with you. So why was she in your offices? I slam the journal closed. I'm woozy, but not in a nice way. Vodka usually mellows me, but this is one of those nights. I just know it. I pack everything away and push it under the sink.

Of course she didn't work with you. I'd seen her in your offices and drawn that conclusion myself when you'd lied. Thinking on your feet, as you called it when you lied about other things. She was in your office to meet you. She was known there. They'd just let her in. My God. They probably thought that she was me. Your wife. My vodka-addled brain is trying to work out how, if they thought Christine was me, had you explained all the others in the Journal?

For some reason, I'd imagined – still imagine even now – that not everyone knew about these women. That you'd kept this big secret from me and everyone else. Otherwise, how could you have defended yourself so publicly? And how could everyone we knew have believed your shit about me being crazy?

Now, as I'm nearly vodka blind, I'm laughing. This was no secret. The only person who didn't know about it was me. All the office parties I'd attended with you, the dutiful wife, everyone there had known. All the nights out with friends. They'd all known, too. They'd probably spent time with these other women.

I glug down a couple of mouthfuls of the vodka and wait for the sweet release of nothingness to close over me.

Chapter Three

I wake up in a Premier Inn hotel room. I know it's a Premier Inn because of the purple curtains and the strip across the bed, which is now thrown over a chair opposite. Premier Inn Purple. It's still dark but I can see a shape lying next to me. Very still. Stinking of alcohol. He's covered in wiry black hair and smells of stale aftershave and body odour, and my stomach heaves.

My head hurts but that's nothing new. I creep to the bathroom and pee. I quickly dress and marvel at the fact that each time I end up in a stranger's hotel room, so pissed that I can't even remember leaving my house, I leave my clothes in the bathroom. I have a flashback of me laughing loudly and dancing naked to Bryan Adams.

I don't drink anything or clean my teeth because the plumbing in these kinds of hotels leaves a lot to be desired. Very noisy indeed. I quickly go through this guy's pockets, removing the contents of his wallet and taking his car keys. One credit card, just to make him suffer. He might not even realise it's gone for a few days, then when the bank notifies him of a fraudulent transaction, he'll have to remember cheating on his wife with a stranger in a bar who ripped him off.

I look on it as payment for my time. I flashback again, this time to me straddling him and bouncing up and down, feigning enjoyment. It's like that saying, if a tree falls in the forest and no one's around to hear it, does it make a sound? If you drink a bottle of vodka and fuck a stranger and you can't remember it, did it really happen and could you have enjoyed it?

Like so many of the others, there's a picture of his wife and kids in his wallet. I look at it for a split second and he stirs. Is this what happened with you and those women? Did they suddenly see a picture of me and Charlie and Laura and know about us? I freeze, tiptoe across the bedroom. I open the door and shut it gently behind me. I hurry down the stairs and raise my phone to my face as I go through the reception area.

It's weird, really. I never see any of these men again. I don't sleep with them all. No. If I manage to get a small memento in the bar I just leave. They could probably find me if they look hard enough. I seem to spend a lot of what I think of as my in-between time in the bar of some Premier Inn or another. In-between because it's somewhere in the fuzzy boundary. The bit where the worst of my pain resides – the deep visceral pain I feel for my babies. I rely on the rationalisation that they're not going to tell anyone what really happened, are they? How would they explain *that* to their wives?

When I turn the key in my front door ten minutes later, I see a white postcard on the mat. There's a police crest on it and a note that they called around last night. Of course they did. You know me, Jack. And I know you. That would be your next move. You can't come around here yourself because of the restraining order. So you would call the police. You'd want to make a big deal of it to make me look madder. I'd anticipated this so it doesn't worry me.

An hour before I must be at work, so I clear up the debris from last night – smashed glasses from my clumsy drunkeness and the empty vodka bottle – and move the briefcase and the holdall to the buried box at the end of our garden, a fire pit that I'd long ago covered up and grassed over the lid; it's where I keep all my souvenirs. Watches, wallets, before I figured out that a missing wallet was quickly noticed. Much better to delay their guilt and inconvenience as long as possible by making it debatable as to whether they had actually been robbed or just lost or spent everything while they were pissed. All the token items I'd taken from women I thought you were seeing. The perfume. A wheel trim. Yes, it sounds crazy but I was trying to keep my family together.

I pull up a small raised flower bed and remove the piece of soil-covered wood underneath. Of course, I'm fucked if anyone finds this. But really, why would anyone look there? The hole is deep and I'd made a box in it out of some scrap wood left in the shed. A bit damp, but not to worry. It all fits in, and I drop in the remnants of last night's little foray into my other self.

Everyone's got a dark side and a light side, haven't they? Problem with me is when I drink I become someone else. Mild-mannered researcher by day; crazy, hoarding, seeker of revenge by night. Never the twain shall meet. Hopefully.

When everything is back in its place I sit on the edge of the flower bed and call the police. DS Lorraine Percy. She answers on two rings.

'DS Percy speaking. How can I help?'

She doesn't know it yet, but she can help me a lot. She's my communication route to you.

'Oh. Right. This is Caroline Atkinson. I found a card behind my door when I got up this morning.'

'Yes. Thanks for calling back. We had a report from your ex-husband that you had a holdall of his that was wrongly delivered.'

I sigh heavily for effect.

'Mmm. His cases were delivered to my house. But I called the delivery company and they picked them up again. They did call back to check.'

'So you haven't got the holdall?'

'No. Look, would you like to pop round and check? I'm not setting off for work for a while. I mean, after what happened before ...'

She pauses.

'Yes. I've read your file. All right. I'll pop round now, with a colleague.'

'Thank you. I'll put the kettle on.'

I end the call and go and clean my teeth. I think about the journal and that guy last night. I only remember snippets, but I'd arrived completely trashed at a local bar and he'd jumped at the chance. All politeness and paying for drinks, but his hands were everywhere. No. It wouldn't have been like that for you. You would have been upfront about being married. You would have made them feel special, as if they were so fucking wonderful that you had cheated on your wife for them.

I hurry back downstairs when the doorbell rings. I look around at the boxes, looming over me, and smile. She'll think I'm crazy. But everyone's got to have a hobby, haven't they? I let her in. She's short and compact and stern-looking in her black trousers and jacket. She's come alone.

From the first moment she steps into my hallway she's shocked. A pile of Thomson Locals tip over at her feet and she looks to me for guidance. I show her through to the kitchen, where I've made a space amongst the section with all the small white goods. Toasters, bread makers, waffle irons. I don't even like fucking waffles.

She opens her notebook.

'Right then, Mrs Atkinson.'

She sounds bored, like this is just duty. I smile.

'It's Dr Atkinson, actually.'

'OK, Dr Atkinson. As I said on the phone, your ex-husband has made a complaint that you have his property.'

I look around.

'Please. Have a look. Whatever it is, it should be easy to spot in here. Unless it's in an Amazon box.'

She doesn't laugh. In fact, she looks horrified. She follows my gaze and frowns.

'You can get help with this. You don't have to live like this.'

'Yes. And I will. But it's taken me a long time to recover from my divorce. Things are getting easier. I'm hoping that this won't be a setback. I don't really want any contact with my ex-husband, you see.'

She's nodding and writing it all down in her little black book.

'So you say you rang the delivery company? Did you ring them straight away?'

'When I realised what had happened. And they came as soon as I got home from work to pick the cases up. I honestly can't see why he's being like this. I didn't ask to have them delivered here. And I'm sure you have more important things to investigate than a missing bag?' I pull my cardigan around my shoulders. 'This is just time-wasting. And to be honest, it's brought back memories. Set me back.'

She bites. Her head tilts to one side and she's in sympathy mode.

'Look, I wouldn't usually be around here investigating this sort of thing. It's just that your ex-husband has instructed his solicitor and he says there are personal documents that could be used for identity fraud. So ...'

I stare at her just long enough for her to blink.

'I'm sorry. I just don't have the case.'

'Well, that's all for now. Look, if I just have a little look around I'll be able to go back and tell him that it's a mistake and ... Well, just promise me that you'll see someone about all this.'

She makes her way through the dreamcatchers and candleholders towards the lounge. It's piled up with dinner services and cutlery near the door, then unopened novels and self-help books further in. She cranes her neck to see into the corners and suddenly turns to face me. We're a little bit too close to each other and I'm glad I scrubbed my teeth.

'So how do you afford all this?'

I'm still thinking about your bent fucking solicitor, and how he's insisting the police take this further than a fucking crime number. I stare at her and we connect.

'I've got nothing else to spend my money on. Nothing else at all.'

She's read my notes and seen my entire file. She knows my children are gone. She knows exactly what I've lost. She turns and lets herself out.

I go to work and spend all day researching the trigger point for people to snap. A bit like in that film with Michael Douglas. *Falling Down*. A lot of people who have committed shoot-em-ups were interviewed about what made them do it. The obvious flaw in this is that they're probably going to say whatever makes them appear in the best possible light, because psychopaths are liars and do have a sense of what they have done wrong, they just don't believe it. And they just don't really care. Not deep down inside. So lying is of no consequence to them. More second nature, isn't it, Jack?

When I get home I go up the garden and retrieve the journal. I thought that I'd made my decision. It had upset me so much that I knew the only sane thing to do was to get rid of it. But it's too compelling. The knowledge that I was right all along makes the suffering worthwhile. Even though it's torturing me, I open it and read it again.

High fucking Fidelity? You were always a *War and Peace* man. You liked to tell everyone that you had read Dostoevsky. You hadn't, but you had read every Martin Amis. And Will Self. Not that there's anything wrong with a bit of lad lit. But it just isn't you.

The more I read of the journal, the more I see that you moulded yourself around those women. If they liked classical music, you'd take them to the Proms. If they liked rock you'd buy concert tickets. It was clear that you went to massive lengths to make them feel special. Even more than I thought. Special. You didn't want me. You wanted them. Special.

I reach for the vodka again. But the cupboard is bare and I'm dry. I could go out to the off-licence and buy some cheap stuff but I'm not cheap. Somehow I need to work out what I should do and how I'm going to get my mind off your fucking cheating. I almost throw the journal across the room, but I know that's pointless. My phone rings and it's your mother. Of course it is.

I leave it to go to answerphone because I know what she's going to say. I watch the message icon flash on the screen and then I press play.

'Caroline, it's Missy. I've had a call from Jack.'

Of course she has. If you can't get to me through the police, then you'll send in the fucking cavalry. Who you convinced that I was totally insane. Although Missy didn't need much convincing.

'I hope this isn't any more of your nonsense, Caroline. You need to think about the consequences. For the children. For all of us. If you've got that bag, give it back to him. I'll call you tomorrow.'

The children. She's complicit in this. Every time I think about what happened I start to cry. I feel delirious with grief. She gets to see my beautiful children every day and I can only watch them from a distance. I do, though, I make sure I see them every day that I can, even the bad days. The more I think about it, the more I realise that I need to do something about it. It's not right or fair. And I miss them more than life itself.

So I close the journal and open my laptop. I check my Facebook messages and check your page, as I do every day. You're absolutely unable to make your Facebook private because who would worship you then? You need the adulation, clearly. You'll have weighed it up carefully. The chances of someone – me – stalking you against the opportunity to tell everyone how wonderful you are and how perfect your new life is. A no-brainer.

Naturally, I click on your friends list and slowly, letter by letter, type in Christine Dearden. There she is. Staring lovingly into her husband's eyes on their wedding day in her profile picture. I try another one. She's there too, with her three kids. I open the journal again and look through your list for most of your ex-girlfriends. All spectators to the demise of our marriage, which they contributed to.

Still wishing you *Happy Birthday Jack* and still liking your posts. Whereas I was barred from your life. Julie Carson lives in a beautiful architect-designed home. Spotless white. She's a marketing director. I wonder if their husbands know what they did? Had an affair with a married man? Slept with you in the full knowledge that you had a wife? There's no reason why they shouldn't know. They made me suffer, so why shouldn't they suffer now?

High Fidelity. You like that. You like the premise. But, like you said, there's too many of them. Well, how would you like it if I helped you out, Jack? If I hunted down each of your exes and made them aware of how much I had suffered?

I get my car keys and drive down to the local PC World. Like always, it's a toss-up whether I make it to where I'm going or just to the Tesco booze department. But, by ten o'clock, I'm the proud owner of a top-of-the-range notebook. Large memory, small enough to be portable. Long battery life. I drive to the centre of Manchester and park up on Dale Street. The laptop's partly charged when I switch it on and it searches for Wi-Fi. Searching, searching, searching until it identifies a nice, anonymous cloud network. Manchester Free Wi-Fi. An hour of free internet time every night.

I sign up as Monica Bradley. The name just came to me out of nowhere. I make a Facebook account and a Twitter account and search Facebook for an anonymous face. Someone the opposite of me, dark and sultry. Someone attractive, with lots of friends and an open profile that I can steal photos from. Sally King from Halifax will do. I give Monica a relationship. Married. For four years. She went to our local school and she's got a degree in computer science.

I send friend requests to some of your friends and some from my own friends list. I send one to myself. My real self.

Then I drive over to the university. A security guard waves me through when I explain I've forgotten some seminar papers that I need to copy for tomorrow. I go straight to the print room and take the journal out of my bag. I carefully scan each page. Each receipt. Each condom wrapper. Each narrative on how you scored them and why you scored them. Where you met them. What each woman's 'speciality' was. Pictures of you together.

I always get a split second where I doubt myself. Wonder if I'm doing the right thing. Usually self-preservation, knowing that no matter how wrongly accused I was, if anything else happens I'll end up in Holloway. But, like every other time, it's diffused. This time my fear is reframed when I'm about to scan a photo of you and Alicia Turnbull. It's one of those sickly-sweet end-of-the-bed poses, her head upside down. All black underwear and legs in the background. The background of my bedroom. Our bedroom. That's my bed she's lying on. My blue dressing gown hangs on the back of the door and that's my mini Tiffany lamp on the bedside table.

You fucked them in our bed. Somehow I didn't think it could get any worse. I look at the date on the photograph and my head's spinning. Two days before your twenty-eighth birthday five years ago. Two days before we went out to the Yang Sing and then came home and made love in that bed. You must have been thinking about her all the time. Laughing at me. I quickly scan the picture and finish the rest of the pages. I pull the flash drive out of the machine and push in my staff key to reset the counter to zero. As I walk away from the university, 'Shout Out to my Ex' is playing in my head and a *High Fidelity* cheating bastard playlist is forming – but this time it's revenge instead of apologies.

Back in the car a flutter of excitement flows through me and I look at Christine Taylor, née Dearden's profile again. At least I have the advantage of knowing exactly what she looks like. Like you, she seems to be unable to keep anything secret. Apart from the things about her that her husband doesn't know. Maybe she's still doing it? Sleeping with other people's husbands? Well. We'll soon see, won't we?

Chapter Four

It was difficult to sleep in that room, knowing what you'd done in there. I haven't changed a thing and now I wish I had. All I could imagine was your laughter and her touching my things.

But I need to start from the beginning if I'm going to do this right. With Christine. Because I couldn't sleep, I had a chance to think about where I could get free Wi-Fi. The university, obviously, but that was too obvious. Too me. Monica Bradley with her high-powered job in computer science wouldn't hang out there. I need somewhere that couldn't place me, or at least place me in the wrong location. About 3 a.m. it came to me. Wasn't there Wi-Fi on the trams now? And the buses. I could run Monica Bradley's life on public transport.

So after I have my coffee I go down the garden to the hole. It's a misty morning and at least I don't feel hung over. But I do feel that you must pay for what you've done. You've ruined my life. I lay awake reasoning with myself that I could move away, start again. But it's an overwhelming task. I'd have to sell our house and move all the things I had bought. Besides, I couldn't leave. My life stopped a year ago, but that doesn't mean that someday things can't just turn around. All I need to do is show everyone that I was right and you were wrong and then I'll have a chance of getting Charlie and Laura back.

Lots of people have misunderstood the situation. They think I'm upset about you and your philandering. They don't understand what has happened here and they tell me to let it go. Let it go. Let it fucking go! Don't they think I've tried that? I gave myself all the advice that I would have given someone in my position. Have a break. Go on holiday. Move house. Get rid of all their stuff. Ice cream. Watch sad films. Cry it out. Sleep. Care for yourself.

I knew exactly what to do. I did all those things right at the beginning, when I felt like it was the kind of normal split-up some of my friends had gone through.

You had to draw it out, though, didn't you? You walked away with a piece of elastic that was my heart and pulled it as long and as far as possible until, finally, it broke. I would feel like I was 'getting over it', then you would come around again to see the children and drop another bombshell that ended with me in tears and you herding the children out as if you were scared.

The worst one was that time you said you were taking them on holiday. I was fine with it. Well, I wasn't because I suspected that you were going with your current girlfriend, whoever that was, and I was upset because the children would spend time with her and not me.

I told myself that I was still their mother and no one could ever replace me. It was only for a fortnight. I planned to decorate their rooms while you were gone. Two days beforehand you called me to tell me when you would pick them up. I thought we'd already arranged it and was confused. Midday Saturday. No, you said, you'd need them earlier.

I'd told you fine. That's OK. I'd already packed and I would have their suitcases ready. There was a silence. An awkward silence, the kind where I knew something horrible was going to spill out of your mouth. Something hurtful. You did it for effect. So I braced myself. It was the beginning of what you would eventually hold up in public as 'bad motherhood'.

'Right. That's …er … well, it's a bit awkward.' Exactly as I thought. Awkward. 'The thing is, I need the extra two hours to go and buy them a complete new wardrobe. I might as well come out and say it. You haven't been … coping, have you? I mean, they're not … clean.'

I rallied. Fuck off, Jack.

'Clean clothes? Is that what you're griping about? Yes. They are clean. I wash them. Just like before.'

More silence. What could possibly come next?

'I didn't just mean the clothes. I mean them. And, let's be honest, Caroline, you. You're looking rough and … not well.'

I returned service, but it had already stung me.

'I'm fine. The kids are fine.'

As I said it, I eyed myself in the hallway mirror. I did look fine. A bit tired, but I was a full-time single working parent, for God's sake. I'd lost weight and my cheekbones were more defined. My hair was more blonde and my eyes brighter. Yet the doubts, as ever, crept in. To me, yes, but how did I look to everyone else?

Depression is usually more obvious to significant others than it is to the person suffering. Things can seem perfectly normal until a relative mentions that they aren't washing enough or they are staying in bed all day. I checked myself mentally on the HADS depression scale. Was I depressed? On you went.

'I'm taking them to Italy. We'll be eating in some smart restaurants and I can't possibly take them there in those kinds of clothes. Washed out and—'

'I thought you said that they weren't washed? Make your mind up. Washed out or not washed?'

Another fucking elongated pause. Then the triumphant pitch that I know so well. The tone of victory and superiority.

'Dirty. Dirty, Caroline.'

It stung. It's every mother's worst nightmare: that someone criticises the way you look after your kids. I felt something about me shrink. When my voice finally escaped, it was involuntarily raised several octaves.

'They're not dirty, Jack. They have a bath or a shower every day.'

'I meant their clothes. Laura had the same socks on two days running last week. Those red and yellow stripes.'

'Yes, she did. And I'd washed them in between.'

And there it was. I'd engaged. That engagement lasted from that moment until the next thinly guised complaint. You picked them up at 10 a.m. on Saturday morning with a cheery, 'Come on, kids, let's go shopping,' and a sly side glance at me.

I was going to paint their bedrooms. I'd already bought the paint and had the rollers ready. Instead, I drove to the local Asda and bought a trolley-load of cleaning stuff. Bleach, detergent, floor cleaner, polish, washing powder, toilet cleaner. You name it, I had it.

I spent the next week either cleaning or sitting in my office thinking about cleaning. I scrubbed until my hands were red raw. On the Friday afternoon I checked into a local health spa and had my hair and nails done. Then I went late-night shopping in Manchester and bought the kids a full wardrobe of new clothes each and myself new black jeans and a white top.

Early on Saturday morning I was sitting in new clothes in my newly sterile house. I remember looking around and thinking that it didn't look lived in. I told myself it was just until you dropped them off, then Charlie and Laura would immediately make their mark on the house and it would all feel normal again. Whatever that was.

You left it until the very last minute. I sat in the kitchen all day, on edge. I hadn't eaten properly all week and when I heard the front gate click and hurried to the door I had a head rush. I ran through the hallway and, on the way, glanced at myself in the mirror. Somehow I looked worse! How could that be? I had new clothes, new hair, smooth skin and carefully applied make-up.

Charlie and Laura ran to me and hugged me, then ran past me and upstairs to their rooms. I panicked a little. Had I promised them that I would decorate their rooms? I thought I had meant it to be a secret, but everything had been so confused this week that I couldn't remember.

You sniffed. It was almost imperceptible, but I saw it. You looked around the kitchen and there I was like a fucking dog, begging for approval. Ever the ambassador, I made the first awkward move.

'Did you have a good time?'

You didn't look at me. You looked past me.

'Yeah. Great. Been busy?'

Temper rising, but I kept it down. I willed myself to not answer. If I don't say anything, I can't sound mad, can I? You walked around the kitchen, some kind of cruel inspection. I could hear the kids upstairs, but I couldn't take my eyes off you. Fear that you would find something out of place. Another stick to beat me with. Finally, you stopped in front of me and lifted my chin until I was looking into your eyes.

'That's better.'

It was a murmur. Despite my extreme stress and fear, which at that time I hadn't really understood, I felt love. I felt love for you. Care, the old kind. You touched me and my body bent to you, just as I thought it would do for the rest of my life. For a second I held the hope that we would get back together. That you would come home. For a second I wanted you to.

You turned and walked away, leaving my soul wrecked once more. This process would be repeated weekly, sometimes daily, for months and months. I know now that when I looked in the mirror that day, it wasn't my clothes or my hair that made me look worse. I was being worn down from the inside out.

That was until the children were gone. I worked harder and harder to keep the house spotless for your weekly inspections. I bought complex washing powder and endlessly researched fabric conditioner to find out which would make their clothes smell nice after you said they were musty.

I'd asked the children why they had new clothes. They'd looked at each other and said that Daddy liked to buy them things. I'd asked them who chose the clothes and they stared at me. Charlie's arms were very straight by his sides. Laura was blinking at me.

'Daddy says we can't tell you. It's for your own good.'

I sat on my haunches in front of them.

'Look, you two, whatever Daddy says, I love you. For ever. It doesn't matter who chooses the clothes. I'm your mummy and I love you.'

I gathered my scared-stiff children towards me. They didn't bend in my arms; they were just waiting for me to let them go. It made me worse, knowing that you were turning them against me too. I'd told myself that whatever you did to me, eventually you would get bored and leave me alone. It would be over and then I could start the healing process. Get over it. *Let it go.*

It just carried on. The judging and the thinly veiled threats. Wiping your finger across the top of the lounge door as you stared at me. Picking up a hair from the stair carpet. Looking me up and down like I was a piece of shit. Then making me believe that it had all been a big mistake and that you loved me again.

I ironed into the early hours and got up at six o'clock to clean.

Even through the divorce proceedings, when I realised that you were trying to drive me mad. Even though I wasn't, you'd made me look like I was. You even told the courts that I had obsessive compulsive disorder. That I was an obsessive cleaner.

In the end, the thing that lost me my kids was me. I can picture myself in that room, crying and wailing. Shouting out my denials and my solicitor telling me to calm down. In fact, I was a mirror to everything you and your mother were saying. Unbalanced. Neurotic. Obsessive. You didn't produce any evidence at all, but the state of me that day was enough.

All the hard work you did, wearing me down, bullying me, hurting me, manipulating me, it all paid off that day. It was all left open, of course. No one said that I couldn't see my kids, which only leaves one conclusion, doesn't it – that I chose not to.

Nothing could be further from the truth. I was scared. Scared stiff. Yes. Dr Caroline Atkinson, Ph.D. With the nice house and the nice car. I was scared and confused and you made sure I had no one to talk to. I couldn't even tell the friends I had left, like Eileen and Fiona, because guess what? I was scared. I didn't choose not to see my kids. I made sure I actually saw them every day that I could, from a distance. But I was too scared to go near them because of what you would do to me.

This doesn't wash with people in general. I know this. *Why didn't she leave? Why didn't she call the police? Why didn't she just go and see her kids?* All the usual questions from people who have never been scared shitless of someone who is deeply involved in their lives, who, at the end of it all – after the hearings and the injunctions – will still be there to carry on.

I tried to tell them that you'd made me like that, but it was too late. Much too late. This is a place that I don't like to go to, Jack,

but only you and I know what happened that day when you came
to get the children for the last time.

Chapter Five

Unbelievably, I'd held it together when I came home from the family meeting. I'd gone to school to get them and I was so used to the constant acting over the pain that I smiled and laughed with the other mothers, and sing-songed the children into my car. I didn't start the engine straight away because I was seriously contemplating just driving. Just driving and not stopping until we were far, far away.

I couldn't understand how today I was able to see my children. To pick them up, to take them home and to give them their tea. Then, at the allotted time, they would be gone, and from then onwards I would have to make an appointment to see them – although I knew full well that those appointments would never be kept.

I had to do it. I had no choice. So I smiled through it for their sakes. Then, at six o'clock, I heard the gate click and you were here. I was at the top of the stairs, watching you through the little stained-glass window that throws shadows onto the landing. You were confident. Tanned and lean, fighting fit, jubilant from your victory. Here to collect your prize.

My stomach flipped for the millionth time and I went to open the door. It would be just like they were going out with you, wouldn't it? Except they wouldn't be coming back. My chest heaved and the bile rose, but you were in the house with your key before I could open the door.

You looked past me and into the garden where they were playing.

'I'll get someone to pick up their bikes.'

It wasn't enough. And what did I have to lose. I turned to look at them. They couldn't hear what was going on in here so I asked you the question that I had wanted to ask since you started this.

'Why are you doing this to me?'

You fixed your gaze on me and stepped closer.

'Doing what? What, Caroline?'

'I know what you're doing. I know. You might have everyone else fooled, but not me. So why? That's what I don't understand. Why?'

You smiled, but I could see the irritation in your eyes. You picked up one of the white marble balls out of a bowl on the table and rolled it around slowly beneath your palm.

'You made me. You wouldn't leave it. You tried to ruin my life.'

I stared at you.

'How? How did I ruin your life? Surely it's the other way round?'

'Yeah, I suppose it is. But you know, lovely, none of this would have happened if you would have just ...'

'What? Turned a blind eye? Left you to it? What, Jack?'

'Stayed quiet. It's all a game, Caro. But it turns out you don't know how to play.'

You threw the marble ball to me, but I didn't expect it and it smashed into a thousand pieces on the stone kitchen floor. You calmly opened the kitchen door and called Charlie and Laura in. I knew I had to stay composed. I knew you were taking my babies from me and I musn't cry.

But they knew too. When it came to it, you hadn't done the thorough job you thought you had of brainwashing them. Later you would tell me that they were crying because they had to leave their bikes and their toys, but it wasn't like that at all. You'd been priming them for ages, telling them that they were moving out to give Mummy a break, that they would be living with Daddy for a bit.

The mistake you made was telling them that I was ill. You were pulling on their coats and suddenly Laura ran to me.

'I want to stay with Mummy. Make her better. If she's ill, I can make her better.'

She started to cry and Charlie's beautiful eyes filled with tears that he tried to bite back. He came to stand beside me and we all stared at you. We stared and blinked at you. You never flinched. Your face was set in a determined expression. I'd started to recognise that look. I'd seen it when I spoke up in court. It was when you clouded with rage.

I held my children, one on each side of me, and willed all my love to filter into them so that they would know that I would never let them go entirely. You took Laura first, huge tears spilling as you picked her up, and she looked at me over your shoulder. As you got near the door she started to cry and kick, but you held her firmly.

While you were putting her in your car, Charlie held my face and kissed it. *Don't worry, Mummy.* That's what he said. *We'll come back for you. You won't be on your own.*

You came back and took him by the hand. He resisted and you picked him up as he punched you and kicked you and shouted, *Bye, Mummy. Don't worry, Mummy.*

Then you were gone. I ran up to the top of the stairs and watched as you struggled with Charlie. He was still punching you as you strapped on his seat belt. I could see them both sobbing, looking up at the house. Looking for me.

I hid behind the curtain so that I didn't make it any worse. Then I slumped onto the floor and cried and cried. It's hard to explain what happened next. Something inside me shifted and I lay on the landing for a full day and night.

When I did eventually get up, I was different. Or I might have always been like this but it was covered by my idealistic life. I don't know. Something had drastically changed and I was a more visceral version of me. The love was stronger, the pain was deeper and the hate was keener.

Every time I closed my eyes I saw my son's little worried face, telling me not to worry. My daughter crying and screaming. I retreated into a world where it would no longer matter if I expressed my feelings. Howling, crying, vomiting. Pushing the boundaries of my sanity.

You'd left some clothes at home. Lot of clothes. I spent days cutting them into tiny pieces. I took your beloved vinyl and scratched them all up with a school compass. Then I stamped on the pieces. Then I took a hammer to them and ground those records until they were almost powder.

As an undergraduate I read about people who put on a mask all day then cried all the time they were alone. I queried this, naively asking what could be so bad that this would continue for years. But that was before I had my children ripped from me by someone who was supposed to care about me and them.

Now I understood what goes on behind the closed doors of those in pain. The elastic nature of time, where keening takes over and what seems like hours can be minutes. I lost track of the days and nights and kept my curtains closed. I turned off the phones and either unplugged the TV or watched it for twenty-four hours solid.

The drinking began after the first week. I needed to eat so

I ordered a pizza. While I was waiting I drank two bottles of Budweiser that were left over from a barbeque we had had. They were years old but I still drank them. Then I found the bottles of vodka you'd brought back from Russia.

You'd warned me that they were very valuable. When I thought about it, you'd spoken to me like I was a child. Or stupid. *They're valuable, Caroline, so don't drink them.* It had been the same with everything. Don't drive too fast, Caroline, or you might crash. Don't wear that dress, Caroline, or you'll look fat. Don't walk to work, Caroline, you'll get tired.

Everything had a patronising explanation tagged onto the end of it. You tolerated me. You were impatient with me. You never wanted me really. You just put up with me.

You came back on day ten. I heard the gate click and it was too late for the postman. I was sitting in the hallway, behind the door, just staring into space and listening to the world outside the door. People walking up and down the pavement. People who could still function. My neighbours coming and going. The postman. The window cleaner.

I heard your footfall and I knew it was you. You don't live with someone all that time and not recognise all their intricacies. In the instant between you opening the front door and me crawling into the cupboard under the stairs I looked into the house. It was a fucking mess. Suddenly I could smell the week-old takeaways and the stale alcohol. I panicked about the clothes and the records but then realised that if you'd really wanted them you would have already taken them. That wasn't what you were here for.

I was in the cupboard. I could just see out of the crack as you passed and went into the kitchen. *Caroline.* You called me. Again, *Caroline.* You went upstairs and checked the bedrooms. Then you checked the lounge. Then you stood in the kitchen, arms on hips, smiling. You surveyed the chaos and nodded. I'd seen that nod before, when you'd finished felting the shed roof, or painting the landing. I knew what it meant. *Job done.*

You left. Your visit had kick-started my insight into what was happening and although I was still rock-bottom, I was standing up and not lying down. The most painful realisation hit me at that moment and I stood in the hallway and watched you drive away. I was going to have to endure this every day of my life. Every morning I was going to have to wake up and remember what had happened.

There was no way to stop it. I couldn't kill myself. It would just make things worse for Charlie and Laura, and prove you right. So I had to get on with it, somehow. I emailed work without checking my emails and told them that I was sick. Even that seemed like a betrayal of my children, as if I knew that at some point I would be better. *Better.* I never was better. Just different.

So you can see why I have to do this now, can't you, Jack? *Fight fire with fire.* In the garden I take out Christine's perfume and spray a little bit on my wrist. Still good after all those years. It's a deep hole and there's a lot of stuff in there. It's like an unlucky dip of everything that's gone wrong in my life. I push my hand deep into the wallets and watches and credit cards and photographs and pull out an item at random. Mrs Simister's business card. It had to be, didn't it?

It's like a warning. As if to say, *Be careful, Caroline, because you know what happened with this.* God, I did feel sorry about that. I was just trying to find out what you were doing, because you wouldn't tell me. I was following you. Yes. But only because you were lying. I saw you with Lorna. I was watching you, but she said I was stalking her. They saw me on the cameras in the car park.

Now I know I'm right because she's on your list. You leaned in and I couldn't quite tell if it was a kiss or not. Obviously I went straight from zero to ten in one second. I knew that, if I asked you, you would say you weren't having an affair with Lorna, no matter how it looked. I know now you gave her three out of ten but that's not how it looked that day.

She looked hot and you were all over her. The mist descended and I stopped crouching behind the bush and started to walk across the car park, towards her Audi. It was anger that drove me. I admit it. I imagined her and you exposed, trying to explain something that couldn't be explained, cancelling out the pain I was feeling right at that moment.

But she drove off and I was left standing in a deserted car park. I thought she hadn't seen me. Instead, I had the police knocking at my door three days later. Lorna had complained that I was harassing her. They had a file. 'Several instances of you approaching Lorna Kershaw.' The policeman said he was there to warn me and asked me if I was planning on doing it again.

I told him that I was, if she carried on sleeping with my husband. I actually said that to them. *Yes, I'll keep following her. I'm not going to stop.* That's all they heard, not the bit about her sleeping with you. Their silent shock shook me into reality and I realised that I was in trouble. They took me down to the police station and cautioned me.

You arrived to bail me out. I wasn't charged because you persuaded Lorna to drop the charges. You got me a solicitor and I asked to read the file, which was when I found out exactly what your tactics were.

Caroline is a little bit disturbed. She's imagining that I am having affairs with women I work with and with friends. Lorna has agreed to drop the charges on the condition that Caroline gets help.

Even then I convinced myself that there had been some massive mistake. That you were just doing it to get me off. That we were still in it together. You were on my side. But soon afterwards I found myself sitting in a counsellor's office. Of course, I knew her techniques. People-centred counselling. Everything out in the open. It was my chance to finally make someone understand what you'd been doing.

I told her all about Christine and Lorna and Julie and what I had seen. She had the case notes from my solicitor and her recommendation was that Jack and I had considerable difficulties and that we should go to marriage guidance in order to resolve them.

Obviously, I didn't think you were going to immediately admit that you were having an affair. Or affairs. But I did think that you loved me. That we were a family. That you would protect me. That you knew what you had done and you would at least keep quiet and just not deny it outright. Do the decent thing.

But you have to be right. And you know me; I'm going to defend myself to the death. So we were at loggerheads and you had the advantage. The marriage guidance was a disaster. Mrs Simister, a tiny, middle-aged woman, sat between us. I accused you of having an affair and you denied it. Not one single new situation came out of it. I got more and more upset and annoyed as you insisted that I was imagining everything.

As a result, my feelings were pushed deeper down and Mrs Simister's report on my neurotic, jealous tendencies just made me feel like the world was completely unfair and that I had to do something about it. So really, what I'm doing now is just an extension of that. Of putting everything I have into not just proving that you were wrong, but into showing everyone that I was right all along. It's the only way I can get my life back.

Of course, up until now there was no way that I could do that. But finally I have some proof: I have the journal. You'll be seething. Ringing around everyone you know, trying to talk it round, make me out to be a liar, paving the way for the inevitable. Because you know full well what's coming next. *What goes around comes around.* It worked before, canvassing my sanity all over town. And I had nothing solid to defend it with. Only hearsay.

Naturally, those in the know weren't interested anyway – they'd already nailed their colours to the mast. But the others were gently lulled into believing the possibility that I wasn't the lovely academic they worked with. That I wasn't the calm friend who was always there to listen to their problems. That I wasn't the trusty PTA member who never missed a meeting. You whispered your lies to everyone.

Naturally I tried to explain, told them that the only reason I was acting like you were cheating was because you *were* cheating. Some of them looked full of pity and touched my arm. Some of them looked shocked and shook their heads. Some of them came right out and told me to get help because Jack Atkinson was a hardworking, decent man. Occasionally, someone would ask me how I knew. I suppose they wanted evidence. But I had none. Only what I had seen and felt.

But I have it now. Not just a few scribbled diary entries that could be written off as fantasy. No. I have photographs. And now I'm going to post them online. I'm going to post them on Christine's profile and on your profile.

Before I know it I'm on the bus with my laptop open. Back seat, beside two men working frantically on spreadsheets. I'm Monica now, in her head, checking who's accepted my 'friend' request. I see myself there, along with Jack and Christine and twenty-three other people.

Then there are another twenty-five friend requests. People who think they know the imaginary Monica. I wonder if that's worth a psychological study as I slip back into serious day mode, then I focus on the task in hand. I push the flash drive into the USB and flick through the photos until I find the one. You're in her room at the Ibis. I stare into the background. It's exactly as I remember it. A spike of temper rises but I push it down, down into the depths.

Select. 'What's on your mind?' Facebook asks me. I'll tell you what's on my mind, Facebook. Revenge. I type: '#ThrowbackThursday #London #Backintheday'. I've already saved some pictures of made-up Monica to her photos, and I post some more of her in London just to make it look like these are just part of a series of pictures of Monica's past. Only three people will know the truth. Christine will know. I'll know. And you, Jack. You'll know.

You know me, Jack.

Chapter Six

I arrive at work early, and I log into my own Facebook account on my office computer. More people have friended the lovely made-up Monica and I flick through the profiles of people who I haven't seen for more than fifteen years. Then back to the picture. It's there, sitting in the middle of my screen. You're laughing. Jack and Christine. It's obvious from the series of pictures you stuck in the journal that they're taken using a camera's timer.

Jack and Christine, laughing at first, then undressing each other. Then naked. Then fucking. But to anyone looking at this single picture, it just looks like Monica was with them in their hotel room, perhaps getting ready for a night out. She took the picture of them together.

I check the 'number of views' digit and it's moving upwards, ever upwards. The picture's been shared three times. Simone Lawrie, one of your sister's friends from school, has posted a question mark in the comments section and your name so you are sure to see it.

My mobile phone rings and it makes me jump. I snap out of this fantasy world and see that it's DS Percy.

'Hi. Caroline Atkinson speaking.'

There's a slight pause. I know she's assessing my opening. But I'm calm as can be.

'DS Percy. Look, Caroline – if it's OK to call you Caroline?'

Of course it is. Be as personal as you like.

'Sure.'

'OK. Mr Atkinson has been in touch. He's made a further accusation. About a picture on Facebook.'

I intentionally wait.

'Oh. Go on.'

'Well, that's it. He feels that you have posted a picture from his personal journal, which was in the bag that he claims was left at your house, on Facebook.'

She sounds pissed off. I expect this isn't really her crime domain, Facebook posts, but your cheating fucking solicitor would be ranting and threatening and insisting that she follow it up. I pause again.

'I don't understand. A picture? On Facebook? But surely you've checked my Facebook account? Surely you can—'

'Yes, yes. Of course. But you are friends with the person who posted it.'

'Am I? Just me? Only I ...'

She's getting annoyed now. I can hear the tension in her voice as we reach the null hypothesis.

'No. Not just you. But you added this person yesterday.'

I tap some keys to imply I'm logging into my Facebook account.

'Oh, Monica Bradley? Yes. I did. I thought she was someone from school as everyone else added her.' I tap, tap, tap to prolong the suspense leading up to my discovery of the picture. 'Oh. Oh.'

'So can you see why he's upset?'

I smile to myself. She's neutral.

'Yes. But what about me? That's not exactly pleasant for me. Seeing him with someone else when we were married.'

'And that's why he feels you posted this picture.'

'Of course he does. He feels that I'm responsible for everything.

To be honest, DS Percy, I don't think I'm the person in the wrong here. I would say that he's the one who's caught out. So, as you say, I can see why he's upset. But it wasn't me.'

She's breathing into the phone. I try to be as helpful as I can.

'Perhaps it's something to do with the woman in the picture? Look, I absolutely insist that you send someone round to my house to confirm I don't have the bag. And you are welcome to look at my computer records. But you're wasting your time. It wasn't me.'

'That won't be necessary. Not at this stage.'

'OK. Well, I'm at work right now so ...'

'Of course. And thank you for your help. I'll be in touch.'

I give her my work number and she thanks me.

'You're welcome.'

Very welcome. Because she's going to end the call and call you. Tell you that she doubts that I'm behind this. That it must be someone else with a grudge. Ask you more about this photograph. About Christine Dearden. Look up her Facebook profile and see her lovely husband. He loves her. It's clear. Loves her so much that if he found this photograph he could possibly make a fake profile to make her and Jack suffer. Make the world see what they were really like.

By teatime DS Percy will be knocking on Christine Dearden's door. Asking her husband if he knows anything about the picture. Doing my job for me.

I press on with my work and before long it's lunchtime. I can't help but check my Facebook again. I can only get a limited view from my own profile, but I dare not check Monica's from here. Lots of WTF comments under the picture. Christine Taylor (née Dearden) has over-explained that 'we were at a party' and 'can't everyone see that this is quite innocent'. I suppose it does look innocent in this picture – they haven't seen the rest. But they're picking up the clues. Her sister-in-law has helpfully told us that 'Barry bought you that necklace so this must have been after you two got together' and 'what the hell do you think you're playing at?'

Every psychologist must have supervision. I'm no exception. If I want to practise, and I do, I need to go to a session with a senior colleague every month. Irritatingly, just when Monica's picture comments are hotting up, a reminder flashes onto my screen. Supervision is this afternoon. Room G43.

I hide Monica's laptop in a ceiling tile (you never know when people like DC Percy will take it upon themselves to pay a visit) and go to meet Eileen Simpson in G43. She always brings cake, and I haven't eaten.

I open the door and she hasn't let me down. A tray of assorted doughnuts glimmer on a low table. She's typing away, but she turns and smiles.

'Caroline, I can hardly believe it's been a month.'

Her voice is smooth and soothing and puts me immediately at ease.

'Yeah. Gone quickly.'

'Have you seen your …?'

'Children. No. His mother is still resisting. Not answering my calls. Social services keep making appointments, she keeps cancelling.'

'God. How are you coping? It must be awful.'

Awful? It's indescribable, the deep pain. The grief.

'Not good. But I try my best to get through.'

It comes out much more jolly than the deep sorrow that I feel inside. She nods and sits at the table as I munch a chocolate doughnut.

'So. How have things been?'

I smile a chocolate smile.

'Good. Great, in fact. Except there's been an incident with my ex-husband. Just yesterday, in fact.'

She picks up her notepad and flicks a switch on her Dictaphone. Good. I want everything recorded in multiple places. That's where I went wrong last time. I didn't drop any breadcrumbs. Or cake crumbs, I almost laugh, as I scatter remnants of doughnut on my lap. Eileen's staring at me as I suppress a giggle.

'Sorry. It has this effect on me. Severe stress. Humour. As we know. It's a coping strategy.'

'Yes. It must be very stressful. So what's happened?'

She leans forward, a mixture of professional interest and gossip gateway, listening to my perfectly related sorry tale. Official version, obviously. I end with the call from DS Percy and Eileen places her notebook on the table in front of her.

'Good God, as if you haven't gone through enough. All you're trying to do is build a new life and this is what you get.' She pours another coffee. 'You'd think that they'd have better things to do.'

I stare at her. Yes, you would. But I know you, Jack. I know how you would insist, get your fucking bent solicitor to push the police. I'm choosing another doughnut and when I look up Eileen is holding out a brown A4 envelope. At first I think it's bad news, but she's smiling. 'This came for you. It was left in the common room.'

She watches as I open it. I make sure that it's raised and facing me and it's just as well because it's some pictures. Of me. And the guy at the Premier Inn. Not just the guy from last night, though. The one before him. From what I can remember. How the fuck has someone taken these? I feel my pulse quicken. I flick through them and thank God that they haven't gone as far as you.

They're of me and the men dancing and kissing, still bad but at least we're not having sex. They're all taken before we go to the purple room.

'Thanks, Eileen. Just some research I requested.'

I'm guarded. Previous experience of talking while shocked has taught me to only ask very basic questions.

'Oh. Right. So. Shall we get started?'

I pick up another doughnut and begin to eat it.

'Yeah.'

I'm chewing and thinking. Casting my mind back two weeks. Four drunken excursions ago. Walker Street. The one with the cheap crystal light fittings behind the bar. Pissed-up me feeling like a million dollars. I'd even ordered champagne.

I swallow the last of the doughnut. Naturally, I haven't told Eileen about my penchant for married businessmen when I'm pissed. How I sometimes drove to my destination. How I exchanged my Boden clothes for online trashy underwear and mass-produced throwaway tat, courtesy of eBay. None of this would help me keep my job, and this is what I'm here for.

Eileen fills me in on the research project and I nod in the right places. I'm itching to look at the photographs, examine them. But I need to get through this first. Eventually she's done.

'Right. Back to you. So what will you do about this mess? With your ex?'

'Oh, like last time, there's not much I can do. I expect they'll find the culprit in the end but, again, everyone will still think it's me as I was the first accused. I'm so used to it, Eileen. But as long as it doesn't affect all my work here ...'

She makes a stern face.

'Oh, no no no. No, it won't. You've been completely upfront and that's all we ask. Obviously, if you were convicted of a crime. But hearsay is just that.'

We sign the forms and I watch as she ticks a box on her computer. Fit for practice. I manage to remain calm just long enough to leave her office and lock myself in the disabled toilet at the end of the corridor. I open the envelope. A face stares out at me. I look closely and see thick, wiry hair escaping his open-necked shirt.

I feel sick. How did that happen? How? From the vague, out-of-focus memory I had of him, he'd been as pissed as me. Rowdy. I remember rubbing up against him and laughing loudly as I practically dragged him to his room.

There'd been a sobering moment when he'd asked me how much I charged, but, apart from that, all I remembered was having sex then passing out. I read the writing on the back of the photo carefully.

I'M WATCHING YOU, CAROLINE.

Chapter Seven

Made-up Monica's phone is beep, beep, beeping as I make my way back to my office. It's a notification beep that reminds me to put the phone on silent and I soon see what the fuss is about. Christine Dearden's husband is on the warpath. He's seen the picture and he's posting threatening comments aimed at you.

Someone from school, Trevor Dane, had chipped in, telling him to 'calm down, it was years ago'. So he's threatened him as well. A sub-post has started about Monica, some girls I hardly knew wondering who she was and did anyone actually remember her?

Someone does, of course. Auto-suggestion powers much of social networking and someone posts that Monica was on the running team and good at geography. Someone else posts that she was the best friend of another girl who doesn't appear to be on Facebook and wonders if Monica still sees her.

I flick between the photos and Facebook. I'm getting no work done and I'm dying to check Monica's messages, so I call it a day and set off home. At the tram stop I wonder if the police will be waiting for me at home. If that guy had reported his credit card missing and now someone knew I had been at the hotel with him. Had proof. If I'd left something in the hotel. A hair. Likely. DNA. Almost certainly. But surely that would take a while to determine? I damn myself for being so fucking stupid and breathe deeply as the familiar feeling of inevitability sinks in.

Obviously this is your doing. *An eye for an eye.* Is this the way you want to play it, then? You know I have the journal so you're threatening me with my pissed-up performances. It doesn't explain the photos from my previous excursions. Have you been watching me for a while? Building evidence against me? The thought shocks me. All the more reason to prove you were lying. And quickly. It's all happening for a reason, this, and it's to make me hurry up and prove my innocence.

I hop onto the tram and take the single seat near the door. I can't open made-up Monica's laptop quickly enough and log on. When I do I'm delighted to find an inbox full of messages from school friends, all claiming to remember her. Asking if she was on the school trip to France, if she was on the hockey team? Some couldn't quite place her. I marvel at the power of the human brain to fill in the gaps. Schema theory. It works both for me and against me.

In this case, for me. Give them five facts and they'll find a sixth degree of separation. But it'll probably work against me when the police go sneaking around the Premier Inn.

I open Monica's timeline and Christine's got involved. She's made a comment under the photograph.

'I just want to make it perfectly clear that this photograph is completely innocent. I met Jack at work and we were about to go out for a meal. I'm sure "Monica" will confirm this, as she was there to take the photograph.'

She's trying to protect herself. Naturally. I wouldn't expect anything less of the scheming, cheating bitch. She's forced my hand, really. I was going to leave it at that, but it's like a game of chess. Some people might actually think that the situation was innocent. And I don't want that at all. I want them all to know that you fucked her.

So I open the flash drive and find a picture of you having sex. Of course, it's very painful for me to look at. You're in the bedroom at the Ibis and obviously having a lot of fun, before I spoiled it. I think for a moment, think about what it would have been like if I had just walked away from you when I realised you were being unfaithful. If, that day in London, I had gone home and packed a bag. Where I'd be now. But all I can see is ... nothing.

When I look up at the screen, I've uploaded the photograph. It's there, right on Monica's page. Can you see it? Can you see yourself being unfaithful? Are you shrugging and smiling now? Or are you uncomfortable and pissed off? I know you, Jack. You'll be livid. And you'll know that this is just the start. And you know me. You know I'll stop at nothing.

I log off and I've missed my stop. I'm fuming and still a little bit afraid that someone will be waiting for me at home, so I get off at the next stop and walk through the park. There's a huge glass greenhouse at one end of the park where they grow exotic plants and I hurry inside. I need to think.

The windows are steamy and I take off my coat. I love places like this. Completely anonymous. And safe. No one can know I'm here and no one can persecute me. The plants nod at each other, weighed down with droplets. Their leafy hands wave slowly and I almost smile.

Everything has a price; I know that more than anyone. It's almost as if when you do something good, something bad happens to balance it out. My good for today is exposing you. The bad is that someone is watching me. Here, in the quiet, steamy hothouse, I flick back through the previous night, in stills, and then, as I focus deeper, in scenes I would prefer to forget.

I run through what isn't still vodka-soaked and I can't find a single moment when I was aware of someone following me. I didn't notice anything. I cast back, weeks ago, to another purple room and another married businessman. Same. No memory at all. Would it be too much of a coincidence for them to be just CCTV or something?

Of course it fucking would. But why would someone do this? None of it makes sense. There's always the possibility that I completely blacked out and someone took the pictures then. But some of them were taken in the bar, at the end of the night when things were getting really steamy. I usually remember most of the night, even if it is fuzzy, the next day. I would have remembered if the same person had been there, wouldn't I? I don't deserve this. I don't.

I wait for half an hour, until I would be due to get home, and then I hide Monica's laptop behind a plastic panel in the greenhouse. I don't want whoever is waiting for me when I get home to find it. Even if I am arrested, there will be nothing to connect me with Monica.

It's about a quarter of a mile walk through the park and then a nice housing estate to my house. No one is waiting for me when I arrive, so I just let myself in. I stack up today's takeaway menus on top of the enormous pile at the end of the hallway and then I flick on my own laptop and look at Christine's timeline.

Oh dear. Christine's marriage seems to be going the same way as mine now it's all out in the open. Her husband is furious and he's threatening to kill you and Christine. And Monica. I'm suddenly alert to the fact that if you've reported Monica's profile to the police and Christine's husband brings it to their attention, they might, just might, start snooping. I'm covered so far, but I'd better be careful.

I look at the photos again. I'm in deep shit here. This isn't just blackmail. I only ever used the credit cards I took once, just to make them know they had done something wrong. To punish them, I suppose. I check the background, so familiar, but now I'm looking for cameras. I spot one, the bulb panoramic type, and another by the fire exit. They'd be everywhere and I'd definitely be seen leaving. But no one can prove I took those cards. All they can prove is that I was there.

I need to think about this. I can't just sit here and do nothing about it, but I need to turn it over and look at it from all sides. You're setting me up. Pushing me to do something rash. Something that will implicate me. Or maybe you're not. Maybe this is meant to scare me. Which is quite funny in a way because, after what I've been through, you would need to try a lot harder.

I know you, Jack. You think like me. You would have taken those photographs thinking that I would never, ever report you because of, you know, the shame. The shame of being caught. That's where you are wrong. Maybe I would have been ashamed if we were still married, but we're not, are we? I'm too far gone now to be ashamed. Too numb from missing my babies.

No. I'm going to call your bluff. You've upped the stakes, thinking I will back down now. Thinking I will give the journal back, drop trying to get my kids back. But I never will. No. What I'm going to do is play you at your own game. Two can play at this little fucked-up game. Tit for tat, is it? There's only one thing for it. It's risky and I don't really want to do it but you've left me no choice. You have to take risks to get what you want and I want retribution. I take my mobile phone and dial.

'DS Percy.'

I take a deep breath.

'Oh, hi, Lorraine. That's OK, is it, Lorraine? I just wanted to ... Well, this is all a bit awkward.'

'Go on.'

I know the rules. Take the risk. Always pre-empt.

'Well, the thing is ... I've received some photos. Of me and ... and ... some men.'

There's silence as she processes it.

'OK. What sort of photographs?'

'They're the type of photographs that could be used to blackmail me. Sexual. And there's a message. Saying someone is watching me. I'm quite scared.'

It's not a lie. I am quite scared. But that's nothing new. And when I'm scared I spiral off at a tangent, but not this time. Not when DS Percy can be so useful to me.

'So do you know the person in the picture?'

'Yes. Yes. Well, I, er, I slept with him last night. And there was one from a couple of weeks ago. Look, I want to make an official complaint. This is harassment. I'd like to make a statement.'

She sighs. 'Of course you do. And your husband is complaining about some missing bag. The thing is, Caroline, this isn't the sort of thing we spend a lot of time on. I can give you a crime number and you can come and see me tomorrow. Just give me some details now and I'll give you a crime number.'

She's not biting. Damn.

'Well, I was at the Premier Inn on Halton Street last night with this man. And the other week I was at the Premier Inn on Walker Street.'

'With a different man?'

'Yes.'

There's a silence and the flip of pages. The tap of keys.

'Was this man last night called Peter Daubney?'

I flash back to the credit card in my hand. His introduction.

Peter. Daubney. Shit. Fuck. Fuck fuck fuck. He's reported the credit card. She's already linked it.

'Yes. Yes, it was. How …?'

I hear rustling and a chair scraping roughly.

'OK, look, are you at home? I'll come round. Stay where you are.'

She's gone and I sit at the table and wait for her, knowing that you'll be trying to get hold of her as well. You'll be trying to report me for faking a Facebook account. So I go outside and take a pay-as-you-go mobile out of the hole. Its battery and chip are tied to it by an elastic band, and I quickly set it up and log into Monica's Facebook. I set it up ready to post a comment under the picture. 'Sorry. I didn't mean to cause all this fuss. It was just a laugh.' And a smiley face, naturally. Then I slip it into the bottom of the grill pan that's resting on top of the cooker. This is working out well. I can use the police to set you up and after this they'll be absolutely sure it's not me posting because they'll be here when made-up Monica presses the button. God, this is tricky, but it'll be worth it when they don't believe anything you say.

The doorbell sounds. She's already here. So quickly. I flick on the kettle and let her in. She's got a younger plain-clothes officer with her.

'Hello, Dr Atkinson. This is DS Smith. So, can you tell me exactly what happened last night?'

DS Smith goes to stand by the back door, presumably to stop me making a run for it. But I'm staying right here.

'Oh. Caroline, please. It's a little bit embarrassing really. You see I … I … look. Can I make you a coffee?'

They look at each other and she raises her eyebrows at him. Then she nods.

'Yes, OK.'

I flick the kettle back on and it takes only a second to boil. Meanwhile, I'm putting coffee in cups, enquiring about sugar and secretly posting Monica's comment. They're so busy checking out the shit that I've piled everywhere that they don't notice me lift the grill pan slightly and push the send button.

'There. So, as I said, it's a little bit embarrassing. I was in the Premier Inn bar and I got talking to this man. Next thing I knew we were in his room. Having ... er ...'

'Intercourse?'

She looks mildly shocked.

'Yes. Yes. I was very drunk, I'm afraid.'

'Right. And what time did you leave?'

I pretend to think.

'About six o'clock. I ordered a taxi and came straight home. Then when I got to work these pictures had been left in the common room. So how did you know it was him?'

She looks puzzled. As if she was expecting to ask the questions.

'We had a report from him earlier today. So I have to ask you—'

Her phone rings. She looks at it and sighs, looking for somewhere more private to take the call. Not much space here, so she moves into the hallway. I smile at DS Smith but he doesn't smile back. He just stands staring at me, hands in front. I can hear her, though.

'Yes, Mr Atkinson. So you said. And when was the last activity?'

A pause. I hear her sigh. She's getting more and more pissed off with this by the minute. I wait for it. I know you, Jack.

'Well, that's impossible. Because I'm with Mrs Atkinson right now. In her home. I've been here for the past fifteen minutes so it's impossible.'

Another pause. I know you. You'll be one step ahead, wondering how I did it. You'll be Googling timed comments and wondering if I got someone to do it for me. She returns.

'Right. Someone's been posting pictures of your husband on Facebook without his permission and he wants to press charges. Invasion of privacy.'

I frown at her.

'Who is it?'

'Well, he thinks it's you. He thinks that you have his bag and you're doing it. But here I am. You don't have the bag and you're nowhere near Facebook.'

I nod.

'Oh dear. This is a proper mess. What's going on here?'

She doesn't know. I can tell by her face. But she persists.

'Look, I have to ask you. Do you know anything about some property taken from Peter Daubney?'

I shake my head.

'No. Of course not. What property? Shouldn't you be asking whoever took these photographs? I phoned you about these photographs and now you're accusing me?'

She and DS Smith exchange glances.

'Not exactly. Anyway, could I ask you to stay around? We might want to ask you more questions over the next few days.'

'Oh. I hope I'm not a suspect.'

She shakes her head. 'Not at the moment. We'll have to review the CCTV again, but not at the moment. Like I said, stay around.'

Chapter Eight

Of course I'm a fucking suspect. Even I suspect me. But until they have something on me, I'll carry on as normal. Or as normal as I can be.

They take my statement and leave with the photographs, which naturally I've photographed with my mobile phone beforehand.

The best thing that came out of this mess is that she swallowed the comment trick. Nice work, even if I say so myself. So what now? What, now the police won't take any notice of you? By the look on DS Percy's face she thought you were a little bit hysterical. Accusing your ex-wife of posting pictures of you on Facebook.

Of course, it does add up. The missing bag, delivered here. The pictures. The journal. You would have had to go through the embarrassing motions of explaining what was in the journal. Who knows? They could look back over the old casenotes and see that, in fact, I was telling the truth. What then?

But it doesn't quell the horrible feeling that my time is up. That I'm eventually going to be arrested for theft. Fraud, probably. I grab a bottle of very cheap wine from my cooking rack and sink down behind the front door. I open the wine and gulp it down. The lull washes over me, then the sharpness hits. I take another big swig and someone's banging on the door.

I sit stock still with my feet on a pile of unopened DVDs. Another hard knock. The footsteps around the side. Oh God. What if that's them? Come to arrest me for spending someone's cheating fucking husband's money? But it isn't.

'Caroline. Caroline, I know you're in there. Open the door.'

It's your mother. No doubt she's here to side with you like she did before. Telling me I've always been a bit unbalanced and why don't I keep my mouth shut, or you will leave.

'Caroline, open this door now. I need to talk to you.' Silence for a moment. 'I've got the children here.'

The children. That old chestnut. Most of me knows she hasn't got the children there. But it's positive reinforcement and I'm reaching for the switch that flicks on the CCTV screen across from the door. It's one of the only Amazon purchases that I've actually used. I search the screen for my children, but, of course, they're not there.

I take another, larger swig of the wine and she's banging again.

'Have it your way, then. But you're in big trouble, lady. Big trouble. Jack's going to press charges this time. Properly. Not the civil courts. No injunctions. You'll end up in prison.'

I tell her to fuck off under my breath. What does she know? Her cosy little chats with you will have, like always, opened up only one side of the story. Your side. No doubt Charlie and Laura have been brainwashed by how great their absent father is and how bad their crazy mother is.

They said it would only be for a few months. Till I got myself sorted out. It's been a year. A full year. As if to confirm it I glance at the calendar, which is, like everything else here, and my whole fucking life, stuck on that day a full year ago.

And she's enjoying it. She's always been a martyr and she's always sided with you; even when she knows you're wrong. Oedipus and all that Freudian theory has a lot to answer for. I wonder how she'll feel when she finds out you've been shagging my sister?

She knocks again and then I can hear her talking on her phone. I press my ear against the door but I can't hear what she's saying. It's getting fainter and then it disappears, leaving me in the free-falling void that everything I do is carefully designed to avoid. The children. Charlie and Laura. I could have faced everything else, but not that.

When your solicitor's threats didn't work, you began to work on them, didn't you? Insisting on taking them for half the week and spending the entire time auto-suggesting that I'm a piece of crap who's off her rocker. Laura told me Daddy asked her if Mummy talks to herself. You gave them both emergency phone numbers to call if they didn't feel safe.

You knew that you had no chance of getting legal custody of them, so you bided your time. Eventually, after several months, long enough to have built up evidence, you went to the family courts with a claim that I wasn't coping. I opposed it, naturally, citing that you were about to leave the country on a year-long contract. There was no big courtroom drama like you would imagine it to be. It wasn't even a custody hearing. The hearing was held round a table in chambers.

I was so stressed that I was crying and, despite my own counsel telling me to pull myself together, I couldn't. You had put me under unbearable pressure. Broken me down little by little. And all I could imagine was that I was going to lose. That you would weave a wider web of lies and catch my children in it. My solicitor had told me that you stood no chance as you were working abroad and had conceded the marital home, and the children would be awarded to the parent who was most reliable.

What I hadn't banked on was your mother. We've had an up-and-down relationship, with her classic 'you're not good enough for my son' attitude mixed with a 'you're my confidante' when she wanted something from me or needed to get to you through me. She had always assumed that when Charlie and Laura came along I would give up work and stay at home. Like she did. When that didn't happen, she subjected me to a tight-lipped tirade of underhand comments, all designed to dent any self-esteem I had left after you had done your worst.

Halfway through the hearing she was called to give evidence. I knew at that point that I had lost my children. You sat there, hair tousled and face affable, but long-suffering. She, at pains to show she was über-sympathetic, tore me to shreds. She told them that I'd always had a tendency to 'go into a world of my own'; asked if she thought I was dangerous, she'd theatrically looked at the table, her knuckles white, until she dramatically raised her head and nodded.

Everyone looked surprised as I let out a wail and sobbed heavily. I couldn't understand how they couldn't see through this. How they could even consider her evidence. How, as she sat down lightly, rearranging her designer dress, the judge was asking her if she would be providing residence for my children until 'Caroline's mental health improves'. She knew how much I love my children. How she could, without even looking at me, nod and smile and whisper: 'Of course. Anything to help.'

That was a year ago. What was actually granted was a joint care arrangement with me having them half the time when I was 'feeling better' – which actually meant after an assessment by social services. Naturally, I thought every day about just going to get them back, but how would I explain the state of the house? I'd told myself that next week I would hire a skip and sort it out, but I just ordered more and more stuff. There never seemed to be a right time to contact social services. The truth is that I was scared.

I saw them at first, but it was awkward. They both eyed me suspiciously and after three months of stilted silence sitting in your mother's lounge with her watching me like a hawk, I took them to McDonald's. I was checking my phone in the queue and I asked Charlie to grab the tray. He stood very still, looking at me. Those brown eyes. Your eyes, Jack. He was beautiful. Tears sprung up and I went to hold his hand, but he pulled it away. In a split second I saw that he was clutching a piece of paper tightly.

I admit that I grabbed his arm. I was probably shouting too. Something like: 'Give me that, Charlie. Give me that paper!'

It looked worse than what it was on the McDonald's CCTV. I'd prised his fingers from around the paper and opened it up. Straight away I recognised your handwriting.

If Mummy starts to act strangely call this number. If there is no phone, ask a nearby adult.

Charlie was crying, running away, and I chased him. Out onto the road, leaving six-year-old Laura crying in a fast-food restaurant. On the CCTV outside I could see myself crying and shouting after him as he ran as fast as he could. Afterwards, he said that I was shouting swearwords, but anyone could see from the CCTV that I was shouting, 'I love you, Charlie.' I love you.

It took the police two hours to find him. He was hiding behind a skip at the end of the road that led to your mother's house. Naturally, social services were involved and I attended on automatic pilot, because by then I knew it was a lost cause. You told them that Charlie said he had seen me drinking. That I had a bottle in my handbag and was pouring it into my McDonald's Coke.

The gap between Charlie and Laura and me was widening with a joint effort of nastiness from you and your mother. It was the last bastion of normality for me, a kind of metric that I would measure each day against. The children. I had to be OK for the children.

You knew that. I could see it in your eyes. At the final hearing, when you flew back from Argentina and turned up with your bent lawyer, even though it was an informal, civil matter, I knew that you knew that it was the final crack that shattered me. Everyone said how sorry they were that I couldn't be trusted to see my own children unsupervised, and they hoped that I would get help for my drinking.

The social worker didn't look entirely convinced, and I hung my hope on her until the very last second. The options were that either I could see Charlie and Laura supervised by social services or I shouldn't be allowed to see them until it had been decided they were ready and I had sought help.

My department head, Professor Linda Cox, had written a letter in my support and it was this that flashed a beacon of hope. My not seeing the children was discounted as I had three character references that told the truth about me. That I loved my kids and this blip was because things had been rough. That I would be helped and supported. That I was still doing my job well.

You didn't like that. Just when you thought you had destroyed me completely, someone was sticking up for me. And for your mother it had become a battle. A battle to make sure that her martyrdom reached new heights at any cost. I saw you exchange glances with her and my heart sank as I watched her shift into the familiar attack stance.

She leaned slightly forward, chin out, and set her mouth into a thin smile. To anyone else it would look for all the world like she was some kind of saint, taking on the burdens of the world with good humour. But I know her. She coughed to get attention, then began the onslaught.

'Well, I was just thinking, if it would help, I could supervise Caroline and the children. I mean, I don't want to interfere but it does seem practical as they will be staying with me for the time being ...'

I saw you brighten. You knew then that I would never see Charlie and Laura again. You knew that your mother would control the situation with a rod of steel. You'd be able to see them whenever you deemed it necessary to pop home from your round-the-world jolly, but I wouldn't be allowed. It wasn't legal custody, but you'd found a way to keep me out of your life completely. She would make every excuse possible to avoid me seeing them. It would all seem like she was very busy and it was a terrible coincidence that the only time she was free was when I was working. It would save you the job of having to look after them and of keeping them away from me. A double whammy.

Everyone was nodding their approval and suddenly chairs began to scrape and everyone left. Except me. I sat there in stunned silence. No doubt to the rest of the world it looked like the perfect arrangement – and one that would work in everyone's favour. But they didn't know these people. Not really. They hadn't lived my life and got to know the egos and the motivations.

Not that it mattered now. What mattered was that my children had been taken away from me and that I had to somehow find a way to get them back. Or carry on with my life without them. Or not. I admit that for a brief moment I considered ending it all, but then they would hurt more and it would prove that Daddy and Grandma were right and Mummy was very, very ill and dangerous.

It's hard to explain now, but sitting there in that room, completely alone in the world, missing my children and wanting to die, I somehow still had a spark in me. It was there, deep down, a knowledge that one day this would all come right. Even if it was when Charlie and Laura were adults and could decide for themselves. I had to be there. I had to survive. For them. I had to find a way to put this right. I had to fight for them. I had to.

Chapter Nine

I did survive. Just. For the first few weeks I didn't go to work. I didn't have a shower for weeks and I hardly ate. I was in breakdown mode, but I knew deep down that it couldn't go on. In the end it was a work colleague who pulled me from the mire of pain I had almost drowned in.

Fiona knocked on the door and when I didn't answer, she knocked again. She is one of those friends who you feel like you've known for ever and they stick by you through anything. She works in my department. She knocked and knocked. Then she shouted through the letterbox. Like now, I was sitting with my back against the door, willing her to go away. I wanted Charlie and Laura, not someone from work. Instead of going away, she waited and waited until I opened the door. Telling me I was needed at work. That there was a project starting and I was on the collaboration list. It couldn't start without me, apparently.

Even though I thought it was all bullshit specifically designed to get me to answer the door, it turned out that, in one area of life, I was valued after all. There was a project and they did need me. They'd been waiting for my sick note to run out and when it did and I still didn't come back they sent Fiona.

'So when *are* you coming back, Caroline?'

By this time she was sitting in my foul-smelling kitchen amongst a build-up of half-eaten takeaways, smoking a cigarette. I stared at her. Didn't she know what had happened? *Didn't she?*

'Of course, I know what's happened. It's awful. It is. But we want to support you. I'm your friend. I want to support you. Not feel sorry for you or patronise you. Honestly, Caroline, you've got to get out there. We need you.'

I hadn't spoken to anyone for weeks and I remember being surprised by the sound of my own voice.

'Give me another week.'

It was weak and small, but it was me. I was still there. Much as I had wished myself away, I was still there.

So I went back to work after a week. Fiona was my friend and she was there for me. I didn't see it at the time, but she ignored my disgusting house, my breakdown-vagueness and red eyes, and she sat with me as I drank coffee in the cafeteria. We didn't talk about it. It was round about that time that I realised that I'd never actually articulated what had fully happened to another person. It was all living inside me, festering into my soul until I felt like I was bursting.

I could have told Fiona anytime, she was there for me, but I was scared. Scared she wouldn't believe me. Scared she would think I had made it up. It had worked. Your plan had worked. I'd been treated badly and now I didn't even bother mentioning it because who would believe me? Fiona talked to me about her partner and her dog and her drug-addict brother and her work and generally anything but me. I said hardly anything. But sometimes no words are needed.

I was thinner and I actually looked better than I had for ages. I smiled my way through the back-to-work interview and assured everyone that I was OK, I had just needed a rest and, yes, of course

I was fighting to get my children back. Yes, it had all been a big mistake. Yes, Jack's mother was looking after them. Yes, the best possible scenario.

I nodded and agreed and realised that I would have to hold it down at work. I would have to keep this make-believe world where life went on separate from my catastrophic personal life. Luckily for me, I loved my job. I loved research and I loved the money it gave me to use as a buffer against the world.

It looked like things had improved, but they really, really hadn't. Almost immediately I stopped going into Charlie and Laura's rooms; I haven't been in either room since. It was as if going in would break all the good work I was doing; making myself strong for when the day came that I was able to pick up the phone and ask your mother if I could see them.

I'd need all my strength because I knew she'd refuse and I'd have to repeat it, make a record of it, save it all up for my solicitor. Take it back to the social worker. Hadn't I carried on working? Hadn't I had supervision and counselling? Hadn't I kept my side of the bargain and tried to see them, but hadn't she obstructed me? I had it all planned.

Eventually I did phone. I was breezy and bright on the surface but anxiety was seething inside me as I heard the ringtone.

'Melissa Atkinson.'

I listened to the background for them. For Laura's sweet voice. Charlie's laugh.

'Melissa, it's Caroline. I was wondering if I could pick the children up on Saturday?'

Be nice, Caroline. Play her game. Silence. Then she was chirpy.

'Yes, of course. I'll bring them to you. Shall we say ten o'clock?'

I couldn't believe it. I choked up.

'Oh, thank you, Melissa. Ten is just fine.'

I was already baking scones in my head. Little sandwiches and the lime jelly that Laura loves.

'I'll see you then.'

She was gone and I started to prepare. I cleaned and baked and hid the boxes – there weren't so many of them back then – and it felt like a new beginning.

At ten o'clock on Saturday, I stood at the window at the top of the stairs and waited for her car. She arrived exactly on time, but without the children. She glided to the front door and knocked, checking her phone as she did so. I raced downstairs and opened it.

'Where are they?'

She walked past me and stood at the kitchen table, looking at the food I had made.

'You really are stupid, aren't you?'

My pulse was banging in my ears and I nearly went for her. But I knew somehow that that was what she wanted – more reasons.

'I have a right to see them. Jack wasn't awarded custody. And neither were you.'

'No. No, I wasn't. But you're a mess. Not fit to look after them.'

I moved closer to her.

'I am fit to look after them. But you're right. I am a mess. Your son has done this. And you've turned a blind fucking eye.'

She flinched. But then she turned suddenly and grabbed my arm.

'You come anywhere near me and I'll make sure you are charged with harassment. Come anywhere near those children and I'll have you arrested for assaulting me. You can't win this, Caroline, so leave it.'

I faced it out.

'I'll never leave it. I'll never leave my children.'

She let me go heavily and I fell backward against the table.

'Well, it's stalemate, then. But the problem is you're already disadvantaged. Let's see what else you have. Let's see it, Caroline.'

She left and slammed the door.

But I still haven't been in those rooms a year later. Because I thought I had the strength, but when I phoned her again she wouldn't speak to me. I hadn't included that in my plan. I almost kept ringing over and over again but realised just in time that it was what she wanted. Harassment. Anything she could bring to discredit me. If she wouldn't speak to me, we couldn't make an arrangement so I couldn't say she had broken it.

Naturally, I called social services and asked them to intervene but they just said that they thought we could 'sort it out' amongst ourselves and made appointments that were constantly cancelled because Melissa and Jack couldn't make it.

So on and on it went until I no longer picked up the phone. I planned more and drank more and soon I had a plan but was too pissed to carry it out. I've just been reeling from being so drunk that I've only a vague recollection of what I've done to produce a brilliant piece of work for my department.

I'd love to say that I'm a high-functioning alcoholic, but I'm not. It's much more complex. When Christmas came I was here alone and I'd been sober for weeks. Then, the day before Christmas Eve, I realised what was going to happen. How I would be trapped here, in my own home, with my memories.

I opened a bottle of prosecco that someone at work had given me as a present and the next thing I remember was Boxing Day. I was lying on the kitchen floor. The long kitchen table was cleared of boxes and laid with three full Christmas dinners, with all the trimmings. Cold and congealed. My head hurt and I spotted several booze bottles in the sink. There was more food laid out on the kitchen sides. I'd cooked enough for about eight people.

Then it struck me. Where had the food come from? I had no food in before Christmas. Therefore, I must have been out. I rushed through the box towers to the front window and my car was parked askew in the road. I knew in the back of my mind what had made me do it. Christmas without my children. No escape except the in-between. But I also knew that, equally, I couldn't stop it.

There are periods, though, when I'm so completely engrossed in my job that I don't drink and don't order things online. That I don't go to Premier Inn and pick up strange men. During that time I don't crave alcohol. It's when I'm in my own home – our home – and I'm suddenly confronted by a closed bedroom door or a sock behind a radiator. By my own children and the unfairness of what happened.

Which brings me to now again. I hear next door's dog barking. It never fucking shuts up, like some kind of frantic burglar alarm that goes off when someone even tiptoes anywhere near it, regular as clockwork. Your mother's round the back of my house, peering through my kitchen window. I duck out of sight behind a pile of shoeboxes. She stays there for a while, then she gets her phone out and takes a picture of the kitchen. Then she disappears and I hear her footsteps click-click-clicking up the path. They stop on the front step again and there's an almost indiscernible thud as she leans against the front door.

The dog's stopped barking now. She opens the letter box again and I duck.

'It's pointless, Caroline. If you're in there, you need to listen. And listen good. You're not a fit mother. You never were. So if all this is about thinking you can win, forget it. Forget. It.'

She clicks off and I hear a car door slam. The engine takes two attempts to start. I take another swig of the cheap wine and feel her words drill into me, shattering any hope that was developing. I look into the lounge and see the ghosts of my family life – you sitting at the kitchen table playing snakes and ladders with Charlie and Laura. Me cooking and laughing and telling everyone that dinner will be ready in a minute.

The kids running upstairs to wash their hands, and your hands on my waist, your lips on my neck. I'm slipping back into my deep grief, down into a chasm where it was just you and me between the sheets, back to moonlit nights in foreign countries before the kids, where we talked and kissed and promised our lives to each other.

I gulp down the bottle of wine and stagger upstairs. I change into a tight black dress and heels, underpinned by tarty underwear. I don't bother with tights, but I smother myself in cheap perfume and draw on make-up until I hardly recognise my own, admittedly blurry, face in the mirror.

I'm not too pissed to know that staying in will lead to me falling over the precipice of my own grief, but I am too pissed to consider anything except another night in a Premier Inn with a random stranger. Peter Daubney's stolen credit card doesn't seem so threatening now – surely if they thought it was me I would have been arrested?

Full of bravado I call a cab and, when it arrives, I stumble in. The driver looks at me in his rear-view mirror.

'Where to, love?'

I think. Maybe the Chadderton Premier Inn. Why not make it a hat-trick? I begin to laugh and the driver starts his engine.

'Chaddy Premier Inn, Please.' He nods and smiles and I feel I have to qualify myself. 'Meeting my sister.'

'Whatever you say, love.'

He flicks on the meter and drives off the estate. I suddenly see the glass house in the park.

'Stop. Here. Stop here. This will do, thanks.'

He pulls up at the kerb.

'Are you sure, love? Look, I can take you home. It's remote and—'

'I'm fine. Here's fine.'

I am fine. I suddenly feel sober. I need to stay away from the Premier Inn. But I need to be out of my house. The in-between will have to wait.

So I take off my shoes and pad barefoot through the grass in the fading light. The park gates are still open but the glass house is locked. I hurry around the back and find that the back door is also locked. There's a key in the door inside so I take off my jacket and wrap it around my fist. I smash the window and wait for the alarm to sound, but it doesn't and I grab the key and unlock the door.

Once inside I retrieve the laptop. I sit down breathless and check my phone. No calls yet, but I catch a glimpse of my slutty self in the phone reflection and begin to laugh. Not at the situation, because that's still tragic, but at the fact that this is the first time I've managed to break the cycle. The first time I've actually thought that I was getting somewhere.

The Metrolink is just at the other side of the park and I carry the laptop around to the stop. My fingers are itching to log on to made-up Monica's profile and I almost feel upbeat. The tram rumbles in and it's virtually deserted. I quickly buy an all-day ticket and find a seat right at the back.

I momentarily wonder if the account has been removed. But I haven't done anything wrong, have I? Although you were clearly having sex with Christine, the picture was hardly pornographic. I've seen much worse on Facebook. I click into Monica's account and see she has fourteen messages. I vaguely wonder if the police can see I've logged in, or if they will even be bothered. Someone is robbing cheating fucking husbands in local hotels, so a Facebook post is hardly going to be part of their to-do list, is it?

So you've messaged Monica. I knew you would. All official and Jack-like, of course.

> Please remove the pictures of me you have posted or you will
> face legal action.

So you're having doubts, are you? Getting a bit confused? Wondering if it really is me doing this? It's horrible when you don't trust your own instincts, isn't it? When you feel sure you know the truth but everyone else tells you that you are wrong. If you thought Monica was definitely me you would have private messaged me. By name. I know you, Jack.

Chapter Ten

My head's banging now and I jump off the tram in the city centre and go into Costa Coffee. I buy a bottle of water and a large cappuccino and find a seat.

I log onto the Costa free Wi-Fi as Jane Smith with a 123@gmail.com email address. I read through Monica's messages, which are mainly from mutual friends who think they went to school with me and made-up Monica. Keely Jacobs asks if Monica is Caroline's friend and if they're doing this together. Paul Barrett wonders if Monica was there that night Jack slept with his sister as he's never been able to get him to admit it and he needs a witness. Some very anti-Jack sentiments are being expressed here. Anyone would think you were a serial liar.

I grab the USB from my bag and connect it to the laptop, scrolling through the pictures. I stop at Julie Carson. Something about her has been bugging me since I saw the diary. She always got on my nerves, in any case. One of your work colleagues, so neat and pristine.

Julie had cropped blonde hair even then. She was compact in every way and always wore indigo jeans and bright white blouses. She had natural class and married the head architect at Johnson Weaver, Francis Carson. But you had to have her. I remember the Christmas party when I was wearing a deep-cut scarlet ball gown and every man in the room had eyes for me.

Except you. While they gazed at me, a curvy, come-hither blonde with a hint of Marilyn Monroe, your eyes followed Julie around the dancefloor. I swear I even saw you lick your lips as she passed within feet. And she knew. I could always tell when they knew. It was a self-satisfied smirk and lowering of the eyes around you.

She was focused on her husband, which made you sit up and beg even more. What was this? A woman who didn't yield to Jack Atkinson's charm? Of course, back then I just ignored it; I thought Julie was happy with Francis and that she wouldn't respond to the side glances and the casual touches at the bar.

In fact, I hadn't realised that she was one of your conquests until I saw the journal. Until I saw the pictures of you together in Paris. They were fixed into the journal with Sellotape and I only realised when I was removing them to scan them that some had more pictures taped below. I look at them now, a series of scenes around the Louvre and various cafés, you and Julie kissing – you really got the hang of selfies way before they were invented. Photos of you both at Giverny, gazing at Monet's garden. Then some blurry shots I can't make out until I look closely and see that they are of the top of a cropped blonde head and your brown brogues are in the background either side.

I feel sick. My stomach turns as I realise what I'm looking at. It takes several photographs to understand the full picture, but it's pretty clear. It's made all the more difficult because our sexual repertoire narrowed after we married. Before we walked up the aisle we tried everything at least once, but after the honeymoon you tailored our sex life to suit yourself. I'd often plan a sexual adventure, something new, fantasise all day about it, buy new underwear and try it on with you, only to be rebuffed and coerced into the 'usual routine'.

I blamed it on you being tired, but now I know you were fucking tired. Very tired. Worn out, in fact, from fucking your girlfriends and engaging in what now appears to be oral sex in public places. I can feel my temper rising again and before I know it I've got Julie's Facebook profile up in front of me.

I can hardly see through the mist of tears, but there she is, her and Francis and two little white dogs, as neatly coiffured as she is. Smiling, ever smiling, that perfect mouth that's been around my husband's cock.

Monica isn't friends with Julie so this is going to be more difficult to rationalise. But you're still friends with her. I can see from your profile that she's wished you a happy birthday and that there's a winking smiley. Of course there is. Monica isn't friends with you now either. Not to worry, though. Plenty of Monica's friends are friends with you, so hopefully they'll see the blurry-at-first picture of Julie's head posted on Monica's timeline. Then, when they realise what it is, they'll alert you, won't they? Well, the ones who know you are a cheating bastard will, anyway.

That horrible feeling that everyone knew except me creeps over me. It seems impossible that all your friends were oblivious to your behaviour. Some of them *must* have known but just didn't want to get involved. But they will on Facebook. Just to be sure, Monica has also shared the picture with Julie in a private message.

The impact is almost immediate. The photo is shared five times and I receive a message from Julie.

I know this is you, Caroline. I'm calling the police. Jack's right.
You're completely crazy.

I close the laptop and finish my coffee. Then I hop back onto a tram and travel around the Metrolink for the rest of the evening, watching the carnage as all your friends realise what the picture is and share it far and wide. I think some people are really enjoying this. Some fickle friends who were never sure if you were fucking their wives and girlfriends or not.

I can sense a tone of retribution in some of the comments, as if people have been waiting for you to be found out. I did know somewhere deep inside that not everyone could have the same low morals as you. That some people wouldn't approve. The sad thing is, though, that they'd feel it was none of their business and keep quiet. But Facebook has a habit of bringing out the worst in people, and from behind a keyboard, where you can't overpower with your strong reasoned, almost threatening arguments, it will be easier to join in the finger-pointing and sharing.

I am a little bit worried about Julie calling the police, if I'm honest. I wonder if it's struck her that she's going to have to admit to giving a married man a blow job while he photographs her, in public, while she's on a secret trip that her husband doesn't know about. I know you, Jack; you'll be telling people that it isn't you in the picture. That it could be anyone. That everyone's just jumped to conclusions because of the Christine pictures.

But right now you will know that it's definitely me who has the journal and that I'm Monica. You know it's you in the pictures and you'll go to any lengths to convince people it isn't. The fact that my phone isn't ringing out with DS Percy's number tells me that Julie hasn't made a complaint. I wait and wait and eventually she posts a comment on the picture that has been shared on her friend's timeline that this isn't her and Jack Atkinson like everyone's saying and that she's going to sue anyone who suggests it is.

Which is almost laugh-out-loud funny because no one has actually mentioned your name and you're not in the picture, just as she isn't. It could be anyone, but Julie has just filled in the schema gaps for everyone and completed the puzzle.

You'll be complaining right now, though, arguing that both those pictures are from your missing journal – and DS Percy, who is, as far as I could see from my comments about my Premier Inn activity, fairly strait-laced, will be wondering what exactly is in this journal – and blaming me. Who keeps a journal full of sexual mementoes of their infidelity? What kind of person does that?

It won't just be DS Percy wondering what kind of person you are. If you're shouting loudly that these pictures that are oh-so obviously of you aren't, your Facebook friends who, let's face it, are more hangers-on who are interested in the dramas of our divorce which you were very public about on social media – poor misunderstood Jack, boo-hoo – will be wondering why there are so many pictures of Jack Atkinson having sex in circulation. After all, someone would have had to take them and you're the common denominator in all of them.

I look at your profile now and all this has certainly boosted your number of friends: more than a hundred new friends since this morning. Naturally, you'll think that they are all sympathisers, swelling behind the Caroline-hating ranks like before, all ready to defend you.

But I know that they're ghoulish voyeurs, hooked on the drama already. They love it. Tonight they'll be huddled around the laptop, watching you and Christine and Julie wriggle and squirm your way out of this. Or not. Fair-weather friends, waiting to pounce when you show a weakness.

The same people have sent me friend requests. It's been hard for me, not least because these are some of our mutual friends who dropped me like a brick when it looked like I was crazy. There were a few who believed me, stood by me, but a year later and a houseful of crap means that they don't call round too often. You can only tell your story of heartbreak so many times before their eyes glass over and they check their Facebook. Which is good for me now as they'll all be watching this. I haven't accepted a single friend request. It will just look like I'm not looking at Facebook and I'm not engaged with this at all.

I log on to Twitter and make a profile for made-up Monica and connect it to her Facebook account. *Kill two birds with one stone.* I post a series of tweets and pictures and within minutes someone has made a #teamCaro hashtag, which is slightly worrying as it connects me, but, on the other hand, it's just support. I didn't post it. Good. Someone comes back with a #teamJack, some guy defending you with a pointless argument about open marriages that only fuels the fire. Even better.

So, Jack, who has the edge now? I look at my watch. It's miraculous. A personal breakthrough. I've managed to survive what started out as a desperate evening without sinking into the in-between. Admittedly, I bottomed a bottle of wine but I managed to pull myself out of the mire and I've done something productive. Unfortunately, my good feeling about tonight is spoiled when I pass a Premier Inn and remember that I'm a suspect in a robbery case and someone has pissed-up pictures of me.

Time to go home. No doubt tomorrow I'll have to face the music. I glance at the laptop screen and see that the pictures have been shared more and more widely. Comments are appearing and there doesn't seem to be any doubt that it was you in the picture with Julie. Francis doesn't appear to have a Facebook account so perhaps she's got away with it, but just imagine the stress she will go through, wondering if someone has shown him.

Just in case they haven't, I make a Hotmail account in Monica's name and check the Johnson Weaver website. Francis still works there and I click on his email address. I attach the most obvious picture and a message telling him to look on his wife's Facebook account and press send. That should cover everything. Like Christine's husband, he has the right to know about his wife's fucking around.

I can see a pattern forming. The human brain likes patterns and thrives on making order out of chaos. Kind of arranging similar things into groups. Like cheating husbands and unfaithful wives. Before long people will really start to realise just what a liar you were, and still are.

Chapter Eleven

Someone's banging on the front door and I open one eye and see it's light. My phone tells me it's three minutes to eight, so I've overslept. When I pull back the curtain I see DS Percy talking to the delivery man who is trying to leave a large box in my garden.

I pull my dressing gown on and hurry to the front door.

'It's OK. I'm here. Bring it in.'

I realise I'm shaking. This is it. She's going to arrest me. I stand back and the delivery man pushes the box into the already overcrowded lounge. He stands with his hands on his hips.

'You can get your money back on stuff, you know, love. You don't have to keep them. You just ask for a return label and I come and ...' I stare at him and he stares past me into the kitchen, where the towers of crap provide their own landscape. I know he wants to help but, right now, it's not helping at all. He shakes his head, turns and walks away. 'Or you could give them to charity.'

I could. But I'm not going to. Not at the moment, anyway. Not until I'm in a position to get my kids back. I feel a little bit of bile rise as DS Percy and two colleagues walk up the path. I try to breathe deeply and feel a little calmer when I remember that I stored Monica's laptop in a carrier bag in the hole last night before I went to bed. Just thinking about it makes me want to check the carnage caused by posting Julie's blow-job, but I can't.

DC Percy approaches me. I can't see any handcuffs or anything. I resist the urge to step backwards and cower amongst the boxes.

'Morning, Caroline. I wonder if you could come to the station with us to help us with our inquiries?'

I fold my arms and unfold them. I don't want to look defensive.

'Am I under arrest?'

She looks around and pauses. Then she moves closer to me.

'Look, I know you have a number of problems.' She gazes past me into the house. 'And I understand where you are coming from regarding your ex-husband's accusations, which we need to look into further. But my priority now is to find out what happened at the Premier Inn. And the other man two weeks ago. And if they're linked.'

I just nod. Did I tell her I'd slept with him as well? I can't remember. Her mobile starts to ring and I see her glance at the screen. She's so close that I can see your name flashing. Jack Atkinson. She cancels the call and continues in a very controlled voice.

'We'll need to take a statement and it's best that you tell us everything you know.'

I get dressed and we travel to the police station. I'm left in an interview room. I call the university and tell Eileen that I have to deal with the accusations Jack made. She makes all the right noises and tells me to take as much time as I need.

Then I check my Facebook profile on my phone. I read the messages and all but the one from Julie say things like, 'God, Caroline, we didn't know Jack was such a bastard,' or, 'Did you know about this before, Caroline?' One person has even come out and said it. 'So it was all lies then, about you being a fruitcake? He really is a philandering prick? So sorry, Caroline.'

I can't help smiling and congratulating myself; but it's still only been acknowledged privately, and this needs to go public. The other thing I suddenly realise, sitting here in the police station with them looking 'into it further', as DC Percy told me, is that whereas the first picture could reasonably have been anyone who knows you and Christine posting the photos for some kind of sick joke, the second set means that Monica has the journal. She must have if she has photos of the multiple exes that are recorded there. If Jack has actually told DS Percy that he kept a journal of his sexual conquests, both he and the police will know Monica has it.

Part of me tells me that it's over. On Facebook, anyway. That I'm going to have to find another way of making you and them pay, something not so public. All your Facebook friends will be focused on made-up Monica now and it will gradually sink in that this is the tip of your cheating fucking iceberg. Meanwhile, I'm making it more personal. Much more personal. I want you to suffer the way I have, the way I still suffer, because me sitting here in a police interview room is an extension of everything you did to me. But it isn't over. If you hadn't treated me like shit then I wouldn't have had to do all this, would I? Oh yes, you'll suffer, all right, not just through some private Facebook messages and some pictures of you and your not even perfect-ten girlfriends, but really suffer like I have. All I have to do is to think of how I can do this even more publicly.

DS Percy comes back with a woman who introduces herself as Linda Jones. She turns the recorder on and identifies me and them.

'OK, Caroline. Here's the situation. The men in the photograph that you've been sent have all reported stolen items: credit cards, money, watches. So we want to talk to you about a substantial amount of property being stolen from the men you met at the Premier Inns.' Fucking hell. I've only taken credit cards. Haven't I? I try to visualise my in-between self but none of it is clear. I need to check what's in that hole. But at least it isn't about your holdall. 'Linda is our tech person and she's going to show you some CCTV.'

I feel my heart beat faster and my face redden. It's going to be me with the first guy two weeks ago. I just know it. The screen opposite flickers to life and I watch as CCTV footage begins. A picture of me and the first guy appears. I'm wearing a tight red dress and high black heels and, actually, I don't look as bad as I thought I had made myself look. The footage moves to another frame of us kissing around the back of the hotel, his hands everywhere.

Then we are inside the hotel, drunkenly stumbling up the corridors until we reach his room. I see myself, head thrown back in laughter, grabbing at his crotch. The time in the corner of the screen reads 2.30 when we go in, and I come out alone at 5.30. I carry my shoes up the corridor and leave.

The screen flickers off, then on again to the next set of footage. Different hotel, same routine. This time pissed-up dancing, then snogging, then to the room around at 2.40 and I come out alone at 5.36. The frame changes to me getting in the lift, then to the street outside and me flagging a taxi at 5.42.

Linda switches it off with a remote control and DS Percy turns to me.

'So. Let's go over things again. Why didn't you mention that you know Brian Patterson? The man in the other picture?'

I force the words out.

'I thought it would look bad. I mean, it already looks bad that I go around picking up strange men and sleeping with them. But I didn't do anything illegal.'

They both nod. DS Percy continues.

'So you knew neither of these men beforehand? This is very important, Caroline, so think.'

'No. I didn't. I just wanted a good time. Being on my own, and all that. Just ... lonely.'

'Right. Did you take anything from either of these men? Or any other men that you ... slept with?'

Fucking hell. Fuck. Fuck. Fuck. *Think, Caroline.*

'No. I didn't. I had sex with them. They didn't pay me. I'm not a—'

DS Percy holds up her hand.

'No. Of course not. For the purposes of the recorder I am not suggesting that Mrs Atkinson is a prostitute. It's just that Mr Patterson's bank card was stolen the same day and used for fraudulent transactions. You must understand that I have to ask you if you took it.'

'No I didn't.' It slips out automatically and I know as I say it I should have said that I did. But how would that look? Like I'm some kind of criminal, that's what. Not like I'm teaching them a lesson. Anyway, he'd be insured, wouldn't he? 'Look, it's bad enough having to air my private business like who I sleep with in public without—'

She holds her hand up again, and it's becoming a little bit irritating. But the screen lights up again. It's the corridor outside one of the Premier Inn rooms. The door opens and I come out at 5.36.

This time the camera stays on the corridor in fast forward. At 6.26 Peter Daubney opens the hotel-room door and walks towards the camera. I see his black wiry neck hair and I can almost smell his body odour. He puts a plastic cup under the ice machine and takes the ice back to his room.

My whole body cringes. I swear to myself that I'll never drink so much fucking vodka that I can't see ever again. I'll stay away from Premier Inns and hopefully, after I've proved you are a complete bastard publicly, I won't ever need to seek revenge.

The film flickers on, now in fast forward again. I watch as a couple of people leave their rooms and pull their cases up the corridor. Kagoule-clad tourists or football fans setting out on a new day.

At 7.10 the entry door to the corridor opens and a figure clad all in black hurries towards room 416, pulling a cap further over their face as they get nearer to the camera. I watch transfixed as someone enters the room. The woman in the opposite room leaves, then, at 7.25, the door opens again and the black-clad figure walks up the corridor. Change frames to the lift area, where they stand with their back to the camera. Then to the exit, where they walk through, again with their head turned away from the camera. They walk away to the right and are picked up on Oldham Street, walking along, head down.

The screen darkens and I'm dumbstruck. DS Percy turns to me.

'So, Caroline, you're not in any trouble. But the same footage was found at the previous scene of crime. And a few others. With what appears to be the same person committing the crime. As this is connected in some way to you, we need to ask you if you know who that person is. Do you recognise the person who went into Peter Daubney's hotel room and came out again fifteen minutes later?'

I still can't speak. The relief at not being blamed for this has washed over me and is now replaced by shock.

The ever-confident swagger, bordering on the Manchester monkey walk, could be anyone. The person who's been following me around taking pictures could be fucking anyone. But I know you, Jack, and I know that you are at the bottom of this.

Chapter Twelve

'So do you recognise him?'

I stutter my answer.

'D-d-do I recognise him? Well, I er ...'

I need time to think. Think what this means. I need to stall. DS Percy forges on.

'Yes. That person. Do you recognise him? Look, I know it's a shock seeing it like that, someone who has been stalking you, but I need to know if you saw anyone like that as you left the hotel? Or the evening before?'

I stare at her. She really has no idea. She hasn't put it together. But why would she?

'N-n-o. No, I don't. It could be anyone, really. A man, obviously. I think so, anyway. It's so difficult to see properly ...' I shrug. 'It's awful. My God. I feel a bit ill now, I'm afraid.'

DS Percy nods and tilts her head to one side. Sympathy. Good.

'Right. I'm afraid we still have to take a statement. Do you want to go and get a drink and come back, or we could do it tomorrow?'

'Oh no. I'll do it now. I want to help out as much as possible. Find out who this person is and ...and ... well. But I'll grab a coffee, if you don't mind?'

She gathers her things together.

'Great. I'll show you where the machine is. And then we'll meet back in reception in half an hour.'

We walk silently to the drinks machine and I get a black coffee. I need to be awake. I need to think about this in a calm way.

I thought you were out of the country. But these photos go back a while. I thought you only got back the other day. Schoolgirl error. Assumption based on the luggage arriving. The woman at the courier company had read out the address the luggage should have gone to: 23 Villa Place. Some posh apartments within a converted stately home up in Saddleworth.

I Google the number for United Utilities and dial. The tone rings for ages and I sip my coffee slowly, seething that I took my eye off the ball. Eventually, after a long interaction with an automated menu, the operator answers.

'United Utilities customer services. How can I help today?'

'Hello. This is Mrs Atkinson from twenty-three Villa Place. OL6 2BP. I haven't received notice of my direct debit payment since I moved in. Can you tell me how much it is and how long the first instalment covers?'

She pauses.

'I'll just have to take you through some security, Mrs Atkinson. Can I have the first line of your address and postcode, please?'

I repeat the information.

'And your date of birth?'

I tell her, but she sighs.

'That's not what we have on the account.'

I quickly interrupt.

'Oh, I think you'll have my husband's, Jack Atkinson. I can give you that or ...'

'No. That will be fine.'

I read out your date of birth and she seems appeased.

'Thank you. OK, I'll just look at the file. Actually, your first payment has gone out. It was £17.05 to cover the first three weeks of the month, from when you opened the account on the tenth. And this month's is due out next week for a full month. £23.17.'

I fake laugh.

'Oh, yes, I can see it now. £17.05. I was looking for £23.17 for a full month. So sorry to bother you.'

'No problem, Mrs Atkinson. Have a nice day.'

Oh, I will have a nice day. I will now I know how long you've been sneaking around. Six weeks. You've been back six weeks. Your luggage must have been lost all that time.

It doesn't make sense. You must have been following me. Watching me, like the note said. Or getting someone else to do it. I cringe to think that you saw me with those men. Knew what I was doing. My habits. My foibles. I can imagine the fucking satisfaction you would have got out of it.

I can even understand why you did it. To make me look bad. Like a slut. What completely puzzles me is how you thought you'd get away with it? You're not stupid. You know hotels have CCTV. Whoever did it disguised themselves but if they ever got caught, even if the police didn't work out the obvious, they'd tell on you? I don't get it.

I suppose it could be one of two things. The first one is that you are stupid enough to actually think there would be no cameras and no one would see. The other one is that you knew I would realise it was you behind it and you actually want me to say it's you. That would be a very similar situation to what had already happened, to me accusing you of all the affairs and of colluding with your mother. Is that what you wanted, for me to make myself look mad again?

But you didn't know I had the means to expose you then, did you? You didn't know I had the journal. A wave of fear washes over me. If you'd do this just to get your own way, what else are you capable of? I know you'd never risk doing anything directly to me as you'd be the first suspect. The accusation I'd made against you would resurface and come true. In any case, that injunction you took out against me works both ways, doesn't it, so you can't come anywhere near me.

DS Percy's back now, walking towards me. She gets herself a coffee out of the machine and hurries over.

'OK, let's get this over with. By the way, your ex-husband is still insisting that you have his bag. And that you're posting pictures online. It looks like we're going to have to come and have an official look.'

She looks apologetic and pissed off at the same time.

'Like I said before, anytime.'

We go back into the interview room and Linda Jones joins us. I go through everything again with DS Percy, letting her take the lead. But all the time I'm wondering how you knew what I was doing, where this person was watching me from. I pause for a moment.

'Did you want me to have a look at earlier? I mean, I might remember something ...'

They look at each other.

'Well, if you're sure.'

'I was a bit drunk but I might be able to ...'

Linda is already running the footage backwards. It starts to play as I come into the Premier Inn, and we watch as I order a drink and fix my gaze on Peter. I'm mesmerised by seeing in-between me, cheap and common but surprisingly steady after almost a bottle of wine and a half-bottle of vodka. But I'm searching the background for the someone common who I even vaguely remember. Each table. The windows. The people at the bar.

I watch a little longer but there are only people doing the same as me: haunting Premier Inn bars for company. DS Percy looks on hopefully. Eventually I shake my head.

'No. Nothing. I'm sorry.'

She sighs. I can see that she's been pinning all her hopes on this. She pulls her chair right up to me.

'Look, Caroline, I'll be honest, we have nowhere to go with this. Is there anyone at all who has a grudge? Anyone who would do this? It's obviously something to do with you, but I just can't work out what.'

The elephant in the room is you, Jack. But you want me to say it. You want me to accuse you.

'No. I just go to work and come home and occasionally—'

She holds up her hand again. She really doesn't like what I've been up to.

'We've been through the obvious. People involved in your divorce. We've given your ex a knock and he has a solid alibi for both times and dates.' Of course you have. 'So we're out of options and that could be anyone.'

I look her in the eye.

'Yes. It could be anyone. It's someone very clever, for sure. I feel a little bit scared, actually. To think this has something to do with me ... that someone's watching me.'

She puts her hand on my arm.

'Don't worry. We're going to get to the bottom of this. It might not even be about you. But you do seem to be the link. And it does seem to be the same person. There have been so many reports and so much taken that we have no choice but to investigate it. And now, with this new development. Look, I can't offer you specific protection, not at this point, but here's my direct number. If anything happens, just ring it.'

Linda runs the footage again and zooms in on the man's face, covered by a pull-down hat. The black cargo pants and T-shirt make him look like a teenager but he could be older. Who is he? Did you send him? We carry on with the interview and when she's finished I sign the document.

'Do I get a copy?'

She smiles. 'Yes. Of course.'

'Only, I think I'm going to have to get a solicitor. All this and then all the stuff with Jack, it's just too much for me.'

They both look sad. Then DS Percy speaks up.

'You know, you could do something about your ex. All this accusing you of things, when it clearly isn't you is, well, harassment.'

I stare at her. She's completely bought it. She's completely on my side now.

'I'll have to think about it. I don't want any fuss. After everything that happened before, I have my job to think about. And the children ...'

I've gone too far. I've said it before I think about it and just the mention of Charlie and Laura brings all the emotion to the surface. I start to sob, big heavy sobs. My nose is running and I'm a slobbering mess in seconds. DS Percy hurries out and comes back in with some tissues.

'It's OK. You have had rather a lot to deal with. Is there anyone we can get?'

I shake my head and pull myself together, blowing my nose loudly.

'No. There is no one.'

DS Percy waits until I've properly dried my eyes.

'So. Well, I know it's not a good time, but we need to come round and check out your place once and for all.' I almost laugh. I've always wanted to say, 'Have you got a warrant?' But it isn't the time or the place. She continues. 'So I'll need to have a look through your computer and bring it here for analysis. We might get your ISP records, if it's OK with you? And a search of the property ...'

ISP. They're going to contact my internet service provider. They're practically building a case to prove my innocence. I wave mid-air to hide the delight I'm feeling at this development.

'Of course. You can do it now, if you want. If you give me a lift home we can all go together.'

She smiles. This is brilliant. She gets her proof to present to you – how annoying is that, Jack? – and I get everything recorded. Perfect.

Chapter Thirteen

We're in the car on the way to my house and DS Percy is in the front, the young PC who's driving us is eyeballing me in the mirror. I'm not worried because they won't find anything. The hole has a thick layer of soil above it and the fire pit was actually designed to be submerged. They'll never find it.

I watch as the city turns to town and the town turns to leafy suburbs, a mixture of terraces and semi-detached like mine. I'm at the better end of town. After all, two generous post-graduate salaries could afford a lot of house round here.

I haven't processed what you've done yet. It hasn't sunk in properly. I haven't had a chance to fully analyse it, and why you did it. It suddenly strikes me that you must have been sneaking around, watching me through someone else's camera lens. For one horrible second I think you've seen the hole, seen me putting things into it and taking things out. Then I remember the fucking dog next door. I would have heard it. Also, the game would be up. You'd have told the police where I had hidden the journal and your bag and I'd be in court by now.

You don't know about the hole. But you know me, and you know that I'll never give up until I succeed. If you did know about the hole, I wouldn't be sitting here in this car now. The rest of it, well, I can think about that later on because here we are. Home.

DS Percy gets out of the car. A police van has followed us and everyone gets out and stands on my drive while I find my keys. I can see the neighbours' curtains twitching, but I don't care because this is exactly what I need to happen. To be seen to be innocent. I turn the key in the lock and DS Percy is behind me. I turn round in the hallway.

'It's a bit ...'

She nods and smiles. She puts her hand on my arm. Perfect.

'It's fine. Don't worry. We'll soon be out of your way.'

I watch as the rest of the officers stare at the hundreds of Amazon boxes. They look at DS Percy for guidance. It's fairly obvious that they're here to search not just for the journal, but for the stolen goods from the Premier Inn rooms.

'Right, lads. Just have a look round. Mr Atkinson claims that five cases were delivered here and that Mrs Atkinson has kept one of them – a holdall. Inside were some papers and some kind of a diary. So that's what we're looking for.'

Three of the officers have a look round and the other one lingers. DS Percy continues.

'Oh. Right. Can we have your computer please, Caroline?'

I pass my laptop.

'I just use it to ...' I let my eyes wander over the boxes. 'And Facebook. You should be able to get right in; it remembers the passwords. There's some work stuff on there too.'

DS Percy stares at me.

'I'm sorry about this, Caroline. You do understand why I have to ...? Anyway, Gary, we're looking for a fake Facebook account. Mr Atkinson claims that Mrs Atkinson is harassing him via a fake Facebook account in the name of Monica Bradley, somehow linked to this lost holdall.' I can hear the sarcasm in her voice and I watch as her eyebrows rise as she speaks. 'But he hasn't said how it's linked.

He's shown me the shared content, some photographs, but it's not clear where they fit in. Anyway ...'

You haven't told her what's in the journal. You've held back, hoping that they'll find something here and you won't have to explain how you are so disturbed that you collect sexual memorabilia and mark your conquests out of ten.

Gary takes the laptop and leaves, telling me he'll bring it back as soon as he's finished and that he'll check my phone records if that's OK. It is. There's nothing to hide. Nothing at all. Not there, anyway.

I make a cup of tea and watch as the other officer pulls out boxes. The dust particles sail through the sunbeams that filter through my stained-glass wind chimes and I'm transfixed. The more they move, the thicker the stream of crap that sails around, settling somewhere else.

I suddenly snap out of it as I hear a door handle turn and the dull thud of a body against a locked door. And again. Footsteps on the stairs and DS Percy appears with Lewis.

'Rooms upstairs. Both locked.'

He's blank. He hasn't read my file. He doesn't know what I've been through. How did I not think about this? That they'd want to look in there? DS Percy nods.

'OK. OK. Right. So, is that OK, Caroline? Only we have to ...'

I feel sick. This can't be happening.

'There's nothing in there.'

Nothing except all my memories of my children. I don't want the dust in there disturbed, flying through the air, changing things. She draws a chair close.

'I promise we'll be in and out. We won't touch anything. And I'll stay here with you. We just have to look round the door. Just to check.'

I feel myself slipping into a panic. I look around for alcohol, but she's putting the kettle on. She pours the hot water and the steam cuts through the dust in the air. I hear Laura's bedroom door open and footsteps directly above me. DS Percy hears them too and sees my trembling hands. She sits down.

'Look, Caroline, completely off the record, is there anything I can do to help.'

I shake my head and wipe a tear away as I hear Laura's door close and Charlie's door open. I can see his room clearly, the Lego constructions carefully placed on the red and blue carpet squares. The Manchester United bedspread and the England posters. Charlie's teddy bears, all in a line on a shelf above his bed, and a squishy rabbit that he'd had since he was a baby and wouldn't go anywhere without. They wouldn't even let me give it to him. She sighs.

'I'll be honest with you, I think you need professional help. With this.' She waves at the boxes and looks around. 'Is there anyone at work who can help?'

I somehow dredge up the words.

'It's mainly research. I talk to my supervisor every month. She knows. She's helping. A little.'

She looks relieved, as if someone had taken the weight that is me and placed it on someone else.

'Good. Good. But the thing that I don't understand is about your children. You're allowed to see them, aren't you?'

I nod. *Stay quiet, Caroline.* This is a dangerous time, when I'm upset. I could say anything. So I say nothing. She stares at me, waiting for me to defend myself. Explain why I've abandoned my own children. When it's clear that I'm not going to speak, she carries on.

'Your ex's mother looks after them, yeah? And you and your husband have split access, with his mother looking after them when he's out of the country?'

I nod again.

'It's not access. There was not a custody order. It was an arrangement but I'm just too ... too ...'

'And they're still living with his mum, even though your ex is back?'

In the middle of all the revelations and shockers that the last couple of days had brought, I hadn't thought of this. I'd assumed – ha – *assume makes an ass out of you and me* – that you had only been back a few days. But why? Why, if you were back and living in one of those posh, spacious apartments, hadn't you claimed Charlie and Laura? Wouldn't that strengthen your case against me, make me look worse? I stare vacantly at her, listening to 'Lewis' close Charlie's door and stomp across the landing. I need to say something or she will start to suspect I'm withholding.

'I don't know. I had no idea he was back. I don't keep up with his movements. To be honest, it takes me all my time to look after myself. As you can see.'

Despite myself, I break down. I might be lying through my back teeth, but some of it is painfully true. I sob deeply and she puts her arms around me. I don't want this. I don't want her close. Taking an interest. It's the wrong thing. But I can't stop the tears.

She gets me a tissue and I blow my nose. She passes me my tea and sips hers. Lewis is in the bathroom now, struggling with the bath panel. I know how he feels, because that used to be a hiding place before I started to use the hole. All cleared now, just like the rest of the house. DS Percy's features are soft and sympathetic and I can see that she's trying to decide whether to say something. She eventually does.

'Look, I shouldn't really ask you this, but it's been puzzling me. And when I saw those ...' She points to a huge pile of unopened mail. I never open mail. Never. I do all my banking over the internet and my pay slips arrive by email. 'Well, the other day when I saw those I wondered if you had contacted social services.'

Social fucking services? This is a new one.

'I have. At the beginning. But they just told me to make an arrangement with Jack and his mother, and they wouldn't speak to me. So ... No. Not since then.' But I do see my children. Every day that I can. Lunchtimes. Spaces between research meetings. I want to tell her that I watch them from a distance, willing them to feel my love. 'Nothing's wrong, is it?'

I know nothing is wrong because if it was your fucking mother would have been telling me through the door yesterday, playing the martyr, reminding me how I'd 'lost' my children because everything is win or lose to her. DS Percy – *call me Lorraine* – panics.

'Oh God, no. It's just that, well, I don't know if I should say ...'

I wait. And fucking wait. While she has a moral dilemma, I listen to 'Lewis' forcing the panel back on and then going into my bedroom. The room where you fucked Alicia Turnbull. He's pulling out the divan drawers, looking for something that he doesn't even have a picture of. I hear him push up the loft door and the ladders come down. DS Percy – *I prefer to keep it formal* – decides to spill the beans.

'This thing is. Well, you've had some letters from social services asking you to contact them.'

I look at the pile of letters. I should have opened them. I should have.

'You see,' she moves closer still and I can feel her breath on my face, 'I wanted to understand what had gone on here. To see if there was more to this. So I requested your file. Your daughter has told her teacher that she wants to see you. Make contact.'

Of all the things it could have been, I didn't expect this. I'd convinced myself that my children completely hate me and have been fully influenced by your bitch mother and their lying bastard father. That they'd never, ever want anything to do with me.

But Laura does. She wants to see me and she's told someone that isn't your mother or you. It lights a flame inside me and this is what I've been waiting for. I dive for the unopened letters, rifle through them frantically. Most of it is, as I suspected, junk mail, but she's right, there are nine or ten from social services. I rip them open and scan the letters.

It's true. They want to see me 'about a family matter'. They want me to make an appointment. I have a rush of despair – is it too late? But it isn't. This seems to have happened recently, the last letter is dated only a couple of weeks ago. DS Percy is enjoying the high, pushing the junk mail into a bin bag and putting the letters in date order.

Lewis appears, along with his colleague Sam.

'Nothing. We've had a good look round. In the loft and everywhere.' He looks through the kitchen window. 'No shed?'

I shake my head.

'Just a lock-up cupboard outside. Where I keep the lawn mower and that.'

I pass him the key and they go outside. DS Percy looks at me.

'So all's not lost. Follow it up. And get this lot sorted out. You'll have the kids here before long.'

Her hand is on my arm again and she's all touchy-feely with me. I put my hand over hers.

'Thank you.' I lie. I'm not thanking her at all. And she's already looking like she shouldn't have broken confidentiality and told me.

I know guilt when I see it. I'm wishing her away so I can think what all this means. You set me up. Got someone to follow me. Take photos. You took my children away. You took them away, but now you don't want them. But Laura wants me. I bet she asked your mother and she wouldn't let her see me. You won't let them see me.

You know me. I'll never give up. And now, now I know there is hope, I'm stronger. A lot stronger.

You know me, Jack. And I know you. And I'm coming to get you.

Chapter Fourteen

It's not just hope, it's hope and anger all mixed into one huge mass of emotion. DS Percy stands in my kitchen, arms folded, watching Lewis and Sam wander around my garden. They look in the lock-up cupboard and then walk up the lawn, stopping almost over the hole. Under normal circumstances I would have held my breath, scared to exhale in case something bad happened, but now I'm too preoccupied.

It's all bullshit. I realise that now. You've been playing a game with me. I suddenly understand. Why you made an elaborate plan to make me point at you and scream like a harpy. Why your mother took a photograph of the inside of my kitchen.

You want to finish me off once and for all. Push me to the limits, accuse you of stalking me, while you stand there and shrug with your alibis. You can't do anything to me because you will be the first suspect. So you're trying to make me do it to myself. Again.

All because my children want to see me. All because Laura has broken out and told on you and your mother, that you won't let her see me, and that she wants to.

The two police officers stand talking at the top of my garden, right over the hole. DS Percy is checking her texts, sipping her coffee. I sip mine and wish they would fuck off so that I can make a plan to get my kids back. To give you a taste of your own medicine. I know you, and you'll be waiting, waiting, waiting for a call to tell you that I've accused you of all sorts. That I've found the journal and I'm raging. You'll be ready to restate your alibi, with your cheating fucking lawyer at your side. Raking over the past, the *she's done this before*s and the *this is what she's like* eye-rolls.

Of course, people will be saying, 'How could she have suspected her ex of all this and never taken action?' Of course they fucking will. It's all the above and more. I'm too scared that I will be wrong, even when I'm right. That's how it makes you. Unsure of everything you say. Suspicious that you are seeing things from the wrong perspective permanently. They'll be the same people who look at women who don't leave their abusive partners and pour scorn on them. 'Why didn't *she just leave*?' Because she's in a psychological prison that they are too single-minded to understand. Because the consequences for everyone, especially her children, are too high. The other person is holding all the cards. Every single one of them and the fear is so deep that it's impossible. You know this, Jack, don't you?

You'll be pushing for another search of our house, more disruption to my life. Pushing me over the edge of my sanity. It's not going to work. You should know this. You're the expert. All that training you did; all the nature/nurture debates you had with people who weren't really interested.

You're the one who lectured me on the unconditional love that mothers have for their children. Your passive-aggressive style of making a point coming into its own as you verbally punished me for wanting to go back to work after having Laura. You never said it outright, so I could never accuse you, but you went on at length about how 'kids who are "farmed out" end up damaged, it's against what nature intended'.

Now it's going to bite you on the arse because just when you think you're wearing me down, when you think I am weak again, I'm the strongest I've ever been. That's the thing about being a mother. Whether you like it or not, you love your kids. Not like romantic love that can change to hate or that you can get over, given time, but a visceral caring that, even if you try to force it, won't go away.

It's a deep worry that your child is hungry, in danger, making bad decisions, crying. I've had to sit here night after night wondering if Charlie and Laura were crying, ill, hurt, happy, sad; and not being able to go to them. I tried everything to forget, to stop the gnawing at my soul. I distracted myself with work and vodka and Amazon Prime and Premier Inn. I tried to convince myself that they had forgotten about me. That they no longer thought about me and their childhood with their mummy.

The only time I actually achieved any kind of relief was in the in-between vodka trance I drank myself into on a regular basis. Now, it turns out, I don't need to. Because Laura wants to see me. I'm still celebrating inside when Lewis and Sam come into the kitchen. DS Percy stands up and they prepare to leave.

'Nothing. We've found nothing at all.'

I nod.

'So will you be bringing my stuff back, you know, the laptop and that?'

She smiles. 'As soon as they've finished. I don't expect they'll find anything of interest on there either.'

'Yeah. Well, at least it'll put a stop to this.' I wave vacantly at the boxes. They all look at the sea of insipid cardboard packaging. 'I'm going to speak to someone about it tomorrow.'

They leave and I watch them drive away. I stand on the doorstep for a while. It's quite exciting really. The thought of calling social services and making an appointment to see them. To arrange to see Laura. I don't even care if your mother comes with her, I can handle anything now. The thought of stepping up my game, of catching you in a trap of your own making.

As soon as they're gone, and they're not coming back, I pick up the phone and dial the number on the letter. My children. I have a chance. The first ring. The second. I look around. What if the social worker says she is coming round tomorrow? What if she wants to inspect the house before she makes a decision? Third ring. Fear sets in. I desperately want this, but I need to sort myself out. And I need to sort you out. I reluctantly replace the receiver and the fear subsides a little.

One thing that I need to do is to move the journal and Monica's computer. A load of random shit in the hole is one thing, but those in particular would incriminate me. Oh God, what have I done?

I wait until sunset then I take my wheelie bin around the front of the house for collection. The fucking dog starts to bark and I make a show of rolling the bin about until he's in a snarling frenzy. Then I creep around my back garden and retrieve the things I need from the hole and go to work.

I'm going to need a car. I know that I've got money in the bank – but when I check my internet banking on my work computer I'm shocked. Even after all the booze and Amazon purchases, all the direct debits and standing orders for things I use once then forget about, I've still got over fifty thousand pounds.

I ring the bank and tell them I want to withdraw twenty thousand pounds in cash. That I'll be calling at the local branch for it at lunchtime. To do my house up. Needs a complete renovation and several skips, I explain to the call that is recorded. My next call is to a skip company who I ask to deliver a medium-sized skip to my driveway and I will pay cash on delivery.

Then I go to the staffroom and find the used cars for sale section of the local paper. I check my post box. I know what's in the A4 brown envelope before I open it. There are pictures of me sitting on the Metro with a laptop on my knee looking very focused. Nothing unusual about that. Except somehow this person has managed to stand behind me at a station and photograph me updating Monica's Facebook page. I turn them over quickly. Someone has written 'STILL WATCHING' on the back. Shit. Shit shit shit. I hide the photos in my bag. I can hardly go to the police with this. I make a coffee and smile as Eileen sits beside me, even though I'm dying inside. She doesn't say anything, but puts her hand on my arm and pats me.

I need to move more quickly. Before whoever is doing this goes public. I wonder why you haven't already. I would have. It just makes me think that you are preparing to return my serve with something bigger.

I find an inconspicuous four-wheel drive in silver. It's compact and functional and has slightly tinted windows, which is perfect. I call the owner and arrange to come over at lunchtime. Just before I leave the university I check my look in the mirror to make sure I look homely and middle-aged. I do. Even I would trust myself.

I go to the bank and collect my cash, mentioning again about my home renovations. Then I buy the car. It's easier than I thought it would be and I even manage to knock the owner down by a couple of hundred. We swap contact details – Jane Smith's in my case, and I drive away with the paperwork.

I toss Monica's computer in my bag, along with her mobile phone and the journal, on the back seat and drive a short way to the side of the park, near to the Metrolink stop. The Metrolink signal is strong here. I check Monica's profile and I can almost sense all your friends hovering over your Facebook account, waiting for the next revelation.

But that will have to wait. My body shakes with anticipation as I sit in the vehicle that I bought in a fake name. I type 'Frances Burrows' in the search box – Facebook is still useful even if it isn't my current weapon of choice – and I see that she runs a lovely little café. I almost click on the map but then remember that the police might well be monitoring this.

Instead, I get out of the car with the journal. I hurry over to the hot house and push it behind the plastic panel. I feel almost sad being parted from it, but I have all I need on the flash drive and if I get caught with it the game's up.

A voice somewhere in my head is saying, *This is dangerous, Caroline. Jack is dangerous*, but I already know this, don't I? I already know you or your crony has followed me and you're moving in for your final attack on my credibility. And that's why I have to protect myself, and to have this car, hidden away, so you can't follow me.

If you're following me to the car park I will see you, either in a vehicle or on foot. It's open and there's nowhere to hide. I'll leave home each way on foot. I'll leave by next door's back gate – I haven't got a back gate; the garden is completely enclosed. But I'll climb over the fence at exactly eight-thirty when I know the fucking dog is being fed.

My own car will still be parked outside my house. You, or whoever you've got following me, will think that it's all getting to me and I'm taking time off work. That's if you dare come near the house, which I seriously doubt as the last thing you want is me invoking the injunction. Not with the evidence piling up, Jack. That would look bad, wouldn't it?

Chapter Fifteen

Frances Burrows. I almost feel sorry for her, but not quite. From her Facebook profile she looks quiet and almost mousy. She's married, no children, two dogs. I check and yes, she's friends with you. Of course she is. She's commented on a picture of you diving in the Great Barrier Reef: *Nice work, Jack xx*

Two kisses. I push the flash drive into the laptop on my knee and load the pictures of you and Frances. She's not your usual type at all. She's not flashy or wearing designer clothes. These pictures are the most hurtful of all so far. I know you, Jack, and you look like you are falling in love with her.

It's like a knife twisting inside me as I load picture after picture of you looking into her eyes. You used to do this thing with me, right at the beginning, when you had to be touching me, looking at me. Slightly smiling. I can see it here. In the art gallery, heads inclined towards each other. Holding hands. It actually stings my soul more than seeing you having sex with them.

I collect myself quickly. No doubt it sank into sexual boredom. No BJ. This woman, like me, thought she was getting your heart, but all you really cared about was sex. In the final analysis, you were out for what you could get. Six out of ten. I almost feel sorry for her until I load the last picture.

She's holding Charlie. Charlie's about six months old and she's cradling him and smiling. You're beside her, arm draped around her shoulder. I remember this day clearly. You said that you needed to go into work on a Saturday, but I had a terrible head cold. I practically forced you to take Charlie with you so I could get some sleep.

You didn't want to. You argued, got a little bit nasty. Inferred that I was lazy. A bad mother. That 'things like this happen and you have to look after your child even when you're ill'.

I still had the strength to fight back in those days. I argued with you, telling you that he was your son, your child, and it was about time you stepped up. You were awkward with him, lifting him stiffly into his buggy and slamming the door as you left. I fully expected you to drop him off at your mother's or my sister Paula's and when you came home at seven o'clock with him I was pleasantly surprised.

Now I know what really happened. You took our son out with your mistress. I click back through the pictures. It's difficult to tell how long your affair with Frances went on, but many of the pictures are outdoors and the seasons change in the background. Charlie would have been six months old in the summer. Some of the pictures before that are in the autumn.

Copper leaves on the trees as you walk hand in hand in the park. There are even some of Frances kicking leaves. Her on a swing. You on a swing. Me fucking pregnant at home.

I throw the laptop onto the seat beside me and screech out of the car park. I speed up the Huddersfield Road, temper tears streaming down my face and I park up in a layby. There's a brew van there and I get a coffee. Then I Google Frances' café.

It's a small tea shop in a small village. Uppermill is touristy, but not so much on a Tuesday morning. The Tea Cosy. I bet it is.

I'm absolutely livid. I want to go round there and shake her, tell her that Charlie is my son and she had no right. Worse than that.

But I know right from wrong. Of course I do. No one must get hurt. Not physically. No.

So I grab a brown real-hair wig that I bought for a fancy dress and some glasses and drive for an hour until I'm in Huddersfield. I'm getting into this playlist thing, like *High Fidelity*, but mine's not a top five because there are so many about cheating bastards who treat women badly. My song of choice today from the comprehensive bastard playlist I made is 'The Snake' by Al Wilson. A classic. And so appropriate. I Google an exotic pets shop and park up. Half an hour later I'm the owner of a cardboard box full of crickets and ten tiny mice – perfect snake food. I always knew my father's love of reptiles and his ceaseless dialogue about them would come in handy one day.

I park up a good walk from The Tea Cosy. I check the wig and the glasses in the rear-view. I'm still shaking with temper when I rock up to the counter. I join the queue and look for my opportunity.

The shop is so fucking twee and the furniture isn't even proper vintage, just replica. It's full of retired people, which suits me just fine as they're the worst complainers. I check out the exit to the toilet and then suddenly I'm at the front of the queue and face to face with Frances.

In real life she's beige. No make-up, hair scraped back and an off-white pinny. She looks happy and confident and I want to slap her. But I don't because I'm not that kind of person. Tears well up, temper tears, and when she asks me what I would like I stare up at the board.

I choose a bacon and cheese toasty. I'd already seen her go through to a tiny kitchen to get some toast, so she would be gone a while. As soon as she is safely in the kitchen, I unzip my tote bag and pull out the box of crickets. I empty them into the side of the curved glass panelled counter, right into the cake section. Some of them fall down the slats in the refrigerated shelf, but some of them are already climbing on the white fresh cream.

I turn and check that no one is watching and they aren't. Everyone is concentrating on their cream teas. So I go to the toilets, which are very country fucking pretty, and release the tiny mice. The toilets are sealed and there's nowhere for them to go, so they run around in the cubical. Perfect.

I flush and leave and my toasty is ready, along with a pot of tea that I ordered. I pass a ten-pound note to Frances with shaking hands and take a seat near the door. I sip my tea and nibble the edge of the toasty. I don't even fucking like cheese and bacon. I watch as the crickets climb all over the lovely cakes and wait for someone to notice. I even manage to get a photo, which I upload to Monica's Facebook page header.

Eventually, two women come into the shop and make a show of putting their bags down at a free table.

The older one orders the 'special' – tea and cake for £3.99 – and my stomach flutters. Frances fills up a teapot and almost in slow motion asks her which cake she would like and – boom – it's all happening now. Frances drops the teapot and the woman screams. I move closer as I head for the door and it's grotesque. The cakes are alive with insects.

I stand gripped by the sight but Frances is trying to flick them off with a tea towel and they splatter against the glass. I make it look like I'm going to help her, but at the last moment, in all the confusion, I take her bag from under the counter. I've seen enough. I'm carried outside on a wave of fleeing pensioners. Someone is dialling the environmental health and my work here is done.

I stand on the cobbles outside the shop and momentarily feel elated. Until I turn around. With the shop empty I can see Frances leaning over the counter, rubbing her face. I step a little closer and peer through the slightly open door. She's crying. Noisy, guttural sobs. Oh my God. What have I done? This isn't what I wanted. I thought she would be angry, full of revenge herself. But she's just very upset.

I want to rush in and hug her and apologise, but I remember that she held Charlie and laughed into the camera and I manage to hurry away, trembling and close to tears myself. I wait to calm myself until I'm far away from the shop. My heart is thudding in my chest and I'm shaking. I feel like I shouldn't have done this. But she deserves it. Doesn't she? As I cross the main road I pull the scarf over my face and hurry to the car. Even if there are cameras around here, which I seriously doubt, no one would recognise me or the car.

I head for the hills. I drive and drive and try to imagine how annoyed Frances will be, losing customers like that and having to fumigate her shop. But all I can imagine is her crying.

I reach a remote picnic area and park up. I get out of the car, still wearing my disguise. The hills are bleak and covered with heather and rocks and I find one low enough to sit on and open Frances's bag. Her phone is in there along with some papers and her purse. I check her purse for pictures. There are none. This doesn't feel like revenge at all. Revenge is supposed to make you feel better. All I feel is guilty. I push on regardless. There isn't a way out now, even if I wanted one.

I take her phone. Is your number still on there? It's fucking locked. But as I try to guess the pattern a notification appears. It's from 'Mum': *Are you OK? Are you feeling better now?* I hover over the keys, wanting to answer but I don't. All in good time.

At least I'll be able to see when you do get in touch with her. She's the next in the journal and I need to monitor what you're actually doing about this. I feel bad, but I need to protect myself. I rustle through the bag for a memento. For my hole. There's a MAC lipstick, unused. A keyring with The Tea Cosy on it. A gas bill. I unfold one of the other papers. It's a decree absolute. I feel another pang of sympathy. She's just got divorced. Then I remember she deserves to be divorced. I hope her husband's cheated on her like mine cheated on me. With her.

The phone rings and I jump. This time it's someone called Claudia. It rings and rings, echoing across the moorland. It doesn't go to answerphone. Another text message appears on the screen, faded behind the pattern. *Just calling on the way to the airport. No Answer. You OK?. Anyway, we'll give you a ring when we get there.* Seven smiley faces. I look around at the bleakness and the low cloud and think that I'd better get going.

Back in the car I leave the phone on the dashboard. DS Percy will probably come and see me about this and my neighbours will tell her that, no, I hadn't been out as the dog hadn't barked and my car had been there all day.

Do I feel bad? Yes I do. This was a step too far. And, thinking about those pictures, no. All actions have consequences and she should have thought of that before she slept with you and held my baby boy.

Chapter Sixteen

I drive home carefully. I don't want to spoil it now. Not when I'm so near to my goal. I keep one eye on the phone but it doesn't ring. There are no messages. Frances isn't so popular. I panic a little and wonder if you or DS Percy have already warned her and if she guesses that it was me? You would have laid it on thick, made me sound dangerous. She would have been expecting me.

When I'm near my house I duck into the back alleyway lined with copper birch that backs onto my garden and climb through the hole in the fence and I'm home. The fucking dog is barking but it doesn't matter now because it's not first thing in the morning and I want people to know I'm here doing a spot of gardening.

I haven't even got my coat off when there's a knock at the door. I pull open a work folder from the top of an Amazon box and grab the cup of cold coffee from this morning. I pop a pen on top of it and kick my shoes off and throw them under the table. I even flick the kettle on.

It's DS Percy. On her own. She looks round at the skip, which I hadn't noticed had been delivered.

'True to your word, I see.'

I invite her in. She looks around then at the folder and pen. Then she places my laptop on the table.

'Clean as a whistle. You can have it back now.'

'Thanks. Doing a bit of work from home today. Not feeling too well. Probably all getting to me. Coffee?'

She nods and I pick up my mug. She looks at my shoes under the table. I go to the fridge for milk and slide Frances's phone right to the back. You know, if I met her in different circumstances, I think Lorraine and I could be friends. She's sitting at the table now, trying to read a report on memory and perception in children under two years old upside down.

'Your job must be very interesting.'

I stir the coffee slowly.

'Yes, it is. I like to keep as up to date as I can. Lots of extra reading.'

I put the coffees down and choose the chair closest to her. She leans back slightly as I settle in.

'So. I'm here to talk to you about your ex-husband,' she begins.

I smile. 'Officially or unofficially?'

I remind her of the information she shouldn't have given me about social services.

'Officially. He wants to make an official complaint against you. For harassment.'

I nod slowly. Of course you do, Jack. That's the next clearest course of action for you, isn't it? Have me arrested so it looks bad. So social services will receive a copy of the court report from your solicitor.

'Oh dear. But I haven't done anything.'

Lorraine smiles. She still feels uncomfortable here, amongst the floor-to-ceiling boxes and the papers piled waist high.

'No. We certainly can't find any evidence that you have. As I said before, we don't really want to get involved in domestic issues, but his solicitor is leaving us no choice. Mr Atkinson has told us a little bit more about this bag he thinks you have.'

I bet you have. I'm all ears. I can't wait to hear this. You'll be adding up the photographs you've had taken of me and me taking the journal and coming up with what you think is the jackpot.

'Oh. Right. But I don't see what it's got to do with me.'

'He's been to the station with his solicitor. He's made a statement saying you definitely have the bag and that the bag contained personal items. His visa papers for his work trips and birth certificate are in the bag and he wants you charged with stealing official documents and harassment. He mentioned libel too.' She looks positively pissed off. 'So that leaves us no choice but to investigate.'

I stare at her. Of course you want me charged.

'But I haven't got the bag.'

'I know. I told him we'd searched your property and that you'd complied with our requests. He asked for another search but we said he would have to go to court to get a decision on that. But he did mention something else.'

'Go on.'

'The diary in the bag. He said that you would be angry if you saw it. It contained details of other women he had known. That two of these women had been harassed on Facebook—'

I interrupt. 'Christine Dearden and Julie Carson.'

'Yes. So you know about this?'

'Of course. Who doesn't? All our friends are talking about it.' All your friends. All your Facebook pariahs. 'As I said before, it's very hurtful to me. But not entirely unexpected. You've read the file. You know what happened.'

She gets her notebook out and writes it down.

'So your ex-husband seemed to think that it would trigger your mental health problems. That you had posted these pictures out of jealousy.'

I look at her. She wants me to explain my way out of this. She doesn't believe him.

'I've never been diagnosed with mental health problems.'

She stops writing and looks around.

'But I thought ... with all this and the divorce papers ...'

She has looked into this. She's read your statement about me. What you thought was wrong with me. The language you and your solicitor used. *Mad. Disturbed. Crazy.*

'You can check my medical records. And ask my employers. I've never been diagnosed with a mental illness. All my colleagues are psychologists. Experts in mental health. Do you think I'd be allowed to work if I had? Go and ask them. So there's nothing to trigger. I'm upset about Jack and his mother stopping me seeing my children, obviously. It isn't fair. That's what this is about. I'm lonely. That's why I pick men up. But I'm not mentally ill.'

She makes a note to check my records. She's frowning and tapping her pencil on the table.

'Look, he's coming after you for this bag. Tell me the truth. Have you got it or not?'

Her eyes say 'off the record'. Her body language tells me that she's on my side. I can understand why she's conflicted – I'm the usual suspect, the most likely person to have the bag.

'I haven't got it. I can't say I have when I haven't.'

I need to get rid of that fucking bag. She shuts the notebook.

'OK. I believe you. But he and his solicitor don't. I'd advise you to get your own counsel. You'll be called as a witness for the Premier Inn cases so it might be wise.'

She gets up and I follow her to the door. She suddenly turns around and touches my arm.

'Look, I'm sorry about this. I don't know what's going on here at all. It all seems interconnected but …'

I feel the anger creep up inside me. Interconnected. I don't want her getting ideas about you being the one who is sending the photographs to me. That you are the common denominator. I want her to keep thinking it's about me, keep the focus on me, until Facebook proves what a fucking lying cheating piece of shit you are.

'I know. It's really spooking me to think that some stranger has been following me around. Then Jack accusing me of this. It makes me feel … vulnerable.'

This is the magic word to all agencies. Vulnerable. It's an invisible signal that you are very near the point where you will accuse them of harassment or abuse. That they need to be careful because you are now sensitive to them and their methods. She stares at me again.

'I'm sorry. I didn't mean to …'

'No, no. You're just doing your job. Perhaps I will get a solicitor.'

Yes, Lorraine, back the fuck off. So I can move my plan to its conclusion and we'll all know where we are.

She leaves and I wait half an hour, then go to work. When I arrive I go straight to my office but Eileen waylays me on the corridor. She's looking very excited. I can always tell when she's got a secret to share because her thin lips stretch across her conspiratorial expression. She's done her hair differently, less 'just got up' and more 'professor'. She hurries towards me.

'Oh my God, Caroline. You'll never guess what. I just got out of a meeting and your latest piece of research has won mega funding. They're so impressed with it that they're using it as the showcase for the department.'

I smile widely, which hides my 'how the fuck did that happen?' sinking feeling inside. That will mean more meetings and less time to research. Or avenge myself against my philandering ex. On the other hand, it also means that, despite everything that has happened, my work is still excellent. I feel a stab of pride, puncturing the anger that had built up since I spoke to DS Percy.

'That's brilliant! Which part in particular? Did they say?'

She beams.

'It was the piece you did on the Hare scale. How psychopathology can be high functioning. They felt like you had an enlightened approach and it was the best piece of reflexive work they had seen for a long time.'

She hugs me and follows me to my office and I wish she would just fuck off, but she doesn't. She sits down. I need to check Frances's phone but I can't. Not here. I need to find out if you are warning people about me, if DS Percy is onto me.

'... so they want you to move offices, into the Dolan Suite. Someone will take care of it, of course. But you might have to work somewhere else for the next couple of days. Is that OK?'

It's more than OK. It's perfect.

'Oh. Well. I suppose so. I'll find somewhere.'

She claps her hands.

'Great.' Her lips purse and now she's serious. 'Of course, there will be a national press release. This is the sort of thing the tabloids love. Psychopaths. They're all over it. That'll give your ex something to think about, won't it?'

I smile and nod. This can go two ways for me. Either it can make me look like I've been working very hard and social services will believe that I am a reformed character. Or it will look like I'm trying to support my quest for revenge. I can see it now. 'Obsessed, she was. Obsessed with trying to prove he's a psychopath.'

'I don't want a lot of fuss. After all, lots of people have worked on this.'

Eileen clasps her hands in front of her.

'My God, Caroline. You are so humble. Such a good person. That bloody ex of yours should be ashamed of himself. If he knew what you'd achieved ...'

That was part of the problem. He did know what I'd achieved. So did everyone else. And that made it all the more difficult for people to believe me. Dr Caroline Atkinson, esteemed senior research psychologist? *Surely, you of all people, Caroline, would have known about and been able to resist the gradual chipping away at your self-esteem until you hardly knew who you were?*

Caroline, professional fixer extraordinaire, would have been able to spot the signs of someone conditioning her into control? It's almost as if no one could believe that Jack could do this to me, as if I had some magical professional shield that protects me from manipulative psychopaths. But at home we were just Jack and Caroline.

You had your little tricks. As well as the emotional withdrawal you criticised everything. You never said I looked nice, you just pulled a little face. Told me the things you arranged without telling me were for my own good. Told me I was a slut if I made sexual advances. It all adds up. The insistence on joint bank accounts. Staying completely calm when I argued with you, and ignoring me.

You carefully calculated the effect it had on me, then you made it worse by implying that if I mentioned any of this to anyone you would leave. Or worse. The paranoia set in as you related stories of 'someone at work' whose wife pushed him over the edge and he just ... snapped. You never hit me. You didn't have to. Award-winning psychologist or not, you scared the shit out of me. That's when I started to give up. What could I do when no one believed me? I'm not doing this because I'm crazy. I'm doing it so everyone will believe me and it can be over.

Eileen leaves and I slump in my chair. I switch on the radio in my office and wait for the news to come on. For them to report that a woman's bag was stolen from her shop. Was that newsworthy these days? I'm so out of touch. But the police would be called and that's mainly where the news comes from, blue-light chasers. I read a paper on it years ago.

One thing's for sure, I need to do an afternoon's work then think of a way to offload your holdall. Once it's found it will all be a big mistake. I'll be in the clear and they'll be looking for someone else. I don't need your fucking journal now. I've got my flash drive and, anyway, the contents are branded into my memory. I know the running order and every infidelity you committed. I could recite them. Luckily no one can read my mind, but I'm going to make sure that someone reads your fucking journal so everyone can finally know what a piece of work you really are.

Chapter Seventeen

By six o'clock I've finished an abstract for a new paper and read over my study ready for submission to the funding panel. They're happy with the outline for the new psychopath scale and they want something more formal. They want to increase my salary. I suddenly realise what the next step is. Professor. It's almost in the bag now.

This is very good. Very good indeed. It proves that I'm a balanced individual who can perform to high levels. That, according to my colleagues, I am in the top 1 per cent of my profession. Not the neurotic bundle of paranoia you labelled me. Not at all.

I'm feeling pleased with myself until I check Frances's phone as I'm parked up in a layby on the way home. Her mother has phoned twice and someone called Elliot has texted her to say he's been round with her scones but she's not in. She must have closed the shop. Good.

I worry for a moment that she knows it's me and she's phoned you. Poor, newly divorced Frances. Just your type. Instead of calling the police, have you convinced her to have a cup of tea and forget about it? With your endless fucking charm and powers of persuasion? Looking into her eyes like in the photos where she was holding my baby son?

I suddenly don't feel worried any more. She deserves to suffer.

She'll lose money. People will be wondering why the café's not open, won't they?

I drive the rest of the way home in despair. Today's been a nightmare, really, despite the funding news. I'm completely exhausted and when I get home my next-door neighbour, owner of the fucking dog, is standing in my drive. I get out of the car and smile at her.

'Police been round. Earlier on. Asking if you were in this morning.'

She's lived next door to me long enough to know that my kids are gone. And to see the delivery man and my early-morning drunken returns. This bodes well. Frances must have guessed it was me and they're checking my whereabouts. I shouldn't have posted the crickets on Monica's header. Damn. Great.

'Yeah. Jack's up to his old tricks again. You know ...'

She rolls her eyes, crosses her oversized cardy over her false boobs and flicks her hair extensions.

'Bastard. Anyways, I told them you were here all morning cos I didn't hear Rover barking.'

Fucking Rover. Good boy.

'I was here. I was doing a bit of work at home while the skip came. Time to get my act together. Having a spring clean.'

She perks up.

'Ooo, throw anything you don't want my way, yeah?'

She's obviously seen the endless procession of boxes coming in and the delivery men walking away shaking their heads. I nod and she backs off.

'Why did they want to know if I'd seen some suitcases going in?'

They're asking around. Fuck you, Jack. You're making them poke this monster.

'Just some mix-up with deliveries. Jack's been away and his cases got delivered here. Then he tried to say it was something to do with me. Can you believe it?'

She shakes her head. 'I can believe anything of him. Shady fucker.' She shifts from foot to foot and kicks some gravel on my drive. Then, avoiding my eyes, 'Tried it on with me once. I said no, obviously. I'm a married woman. Made me think that it wasn't the first time he'd done that, though. Then I saw him ...'

I see red. Blinding fury. I hold onto the skip and clench my fists until my knuckles are white.

'Yeah, I know. That's why we're divorced.'

She nods deeply and does a 'smashed it' fist.

'Stay strong, sister. Stay strong.'

I'll stay fucking strong, all right. I retreat past the skip and scan the kitchen for alcohol. I haven't bought any since all this happened and I'm desperate now. Desperate for something to numb this pain. When it's isolated inside me – hidden – it's manageable. It's the leaking out into public spaces that I find hard to cope with. Very fucking hard.

Now even my neighbours are telling me that Jack is a bastard. I open the drawer and there are the Tramadol you were prescribed when you had a bad back. It's no wonder you had a bad back, is it? I know why now. I stare at the tablets. This is all supposed to make me feel better, not worse. So why do I feel like I'm taking a step in the wrong direction?

The tablets are already in my hand and I'm pouring a glass of water when I stop dead. This isn't going to take the pain away. The only way I can deal with this is to offload the holdall and get the police off my back. Then I can ring social services and set up a meeting with them. Then I can see Charlie and Laura.

Of course, the nagging doubt in my head comes in the form of your mother. She'll do anything she can to discredit me and put a stop to social services' arrangements. It suddenly strikes me that that's the reason she was round here the other day, taking photos through my back window. She's trying to find a reason.

I look out of the hallway window at the skip on my drive. If I can make a start on clearing things, when they come round to inspect the house ready for the kids to come they'll see that I'm making an effort. Because I am.

I drop the Tramadol into the sink and run the water. They disappear in a swirl and the pain is still there. I walk up to the main road and check Frances's phone again and there are two text messages from her friends: *U OK hun?* and *Got that bug?* Of course, the shop would still be shut. But all this has given me an idea.

I cheer up a bit and order a pizza as I walk back home. While waiting for it to come, I Google 'How to unlock an Android phone' on made-up Monica's mobile. It's a choice between losing any data that's not on the SD card and being able to read Frances's messages and listen to her calls from now on. And have access to her social networking, hopefully.

Until now I've had the battery and SIM card out while I'm at home or at work. I know all about 'Find my phone'. So I walk down to the tram stop at the park and jump on the next tram. After three stops I prise open the back and take out the SD card. Fingers crossed all her numbers are on there. I hold the volume up, home and power buttons together, take a deep breath and choose 'wipe all data'.

It reboots and I go through the motions, switching off, reinserting the SD card and switching on again. Yes. The contacts button reveals all Frances's contacts. The call log and texts are gone but never mind, I'll be able to fully see what's going on now. Almost immediately the phone rings and I let it go to answerphone. When I listen to the message, it's another friend.

'Hi, Franny. Just wondered what happened to you today? I thought you were coming round? Give us a call.'

It's someone called Julia. I flick through Frances's pictures and see that she likes a night out. Her with friends drinking champagne. Her in a restaurant with a different set of friends. Smiling. Her with her cat. Her beautiful house in the background. Probably the same house you and she took Charlie to.

I could text Julia. Tell her Franny has the flu. She's in bed. When clearly she'll be frantically trying to get rid of the crickets and the mice before environmental health swoop. Frantic Fran. I almost giggle, but then I remember the pain I felt when I saw her holding my baby son.

As predicted, the phone has a Facebook icon right on the front and I click on it. The app opens and suddenly I have access to all her photographs. As if I hadn't tortured myself enough, I scroll through them and eventually come to the ones of you and Charlie. These are different from the ones in the journal. Those are self-conscious, the look of lovers trying to look their best, but these are more natural. Selfies. Big smiles. Then I find it. A video. I see your face frozen on the front of it with the 'play' white arrow urging me to press it.

I wait a second then I press it. It's you, talking to the camera. Telling it that you are happy. Happy. And you're not the only one. You turn the phone around to Frances and she's there. Holding Charlie. She's laughing, you're laughing and then, Charlie is laughing. His beautiful baby chuckle rings out on the tram. I let it play. She's tickling him and you're tickling her. It's a family scene, except she's not family and I am.

It goes on and on and I have to stop it. I feel hysterical inside with the pain of my son in another woman's arms, but I see myself in the tram window, calm and collected. I look back at the phone and I'm pressing the share button. I'm tagging you in it and writing '#notmybaby #notmyman'. I know this will fucking incriminate me even more but they would have to catch me with the phone to do that.

I take the battery and SIM card out of the phone and jump off at the next stop. I cross the tracks and jump on a tram back home. Adele tells me that *never mind I'll find someone like you* and I fast forward to 'Irreplaceable' and think how right Beyoncé is. It's dark now and I look around, ever aware of you following me. You must have. You couldn't have known about my Premier Inn habit otherwise. I walk across the open ground beside the park and no one is following me. No one is around at all.

Then I walk home. Halfway there I realise that I don't really want to go indoors. My insides tremble and I know that things have got out of hand. Not that it's my fault. This is a means to an end to me, to get my children back. But I never meant anyone to get hurt. I never meant to steal anything at all. I need to remind myself why I did that, because things are certainly becoming muddled.

I double back to the car and retrieve Monica's laptop and the flash drive. I sit in the dark under an oak tree and fire it up. I watch as the bats dip through the last of the sunset and fly back into the trees.

I scroll through the scanned images of you and your women until I reach you and Frances again. The picture of her holding baby Charlie. I was right. The following pictures show you in her house, the same one she lives in now. I reach the end of the sequence and skip over scanned cinema tickets and a receipt for a diamond tennis bracelet. I'm thinking that I'm desensitised to this now until the next pictures flash up in front of me and my mouth falls open involuntarily.

Pam Harding. She's beautiful. I admit that. Dark hair curled right down her back. Ruby rosebud lips. Dark eyes. But in the fifth picture she's wearing a wedding dress. My hands shake as I flick through the pictures. *Wedding dress. Smirk. Smirk over the shoulder. Blowing a kiss. There's no bouquet. I recognise that tiara. Wedding dress undone. Naked in my wedding tiara. In my bedroom.*

I slam the laptop shut. What the fuck was I thinking? Almost feeling sorry for these women. Frances, with her fucking cat and her tea shop. Frances, who held my baby son and smiled for your camera. And now Pam Harding. Nine out of ten. You fucked her in my wedding dress on my bed. And now I have to go back there.

You deserve everything you're going to get, Jack. And so do your women.

Chapter Eighteen

This is a turning point. I can feel it. I know that I'm a good person and my mind keeps making excuses for you. Telling me to leave it, leave it. It's not worth it. But I know this is how you trained me. Telling me I was insane when I half suspected something. *No smoke without fire.*

Now I am sure. I was before with Christine and Julie and Frances, but now smirky Pam is in my room with you, wearing my stuff on my bed. I run home and burst into the house. I don't even check my phone, which, naturally, I left on the kitchen table because I can't be in two places at one time, can I? I run upstairs, past my absent children's bedrooms, and kick our bedroom door open.

I keep my wedding dress wrapped in tissue paper in a box on the top of my wardrobe. I keep it there because I wanted to pass it on to Laura when she marries. Now you've spoiled all that. I can't pass it down to my only daughter because your mistress has worn it to pose for photographs. Then you've had sex with her. In our fucking bed.

I pull down the box and it's crumpled on top of the tissue paper. The zip is still down and I can't believe I never checked it before. But why would I? What married woman would ever imagine that particular scenario? I pull at the side seams where the zip meets the white pearls. It's a beautiful dress and it's a shame. It tears easily and I rip savagely at the rest of the dress, seed pearls flying everywhere, tap, tap, tapping on the laminated floor and bouncing to a halt onto the wool carpet.

The tiara is beautiful. I had it specially made when I still believed that our marriage would last. I supervised the placement of every Swarovski crystal and every pearl. Paula came with me and chose her bridesmaid tiara at the same time. I pull that out of its box as well. We made a pact to save them for our daughters' weddings. All that has fucking changed now. No daughter of mine will ever wear either of these witches' crowns. I twist them into each other, the crystals popping onto the floor and spinning through the tiny pearls. My tiara snaps into bits. Paula's is a little bit more durable and it takes a few hard stamps to shatter it into pieces.

I'm breathless and sweating and I turn to the bed. I can't sleep in there any more. Not where you slept with all your whores. I can't. It was difficult before, but this is the last straw. I rip off the sheets and the duvet and run down to the kitchen. I pull the largest carving knife out of the cutlery drawer but it's not big enough. So I locate the 'kitchen utensil' section of my Amazon stash and open boxes until I find a knife set. I take the biggest, sharpest knife and run upstairs.

I slash and hack at the Tempur mattress and feather pillows. My arms flail and my body takes on a life of its own and I lose control. It feels good again to not have to be the person everyone thinks I should be. Perfect. To do what I feel. I hack away until the whole room is white and I am white and only then do I feel pure again.

I must have fallen asleep with the knife in my hand because when I wake up at 2 a.m. I'm covered in feathers and cuddling a chef's carver. I check myself for alcohol and hope that I haven't been to the in-between with this knife, but it's OK because I remember everything about last night. The dress is lying in shreds and the tiara is bent and broken. Our wedding album is in shreds on the floor beside me, every picture destroyed.

I look at the cover and the stab marks in it. It's OK because I know now that I never should have kept it sacred. That I was right to begin with. Our marriage was a sham and no amount of explaining away your behaviour as stress or boredom or *that's just what men do sometimes* could make any of it right.

It's OK because I know, in that moment, that I have a plan.

I take off my clothes and leave them in the feather-strewn bedroom. There are clothes in the tumble dryer and I walk through the house naked and dress in the kitchen. I catch my reflection in the kitchen window and I look almost childlike, my hair hanging over my face. This feels like some kind of an exorcism, *washing that man right out of my hair*, and I pull out some stray feathers.

I open the back door and go to the hole. Fucking Rover barks but my security light doesn't switch on. I watch to see if my neighbours' lights come on but they're desensitised to this particular alarm. So I lift the lid and pull out the holdall and the journal. The pictures, loose now, spill out and I scoop them up and push them into the briefcase. I feel around until I find a box inlaid with jade and bring that with me.

I go back into the house and sit down at the table. Rover's quiet now and I open the box. It's black silk inside, all compartments for your toiletries, except you used it as a dumping ground for bits of tat from your pockets. I pull out single cufflinks and a tiny chrome spanner. A lighter. Some coins that were your father's. Not that you gave a fuck about your poor father either, come to think about it. You built a case against him too, didn't you?

Right at the bottom is a bunch of keys on a D ring. I pull up the ring and roll a Yale key around it. I zip on a black hoodie and pull on a black beanie. I open the front door as quietly as I can and Rover is silent. I hurry across the drive and around the skip and run over to the park, your bag over my shoulder.

The laptop and the flash drive are still on the floor of the car. I eventually park up in a city-centre back street and hop onto the Manchester free Wi-Fi. I open Monica's Facebook account and find the offending photos. Pam Harding still smirks out at me and she's still wearing my wedding dress. No time to feel angry now, though. I'm on a roll. Instead, I write a status – '#drunkenselfie #notmydress' – and add a picture of the back of Pam with the dress unzipped. In the 'who were you with' section I select 'Jack Atkinson' and in the 'where were you' I tag my own postcode. It's obvious that this photograph is taken in a bedroom, and anyone who knows me will know it's my bedroom because behind Pam is a huge picture of my children looking down on her smirking face. I add the hashtags #notmyhouse and #notmykids and post the picture, knowing it will immediately post to Twitter and be dissected by #teamCaro and #teamJack.

I turn off the computer and I continue on my journey, this time back towards my house but I turn off three streets before. I park outside a three-bedroomed detached house and switch the computer back on again. Because it's night-time not so many people have shared the picture yet, but some of your friends have liked it and tagged you. I can imagine you now, phoning DS Percy in the middle of the night and demanding that she goes to my house and arrest me straight away.

If she is half the copper I think she is she will be using 'find my phone' right now to see where I am. She'll ring my mobile and when I don't answer try to trace its location. She'll see that it's right there in my house and that obviously I am in bed asleep. She'll probably ask the police IT people to trace the IP address of made-up Monica's post and the location. I've helpfully switched on 'location' on this laptop now so that when I post the next picture, the one of Pam naked in my bedroom, with the status #ooopsIdiditagain and tag you, eventually, when I'm long gone, the police will trace it to this spot.

It will take them a while, which is good, because I've got more business here. I leave the laptop glowing in the four-wheel drive and take your holdall from the seat beside me. I tiptoe up the drive of 6 Gimble Lane and push the key in the door. To my relief it turns. I thought it would – only a small percentage of me doubted it. Most people neglect details like changing the locks regularly because we are all hard-wired for optimism.

Your mother is no exception. The key turns but there is a door chain stopping it from opening. Fuck fuck fuck. I lean hard against the wooden door and push and push, and finally the cheap metal breaks. I wait for a full minute, hidden back against the wall outside, in case anyone heard the crack, but all is quiet. I know this house; bedrooms at the back, away from the traffic on the road.

I creep into the house I lived in after we married. It's mostly the same as last time I was here. I hurry through the hallway and push the bag into the cloakroom. Her new kitchen is cavernous and opulent and the low lighting is automatic, so as I pass the doorway it comes on and startles me.

It's then that I see a pair of trainers under the table and a schoolbag slung over the back of a chair. I turn back to the cloakroom and pull out an anorak and bury my face in it. My daughter. It's the nearest I have been to her for months.

I hear a movement upstairs. Heavy footsteps. There's a creak of a floorboard and my muscle memory recalls from when we lived here when we were first married that someone is on the way to the bathroom. I duck into the cloakroom and pull the door closed behind me. In seconds the strip of light below the door disappears and I breathe out. The kitchen is in darkness again and no one knows I'm here.

I wait for the toilet to flush and hear the footsteps on floorboard, tracing them by memory back to your mother's room. It's a treasure chest all around me, with my children's shoes and bags. I open a gym bag and pull out a leotard and pumps. Dirty football boots in another. I hold one of the muddy boots close to me. I'd hoped that they'd kept up with things. These were the minutiae that lined my bigger worries about their health and happiness.

I'd follow them, trying to see their lives. Sneaking around their school and waiting to see them. Peering through the community-centre windows to watch Laura perform her first pirouette. Watching from the sidelines of the football matches in disguise, cheering every time my son kicked the ball. Watching them go to Christmas parties and school trips, all dressed up and excited.

But it wasn't fair. They needed to acclimatise to their new world. I told myself that it was better for them, better that they didn't actually see me for a while. I never really believed it. But I'd see them. Every day that I could. Better for all of us. All this was ultimately about them for me. But not for you, Jack. It was about you. And because of that I've been denied these boots and the pumps and the proud-mummy moments. Worse, so have they.

Chapter Nineteen

I wait another ten minutes – studies show that's the average time for someone to fall asleep when woken in the night. Then I open the door very carefully and stand in the hallway again. I listen but hear nothing. As I walk towards the front door without the holdall I feel like a weight has been lifted from my shoulders. I wonder if I should have left the laptop too. No. That would be too risky. I'm already worried that the journal will reveal my DNA.

But why wouldn't it? I was your wife. I would have been near that bag, touched your stuff. I wore surgical gloves when I took it apart so I'm not worried about fingerprints but a stray hair? Then another more urgent thought invades. My children are asleep upstairs.

My overtired, frazzled brain protests but my heart wins as I turn to go upstairs. I know where the creaks are and I avoid them. My feet make a familiar pattern on the soft carpet and I'm strangely calmed. I pad up the landing, knowing that if your mother wakes and comes out of her room it's game over. I head for what used to be our room and turn the doorknob.

It's like turning back time and looking at myself lying in my bed. Laura is bigger than last time I saw her this close up. She's no longer a tiny child. She's changed so much in a year. Her blonde hair is long and spreads across the pillow. I step closer and she moves, so I freeze. My God. I feel a warmth in my soul, one that I haven't felt for so long. She's moving more now and I back out of the room.

I sneak across the landing to your old room. There's a red 'Keep Out' sign and I realise that Charlie is almost ready for secondary school. I missed it all. I missed this important transition. I push the door open and there he is, in a bedroom full of football posters. There's a computer in the corner and a pile of school books. I feel full of pride. My son's at school working hard.

I start to read a certificate on the wall, squinting in the darkness. He's been chosen for a football trial. I almost start to cry, then my wake-up call in the form of car headlights outside arrives. I worry for a moment that it's the police already, that they've traced the IP address, but the car passes.

I need to go. I'll see my children soon, if it kills me. I will. As I stand looking at Charlie I realise that, if I am going even to stand a chance of getting them back, I need to stop all this. I need to get back to Caroline. Mummy. The pull of revenge is strong, like an addiction, but this needs to be over.

I take a last look at my sleeping son then hurry back across the landing and down the stairs. I take made-up Monica's phone and log it into her Facebook account. Despite myself, I post another status: 'Hope everyone is enjoying my updates. Show your appreciation by texting me on 07924321875.' I switch on the location tab, then I wipe my fingerprints from it and hide it under the pile of newspapers beside the landline. It's Missy's phone now, sitting in her hallway. The screen lights up with texts immediately. It should be easy for the police to trace to here.

I'm out of the front door and into my car. I drive through my tears with a heavy heart, and under the cover of the trees I struggle to put Frances's phone together and I realise I'm sobbing as I check her messages. One call from Mum.

'Pick up, Fran. We're having a great time, don't work too hard xx.'

Seven text messages from different people. None from you. Which probably means that you have called her before I did the factory reset to warn her she's next. I check the local news and still no reports about a tea shop incident. It is the middle of the night, though.

I turn off the location on Monica's laptop, and when I check her Facebook I cheer up a little. The Pam posts have exploded into outright accusation. Quite a lot of 'How could you, Jack?' and a few 'Is this in your house?' One I particularly like says: 'What sort of a man would do this?' Perfect. It's been shared far and wide and when I check your profile you've made a statement: 'This is not what it looks like. This is an ongoing police matter. My solicitor is dealing with this.'

No likes. No shares. No one is paying attention to you now. Everyone's too busy feeling sorry for me. Realising that I'm not mad and I was right all along. There can be no doubt now.

I dismantle all the devices so that they definitely can't be traced back to this car. I hide everything under the seat and sit there for a minute. Where is this going to end? I've set your mother up and she deserves it. I try to recall a moment in my life when she gave a shit about me. I've known her since I've known you, at first just as my boyfriend's mother, then as my children's grandmother. You told me that even when you were a child she was too busy keeping up with the Joneses to notice much. She was certainly like that when I met her. She barely noticed me until it became clear that we would get married.

She mocked me when I told her how I would rather be reading in my room than playing hockey. Or going to discos. She sat impatiently in the audience in our first year at university, just weeks after we met. My Juliet to Jack's Romeo. Everyone smiled on as we appeared to fall in love before their eyes. I did fall in love with you, but inside I was trembling. I pushed it down so you wouldn't see it and so that your mother's warmth and applause would last. She made me feel like that, even then, with her disapproving gaze. I wanted you, but first I had to appease your mother. I should have known then.

The majority of the time she was icy cold. Functional and organised, it was a rare treat that she would laugh and hug you. Her pride lay in impressing other people. Not everyone, just the people she considered to be important.

She never made any secret of the fact that she didn't think I was a good mother. Right from the start she objected to my Primark baby-grows and second-hand prams. Charlie and Laura would come back from a weekend with her wearing designer children's wear and clutching a bag of expensive toys. The most surprising thing was her rationale.

'I just want them to have the same kind of upbringing that Jack had.'

The thing about liars is that they forget who was there. They happily lie their way through life and lose track of the evidence. She forgot that I had you to tell the other side of your childhood. You told me that she spent all her money on herself, and that she rarely bought toys or took you on expensive trips. After your father died she became even more self-centred. I weighed the situation carefully and realised that this wasn't a case of you and her against me, rather that you were using her just like you were using me, and I sometimes felt sorry for her. Her one saving grace, and the reason I didn't, couldn't, cut her off completely was that she does love Charlie and Laura. She used them to point score, but she does love them. With them, her smile is soft and her hand is light in a way I've never seen before. Perhaps she sees them as her second chance to perfect motherhood, but they're my children not hers. When I first had them I was her favourite too. But as they grew and became independent of me she cooled. Later, as your partner, I was so far off her trajectory of expectations that she virtually ignored me. So now, sitting here in a strange car in the middle of the night, I feel a little bit sad.

Even after she's manipulated the situation so far that she took my children, I still feel sad that this will be the end of our relationship. I suppose it's a bit like Stockholm Syndrome. I've been stuck in a destructive relationship with her all my life, but it's always been one where we have related. It might have been via a solicitor or manipulative actions, but we've always communicated.

Now I've won, she will be gone. When the police knock on her door and find the phone and the holdall they will think it's her who has posted on Facebook. It will look for all the world like she has betrayed her beloved son, that she disapproves of your behaviour and has protested by posting the journal. Only she and you will know the truth. Her world will crumble because she really didn't think that I was capable of setting her up.

I get out of the four-wheel drive and go over everything in my mind. I've brought Frances's phone with me, dismantled, of course. Monica's phone is at your mother's and her laptop is in the car, deactivated. My phone and laptop are at home, both with the location turned on.

I don't know how long it will take you to convince the police that they need to take action, Jack. But I know you. You've already tried to deny Pam on Facebook, posting in the middle of the night because someone has alerted you. You're like your mother. You won't wait for morning. You'll call DS Percy, because you like the personal contact. You think it gets you further.

I know you. You'll have done all this already and you'll have made sure that you get an assurance that whatever device is posting to Monica's account is traced. You'll know the location is on because you'll have seen I tagged our home. You'll think it is a done deal.

If I can find out where my mobile is using 'Find my phone', then the police will have something much more efficient. I expect they will trace Monica's phone and the laptop IP address. DS Percy will put two and two together and know that whoever posted the pictures has the holdall and will search her house. And your mother will let them.

I try to imagine her face when they find the bag. I wish I could be there, in the cloakroom, looking out onto the scene. Her working out how it got there, puzzled because she was *so sure that she had destroyed me.*

Watching as they open the holdall in her pristine kitchen and all the pictures fall out, Pam Harding's on top. Their faces as they realise what the journal is. What it has recorded. DS Percy's expression of distaste as she begins to understand the full situation. Asking herself who marks women out of ten? What sort of man takes photographs of himself having sex with his mistresses?

It will all be out in the open. They'll know what this was about, what you were trying to hide. They'll even see what you said about me. That I am stupid. Naïve. Your mother will look like a bitter woman who is mistreating her daughter-in-law. Of course, she will try to turn it around and tell them that she was doing it to protect me. That of course you needed to suffer after what you had done to poor Caroline. That she was helping me with the children. So it all looks good for her.

But the fact will remain that the bag was found in her home and the phone, with recent texts, in her hallway. The only conclusion the police can reach is that she has done it. She has harassed your exes and because you have made an official complaint about the holdall, she will be blamed. Perfect.

I walk slowly home and the sun is just about peeping through the trees. It's still dark, but it's light enough to cast shadows and to see the dew on the grass and the spider's webs that decorate my bay trees. It's easily light enough to see Pam Harding standing in the middle of my lawn.

Chapter Twenty

I sneak around the skip and through the gate at the side of the house and she doesn't see me. Rover is already going fucking mad so I don't have to worry about that. She's shouting something.

'Caroline, I know you're in there. You'd better get out here right now or I'm coming in. Open the fucking door.'

I rush through the back door and upstairs and grab my dressing gown out of the bathroom and change into it. I go into the bedroom and rub some of the feather debris into my hair and onto the dressing gown. I open my own laptop and log onto my Facebook account. Then I go downstairs and open the front door. It bangs in my face as she kicks it.

She rushes at me and I stand my ground.

'You're going to be sorry you did this, Caroline. Very sorry.'

I fold my arms and we're nose to nose.

'I'm going to be sorry? You're the one who wore my fucking wedding dress and slept with my husband in my bed.'

She takes a step backwards.

'You posted the picture online. You.'

She goes to grab my hair but I hold her wrist. I twist it and pull her towards me.

'No. I didn't. That's what he wants you to think. But it's nothing to do with me. Can't you see I'm in pieces here? I've just had to see that picture myself.' I let her go and cover my face. 'How do you think I feel? It's really ... really ... affected me.'

She pushes past me and hurries into the kitchen. She sees my laptop and the picture. She looks in my internet history for Monica's login. It isn't there, of course. She even tries the drop-down login box to see if the auto text is there.

She turns and looks at me.

'So it really wasn't you? Only he said ...' I'm standing there in a scruffy dressing gown with feathers in my hair. She looks past me. 'Jesus Christ, what the fuck is going on here?'

She cranes her neck to look at the towers of boxes, some of them opened randomly last night to locate the knives. I slump onto a chair.

'This is always happening. Jack sending people round. Doing ... stuff. Them somehow blaming me.' I look up at her. 'It's not my fault that he slept with you. Or that he took photos. Or that they ended up online.' I've got her attention now. She's pacing around. 'I think we've both been had here, love.'

She stops and stares at me.

'OK. So how did you know it was me, then? I've changed a lot since that picture.'

She hasn't changed at all. Maybe a little heavier, hair shorter. But it's so obviously her.

'I saw you on Facebook. In my wedding dress.'

She's peering at me now.

'But the picture didn't show my face. It was from the back.'

My God. She hasn't seen the second picture. I scroll down the screen on my laptop. She leans forward, then makes a little noise.

'Holy shit. But I do look good.' She turns to me. 'Sorry. That's really inappropriate. Sorry.'

Yes, Pam does look good. Nine out of ten, in fact. *Couldn't keep her mouth shut.* I'm guessing that she was always blurting out inappropriate things. So let's find out what she knows.

I put the kettle on. She's fidgeting and tapping her foot. Staring at me. She's very intense.

'So why are you covered in feathers?'

I pour the tea. Slowly. Make her wait.

'Come with me.'

She follows me upstairs. I open the bedroom door and she gasps.

'Oh my God. Have you been robbed?'

'No. This is what that picture made me do. I can't bear to sleep in here any more. You weren't the first, you know. My next-door neighbour saw him with all sorts. Brought them here in the afternoons. While I was at work.'

She's looking at the picture of Charlie and Laura.

'Those your two? Are they ...?'

'No. He made sure that I lost everything. Everything.'

I begin to clear things up and she's helping me. She's collecting the tiny seed pearls and the pieces of dress and putting them back in the box. She knows the layout of this room and she knows where the box belongs. When she's collected as much as she can, she pushes it back on top of the wardrobe, which makes me hate her even more.

I fetch a bin bag and we scoop up the feathers silently. Then the smaller pieces of memory foam. Pam piles the bigger pieces on the bed base and we sit there, looking at the room, both tired to distraction. I make my move.

'So what did he say, then?'

She's rubbing her eyes.

'Who?'

'Jack. What did he say about all this? I expect he's as upset as I am.'

'Well, when my sister told me about the picture being on Facebook,

I rang him. Just the sort of stupid fucking thing he would do.'

This surprises me. I expected her to be still in awe of him.

'Oh. Why?'

She takes out a cigarette and lights it with a Zippo lighter. Her fingernails are glittery green.

'Because he's a prick. But I guess you know that?'

'Yes. Yes. He's certainly not treated me well. As you know.'

She points her cigarette at me.

'He told me that you were a bitch who wouldn't give him a divorce. A marriage of convenience, yada yada yada ...'

'So what made you think he was a prick?'

She thinks for a moment, as if there are several things and she has to weigh up the worst.

'Well, he told me you were living separate lives. I wanted him to leave you but he kept making excuses. So I got suspicious and followed you. You weren't living separate lives at all, were you?'

I shake my head.

'He lied right to the end. Made me feel like I was crazy for knowing he was lying. So I got rid and felt immediately better. Until now.'

I hurry her along now.

'So what did he say? When you rang him?'

'He told me you'd posted it. Something about some photos you'd nicked off him. Said you were a psycho. But anyone can see that you're just heartbroken.' She puts her hand over mine. 'Sorry. I shouldn't have done any of it. I shouldn't have come here.'

She gets up and goes to the bathroom. I know as soon as she turns the tap on that she's running water over her cigarette stub. I'd found them in the mother of pearl mini-bin in the bathroom round about the time I'd smelt smoke in our bedroom. When I asked you,

you made up some cock-and-bull story about my hormones making me smell funny things. I even Googled it at the time.

They were hers all the time. She's been here more than once. I stand in the bathroom doorway as she sits peeing. She's used to this. One of the girls.

'So how long did it go on for?'

'Six months.'

Six fucking months. I swallow a little bit of bile.

'Even though you knew about the children? Were they ever here?'

'No. Never. I promise. Look, Caroline, this was a while ago and I'm really sorry. Come on, I'm on your side.'

She's sorry now. Now everyone has found out. Before, when it was your little secret, she wasn't sorry at all. She's eyeing me, looking for any sign that I'm going to turn on her, but I don't. I want her to trust me, so I smile and nod. She follows me back into the bedroom and I watch her settle into what's left of our bed, curled up and drowsy. She's kitten-like, still selfish even though she knows she's ruined someone's life. I lie down beside her and pull the ragged quilt cover over us. It really is a lovely #allgirlstogether scene.

Her breathing slows. I can't sleep. I look at the feathers in the bin bag. I pull down the box and examine pieces of my wedding dress. I loved that dress. Tiny seed pearls make a tap, tap, tap on the floor but she doesn't wake.

I hurry back to my Facebook account and look at all the comments on Monica's pictures. It's light outside now and the world is waking up. Everyone is logging on to see the latest instalment in your downfall, and now they're seeing naked Pam in my room.

It's seven o'clock. Pam's words snap at me. *I'm on your side.* Is she? Is she on my side? Fuck, fuck, fuck. Were they all on my side? Duped, like me? I stand outside my bedroom door. Our bedroom door. The thing is, I know that she is sorry. Genuinely sorry. But there's one little thing that's bugging me. She told me she followed me. Us. So she knew that we were together. Still a couple. Yet she kept on seeing you. For six months. What kind of woman would do that?

In the early days, when I first lost the children, I couldn't understand how people could hurt other people like this and get away with it. How I could hurt so much, have so much wrong done to me, yet I could do nothing about it. It isn't illegal to hurt someone you love. To ruin their lives. You just have to 'get over it'. *Let it go.* Even the kind of cruelty you put me through. *All's fair in love and war.* It doesn't seem like it is right now. Not at all.

I turn around and look at the two doors facing me, both locked. My children's names stencilled on the doors, with ivy frames. I want revenge, but I want my children back too.

Chapter Twenty-one

Pam's suddenly behind me. I jump, wary of the horrible things I want to put her through that race through my mind. But I'm stronger than that. The thought surprises me and I straighten. She smiles.

'Come on. It's been a long night. Let's have a cuppa.'

Her voice is soft and quiet and I wonder if, apart from fucking my husband, she is a nice person. She motions for us to go downstairs and we sit at the kitchen table. She tilts her head to one side.

'I know you don't believe me, but he took me in too. Told me he was leaving you. That he'd leave soon. And yeah, I did feel sorry for your kids. But I thought I was in love.'

I snort. 'But you fucking knew he was with me. You fucking knew.'

'I bet you hate me, don't you?'

Her eyes are pleading. I nod.

'Maybe not hate. Strong dislike? You deserve it.'

She winces. 'OK, maybe I do. But deep down you know that it's not my fault. It's his. I was stupid. So were you. And whoever else he took in. But having a go at me is just going to make it worse. For both of us. The Facebook stuff is one thing ... but all that upstairs, the dresses and that, well, it's a bit ...'

She lights a cigarette and gets a saucer from the cupboard. I think how close I came to taking real revenge. I feel a pang of guilt, a roll in the pit of my stomach when I think about Frances's shop.

What the hell is happening to me?

I study Pam as she checks her phone messages. She looks happy. I wonder how, if she says she loved Jack, she had got over it. How do people do that? For the first time since I saw that fucking holdall I feel genuinely sad. I wonder if I've done the right thing, going after these women.

I can't change it now, but I can do something about it. I can go and talk to DS Percy. I can tell her that I'll help her as much as I can with her inquiries and, obviously, the posts will stop so you won't be able to complain any more.

I watch Pam's cigarette smoke wind through the morning sunshine.

'What you said, you know, we're on the same side?'

She laughs. 'We are. We're both Jack's exes, like it or not.'

I hadn't thought of it like that. It's different for me. I was married to him. I had children with him. But I'll take it. I need to think. Think of a way to get my kids back.

'Yeah. Well, it's just got a bit out of hand. I didn't ask for any of this.'

She looks around and waves her cigarette at the boxes.

'All this. You need to unfuck yourself. You need to think about getting back to who you were before all this shit happened. Look, we're never going to be soul sisters, but if you ever need anything, give me a call.'

She tears off the top of her cigarette box, writes her number on it and throws it across the table. I'll never use it, but I take it. I suddenly remember Sandra Bullock in some film where someone says you have to look after a plant, then a pet, then you might be ready to look after a relationship. Or yourself. The guilt eases a little and a wave of relief washes over me. I was beginning to believe it.

That I was mad. That I was the psychopath. But this chink of regret tells me I'm not. Unfuck myself. Yes. There's still a chance for me.

Pam leaves. I put on my coat and because I've had no sleep I get a taxi to the police station. DS Percy is in a *call me Lorraine* mood. She's talking about the Peter Daubney case, how they haven't made any progress. How they are trying to trace and question everyone in the bar that night. Going on about a lot of things that have been stolen – more than I took, for sure. Had I remembered anything else?

She makes me a cup of hot coffee and we chat about what we did last night as if I am stupid enough not to know she is sounding out my movements. But I oblige and give her a rundown of how I fell asleep early. When I've finished she leaves the room and comes back minutes later with a file and a tablet.

'Do you know this woman?'

It's Pamela. In my wedding dress. For one horrible minute I think she's played me at my own game and told them what I did.

'I don't know the woman but that's my wedding dress. The one that I was going to give to my daughter. Priceless.'

She reads the file. It takes a long time and I worry more about what Pam had to talk so much about. But I'm totally on the wrong track.

'So it turns out that she's contacted your ex about the picture being posted and he said you had done it. Even after I had told him that it wasn't you.' She shuts the file and leans forwards. 'Look, I can see what's going on here. He's harassing you. And you can do something about it. You can press charges. Against both of them. Caroline, do you think that he sent those photographs?'

My God. Just when I was going to spill the beans, she's worked it out. She's put it together. Finally. She not sure, but she's asking me. Perfect.

'I don't know. I don't feel confident. It's one thing after another. I feel ... vulnerable.' I need to get out of here. Now. 'I'm worried what he will do next. I honestly don't know anything about all this. But he's convinced it's me. I don't know how ...'

She gets up and shuts the door.

'I was going to tell you at some point but ... well, it's a bit tricky. We've found the missing bag.'

I can hardly disguise my pleasure. I feel the guilt and regret fading and I try to drag them back, but the pull of revenge is too strong. It's like a wave washing over me. I can tell her later. But for now ...

'Oh. Thank goodness. Did the depot find it after all?'

She's silent for a moment. Considering how to tell me.

'No. It was found elsewhere. But you don't need to worry about that. All you need to think about now is getting some help and getting over all this. We need to focus on finding out who robbed those men and who sent those pictures now.'

That's it. She's completely invested. She stands up and it's time to leave. I can't go home – I can't face it yet – so I ask her to ring a taxi to take me to my office. I wait outside, my backside numb on the hard wooden bench. I check my messages and there's one from Eileen confirming a meeting on the 27th. Another from Amazon telling that, based on my previous purchases, I might like another slow cooker. I almost laugh out loud and look up just in time to see Missy being led into an interview room.

She looks older and frailer and if I didn't know that she was such a bitch I would feel sorry for her. She's still wearing her slippers and I suddenly wonder where Charlie and Laura are. Probably at school. Who would collect them? Rage surges up at the unfairness that it isn't me. I only just manage to resist the urge to phone social services and demand to know what's going on, who will care for my children. But I know that's what you want. Hysterical me jeopardising the meeting. All that shit still in my house. Another black mark against Caroline. It takes me all my will to stop myself though.

There was no chance that I could try to pick them up. Not after last time. I'd waited in the playground with the other mums on my allotted joint day and gone in to help with their coats when the bell rang. The teacher had shielded Laura protectively, even as she darted towards me. It turned out that your mother had rung ahead and told them that 'Caroline is having one of her off days', and that the children shouldn't go with her. But one day I will be there to pick them up. I will.

What will you do now? Now that she is no longer the shining star on the horizon? No longer the strong matriarch who will endure anything? Who will be on your side now to do your dirty work?

I'm just congratulating myself on blasting a huge hole in your defences when I spot your cheating fucking lawyer striding through the double doors and going into the interview room. They're going to claim that I planted the bag there and that Missy is innocent. Of course they are. But they can't prove it. If the police have done their homework, all the evidence will put me at home, aided and abetted by Pam's insistence that I was there to open the door for her, and that I had been trashing the bedroom before she got there, if necessary. And I have her number if I need to prove it.

My taxi arrives and on the way to work I mull over a niggling doubt I have. Where are you, Jack? If you've been following me, tracking my movements, why has that suddenly stopped? Granted,

I have been very careful. Maybe I'm underestimating how clever I have been. But you knew I was at the hotel. You knew I was in Peter Daubney's room. You must have had me followed to know what I was up to. And the photographs going back weeks and weeks. So what about the rest of the time?

Pam spoke to you on the phone but you could be anywhere. If you're not following me, and I don't see how you can be because you would know about the hole and the other car, you must be distracted. I'm overtired and stressed and I want my kids back, but I have my finger on the pulse. I check the news for anything about an incident at a tea shop again. Nothing at all. Not even local news. Nothing has been reported.

By the time I get to the university I'm all worked up about it. I go into my office and close the door. It wasn't that long ago that I was sitting here waiting to send those cases back. For the first time since then I wonder if I should have done just that. Let it be. If I hadn't looked in that journal, I wouldn't be half mad with tiredness. At least then I knew where the kids were. Now they could be anywhere.

There's only one way to find out. I take the social services letter out of my bag. This is the perfect time, with your mother in custody, to make this approach. I press the numbers on my mobile phone slowly, savouring the moment. I have to be strong. Take the initiative. A steely determination takes over me.

'Hello. Karen Connelly.'

For some reason I was expecting one of the team who had worked with me. This was someone different.

'Hi. This is Caroline Atkinson.'

'Hello, Mrs Atkinson ...'

'Dr. It's Dr Atkinson.' Damn. Damn it. Not a good move. I need to wake up. 'But please call me Caroline.'

'Oh. Yes, yes of course. Caroline. How can I help?'

'I'm responding to a letter you sent me. I'm afraid I didn't open it straight away and I've only just had a chance to ring you.'

I can hear her rustling paper. She shuts a filing cabinet and then she's back.

'Ah, right. Yes. So, we'd like you to come in for a meeting. When would it be convenient?'

'What's it about? Only, it's been a while?'

There's a long pause while she reads the file.

'A review of arrangements. We've noted that you haven't been taking your access with your children and we wanted to check that everything is OK.'

I'm not supposed to know what's happened. That your mother has been arrested and you're living in a posh apartment *sans* dependants. I sniffle.

'I just wanted to ask … are they OK? My children. I miss them. A lot.'

She's quick off the mark. 'Fine. They're doing fine. But there are some issues we need to discuss. Nothing negative. So shall we say a week on Tuesday?'

'I was hoping for sooner than that. I really want to make an effort. Things have taken off for me at work and I'm in a much better position now.'

She flicks pages and taps her pencil on the desk.

'OK. Next Tuesday?'

'Great. So who will be there? Is it just me or will Jack's mother attend? Only she's looking after them and I—'

'No. No. I don't think she will.'

I wait a moment, but she doesn't enlarge.

'Jack, then? Their father?'

'As the other parent he can be. If he requests it. Look, I'll explain everything when I see you. Don't worry, Mrs Atkinson, it's just an informal meeting. 2 p.m. OK for you?'

We agree and I end the call. Good. It's underway. It makes me feel excited, but nervous. It's a step forward, finally. What will they think of me? Laura must have missed me or she wouldn't have asked to see me, would she? The only problem is that now I have less than a week to finish my mission. And six more women to track down. I just want to know who they are. Like Pam said, it's gone too far and I feel genuinely guilty about what happened with Frances, but social networking is different. It isn't real. Is it?

Chapter Twenty-two

It's difficult, but I manage to stay in my office all day. I even switch off my phone and I don't check the internet once. I finish off some research for the funding grant and go over the work I did on the psychopath test. I make sure that I leave the door open and log onto the university computer system so that, if necessary, I can prove I was here.

It's teatime before my mind wanders to Pam and the house. I turn my phone back on and there are two missed calls from DS Percy. She's left a message and I listen: 'Have you thought any more about what I said? You might want to think about getting some counselling after what's happened. Give me a call back so I can update you.'

I dial her number and she answers immediately.

'Hi, Caroline. How are you feeling now?'

I almost laugh. She's so concerned.

'Well, I'm tired, obviously. But I had to go to work.'

'OK. With the pictures on Facebook and everything. Have you thought about what I said?'

I have thought. About little else. But it isn't time yet. She wants me to have you charged with harassment. To haul you in front of a poxy magistrate and have you bailed the same day. No. I want more. In that moment I realise that this isn't finished yet. I've memorised the running order of your journal and Alicia Turnbull is next. While *Lorraine* is going on about the procedure to get you to court and what I would have to do, I look on your profile for Alicia, careful not to click anything. No one can sue me for looking at my ex's Facebook profile, can they? She's not there. Expensive tastes. That's what it said in the journal. Must have an expensive-tastes job then.

I log into the untraceable University LinkedIn – the servers are reset every night – and type in her name. There she is, just like in the pictures of you and her. Pale, thin, with caramel coloured eyes. I see that she works for an underwear company. She has lots of recommendations.

> Alicia is a top performer. She excels at everything she attempts. Since becoming the MD Alicia has taken the company from a midlist to a Blue Chip.

And:

> I've worked with Alicia for many years now. Down to earth, funny, yet a top-notch sales person, she prides herself on her grounded attitude and flawless personal and business reputation.

Oh, this is going to be easy. I save it up for later, then scope the next one. Lorna Kershaw. This one is interesting because she was a three out of ten. If I remember correctly, there are no sex pictures, just a couple of nights out. Next: Louise Shaw. In-your-face, footballer's-wife type, if her Facebook profile is anything to go by.

I suddenly realise that *Lorraine* has finished speaking.

'... so it looks like we would be able to charge him with harassment.'

'Oh. Right. Well, he did give me quite a fright.'

'Yes. I know. But Caroline, if there's anything at all you want to tell me ...'

I fake laugh. I know exactly what she means and earlier on I would have. But I need time to think. Make sure I cover my tracks. I took a massive risk going to The Tea Cosy. And Pam knows how fucked up I am from the state of my bedroom. I want my kids back and that wasn't the way to go about it. I face it out.

'Well, I know I need to get the house sorted, if that's what you mean?' I know full well she doesn't mean this. 'By the way, I just wanted to say thanks. I phoned social services and I've got a meeting set up for next week. So ...'

Silence. She's debating whether or not to tell me about your mother. I hold on seconds longer.

'If that's all ...'

'Yes. Yes. Look, I'll give you a call in the morning. There are a couple of other things I need to check out. Speak then.'

She drops the call and I stare at Louise Shaw. I check the comments on Monica's account. Obviously, none from Alicia, none from frigid Lorna – she probably thinks she's had a lucky escape. But Louise is all over it. Liking comments. She even posts a sad-face emoji.

But she doesn't comment anything about why she slept with my fucking cheating husband. She could be agreeing or, like me, just stalking. These women. All so different. Surely they would all want to come out and show you for what you really are? A philandering bastard. I'm actually starting to wonder if we *are* on the same side.

I log out of the university system and flick off my screen. I call a taxi and when I arrive home my next-door neighbour is waiting. She's got a lot of make-up on and she's had her hair done.

'Police have been. Been asking questions. That woman. Saw her when ... you know. Told 'em. Told 'em she was here with Jack.'

She's got a memory like an elephant. I wonder what else she's told them.

'Thanks. That's brilliant. Did they ask you anything else?'

'Only the usual. Who's been here lately? Told them that his mum was round a couple of times. Were you here last night? Which you obviously were coz Brian saw you open the door to that woman. She was shouting for a bit before that.'

Your mother. She told them that your mother had been here. Brilliant.

'Yeah. I was upstairs. To be honest, I was a little bit scared.'

'Well, you had good reason. She's a nutter.'

I take the opportunity to exploit her nosiness.

'So have you seen anyone hanging around here? You know. Anyone?'

She shakes her head and her hair extensions swish.

'No. Never seen anyone round here. All this is proper exciting for us. Brian's got it all noted down.'

I nod. Of course he has. I expect he's been showing his notes to the police, which bodes well for me because I know for a fact that you can't see my back garden from their kitchen window. The only time I've been in there, when my water was off and I needed to fill the kettle, I looked across. To see if they had a view of the hole. But the fence is just that little bit too high. So fucking Rover can't escape. Good boy, Rover.

'Well, I'd better get in there and tidy up.'

She stifles a laugh as she turns away. I know they're all laughing at me. That mad woman whose house is full of Amazon boxes. She doesn't throw anything away, you know. She's an eccentric academic type. Her husband divorced her. She lost her kids.

But I haven't lost them, I remind myself as I grip the side of the skip and smile at her. If I can just get through this, get to next Tuesday, I've got a shot at getting Charlie and Laura back. Your mother's learning her lesson right now and, by the time I've finished with you, you'll wish you'd never been born. The rest of your harem are going to help me in my mission, even if they don't know it. I know I can't do anything that will compromise Charlie and Laura, but I need to get the message through that I'm no pushover.

The inside of my house is a complete mess. The boxes I have opened to find the knives are stacked up against the other boxes. I start to take the stuff out and make a couple of trips to the skip with empty boxes, but I'm tired. Then I suddenly remember that I have no bed. No mattress, anyway.

I go upstairs and survey the damage. As well as what's left of the the ripped-up pillows and mattress, and the dresses and tiaras, the tiaras' metal has ricocheted off the back of my bedroom door. The beautiful wood is damaged. I run my fingers over the rough welds. In a previous drunken temper I'd scrawled on the walls in red lipstick that I deserve everything I got and didn't I know that you never loved me?

It seems like it was someone else who did that now – someone desperate – whereas now I've changed direction and I'm not craving the in-between so much. But how appropriate those words were. These words decorate the very room where I realised that you didn't love me. I'd been interviewing people for my Ph.D. studies. It was about relationships. Most of the women I interviewed had talked about their husbands or boyfriends like they were friends. Many described them as their best friends and the person they trusted the most. It had rankled. One of the questions in the study was: how has your relationship changed after five years?

All but one of the women told me that their relationship had improved. Particularly their sex lives – less often but better. The one quality that stood out in their relationship was laughter. They laughed with their partners. I didn't laugh with you. We went out to restaurants and you talked about your work. I talked about my work. We discussed the kids. Sometimes the past.

We never talked about sex. It was as if it was a taboo subject between us. Even when we were doing it we didn't speak to each other, did we? It was a performance. Worse, it had always been that way. No laughter. No fun. It was as if the kids, the house and I were just a container that you could step into every so often for clean clothes and respectability.

I suppose I knew deep down that you didn't love me. After the study, it nagged at me more and more every day. I watched other people, couples, wearing wedding rings. I sat in cafés in shopping centres in town and watched how people reacted to each other. Was there laughter? Was there touching? Listening? Yes. Yes, yes, yes.

So, I brought you shopping. I wanted to see if it was my imagination or if you really were perpetually distracted. I brought you to the Costa Coffee where I'd been people watching for months. Ever the scientist, I repeated the experiment in situ. A controlled environment where everything that the other couples had was in place.

Social situation. Coffee. Piped music. Cake. Just two people on a shopping trip, treating themselves to some of life's luxuries. You looked bemused right from the start, because I never made demands on your time. You agreed to come with me for the children's Christmas presents. The journey there was conducted in the strained silence that always pervaded when you needed to be somewhere else. It was as if you were under extreme duress.

Once there, I laughed and made light conversation. Some would say I flirted, but how can you flirt with your husband of many years? You stared at me for a long time, until I ran out of amusing stories. You drained your cup and, as I placed my hand over yours, you drew it away.

'Are you feeling unwell, Caroline?'

I laughed again and your expression barely changed. We did the shopping and went home. I suggested that we store the toys and clothes in the top of the concealed wardrobes. You're taller than me and I had to ask you to reach up. As you did, I put my arms around you and drew you to me. I raised my face up to kiss you, but you pushed me away. In that split second I saw your face in the dressing-table mirror as you turned away. I wasn't supposed to see it. You hid that expression from me, but I saw it. It was disgust.

Even though I was shocked, I kept trying. Turning my head so that the brotherly kiss on the cheek became a kiss on the lips. Making the first approach in bed, only to be snubbed and told that it wasn't ladylike. I bought new underwear. It turns out it was from Alicia's company.

It was one day, sitting in this room, that I finally realised. I suspected your philandering but I could never prove it. And you'd never hit me. You weren't especially cruel to me. You gave me money, bought me birthday and Christmas presents. You took me to nice restaurants. We never argued really. I shouted but you rarely reacted. You just withdrew. You were away more and more, and when you came back you played with the kids, then sat in the study.

I suddenly realised that we had no life together. If I disappeared into thin air you wouldn't miss me, as long as the washing was done and dinner was cooked. It has always been like this, except at the very, very beginning. I was a means to an end. Someone to feed the cat, and then the kids, while you were away. If I got too close, you could just push me away without any fuss. That wasn't love. It broke my heart.

Chapter Twenty-three

So the words I scrawled on my bedroom wall are the truth. Yet now, in the aftermath and with the real truth out in the open, they matter less. It just makes me more and more determined to show the world who you really are. This room will have to wait. I'm checking into a hotel where I don't have to think about it. No reminders.

I grab some clothes and push them onto a blue denim holdall with enough spare underwear for five days. I need to have this finished by Tuesday. I send an email to Eileen.

Dear Eileen

I've decided to go on a research trip where I can finish writing up the Naylor abstract and think more about this funding bid. I'm really excited! Be in touch,

Caroline

It's only half a lie – I have finished the Naylor abstract already, but I do need to think about the funding bid.

I sneak out the back way and go to the hole. I need to be anonymous, so I pull out some of the money I had left over from buying the car.

No one is following me. It's getting dark and I wait until the sun has stopped reflecting off its bonnet. Then I drive up across the moorland, purple with heather and shadowed with dusk. Quite beautiful. It's all going well until I pass The Tea Cosy.

I can't help but slow down and stare at the door. It has the closed sign up.

I check myself – weren't the photographs from the journal enough? Why do I need to see this in person? *Unfuck yourself, Caroline, unfuck yourself.* It's as if it's all become one big game and I need to see it with my own eyes. I check my rationale for doing this – revenge. But revenge without harm. I just want them to suffer emotionally in the same way I did. Just a little bit more, I promise myself, then it's over.

I can't think about that now. *Wait, Caroline, wait.* All in good time. It will all come out in the wash. For now, I need to focus on my next task. I park in the gravel area at the back of the Hare and Hounds Hotel. It's hidden from the road, which is partly why I chose it.

I've been here once before on a works outing and it's pleasant, with an open fire and pub food. I check in as Carol Lord and bring in made-up Monica's laptop and the flash drive. I unpack and half an hour later I'm sitting in a Queen Anne chair in front of a log fire. The pub is quiet and I order sausages and mash.

While I'm waiting, I check that location is definitely off on this laptop, then I make three email addresses, one each for Alicia, Lorna and Louise. I prepare profile pictures from the scanned journal photos and make a Facebook account for all three of them. Then I set about making a history for them. I post 'life events' and copy pictures from random Facebook profiles and soon they all have make-believe lives. It takes me about an hour, including eating the sausages and mash, and when I'm finished I'm very pleased indeed with my work.

Naturally, I'll have to be careful, because DS Percy will believe that she's got made-up Monica. Your mother will be in the frame for that and I don't want to detract from the good work I've done there. These will be more of a personal campaign. More of a support group. Instead of working against the tide, I'm going to work with it and give everyone else a chance to say how they feel about Jack Atkinson. Test Pam's theory that we're all on the same side. Why should it be just me?

I make Alicia the poster, as she's the one who hasn't actually got a Facebook account, so she won't see it.

'Never thought Jack was like this #shocked #ifyoucantbeat themjointhem #manshaming,' I post a nice picture of them looking into each other's eyes. I look through the photographs for another suitable one and I stop at a scene in a restaurant. He's there. So is Alicia. So are our 'friends' Lucy and Kieron. All smiling. Alicia is holding up her hand and there's a ring on the third finger of her left hand.

I see red and slam down the lid of the laptop. An older couple in the corner look at me in disgust and I remember that I shouldn't be drawing attention to myself. When my heartbeat returns to normal, I look again. I enlarge the picture and, yes, it's my grandmother's engagement ring. The one that went missing out of my jewellery box.

It was claimed on the insurance and we spent the money on a nice camera. For the family. I never saw the camera again. It was all bells and whistles, timers and filters. Now I know what it was for.

I write another status for Alicia.

'We were engaged. Anyone else? Come on, girls. Let's tell the world what Jack Atkinson's really like #cheatingbastard.' I post the picture and tag Jack, Lucy and Kieron. I wait ten minutes, sipping a frothy cappuccino, and congratulate myself for not choosing vodka. It's nice here, in front of the fire. I feel a little sleepy, but I need to stay awake. I've dismantled my phone so when DS Percy rings me she will get my answerphone.

I log into frigid Lorna's fake profile and post a comment under Alicia's post: 'Me. He wanted more than I was prepared to give him #cheatingbastard #allgirlstogether.'

Then I log into Louise Shaw's profile. I post another comment on Alicia's thread. It's a photograph of her and you. You've got your hands on her breasts and she's pouting.

Lots of people are admiring your photography skills with your lovely new camera. I Google our insurance company, the one we used to use, because I changed it when you left. I go to their contact form and enter your details, our old address and your new address. Then I explain how the ring belonging to your wife that you said was stolen wasn't stolen after all and that you actually gave it to your mistress. Oops. Then I attached the photograph of Alicia wearing the ring and press submit.

When I go back to Facebook, incredibly, Katy Squires has posted her own photograph. I haven't checked her out yet so I'm totally not ready for this. She's standing beside a Christmas tree and I check the background to make sure that it isn't my house.

It isn't. It's a Victorian-style lounge with a Chesterfield and a piano in the background. You're standing behind her. Your hands are stretched around her pregnant belly. I feel momentarily sick, but remember that I'm doing this so I know everything. I scour the picture to try to find some clue to how long ago it was taken. She was at the end of the journal, near to last.

I find her Facebook profile and there she is, with a small child. He's all over her Facebook. Jamie at playschool. Jamie in the snow.

Jamie with a dog. Jamie with a bike. I scroll down and down through her photographs and, finally, about four years ago, Jamie with Daddy.

There you are, Jack, in the hospital, holding Katy's baby. I click through the photographs, almost blind with tears. This was in the years we were together. All the times I asked you if there was someone else, if things were wrong between us. You just stared at me and suggested I go and get some medication. That I was imagining it.

All that time you were having a baby with someone else. You were working away a lot, home about every three weeks to see the kids, then off again. I flick, flick, flick through Katy's pictures and see that you were there when Jamie took his first step. There are even some pictures of you in bed with baby Jamie.

Jamie wearing a T-shirt saying 'My Daddy is a Scientist'. I'm suddenly able to time it. Yes. I remember that day. You came home from the airport with presents. You'd bought me perfume from the airport shop as usual and I remember thinking that you did love me after all. Any little token would convince me. You had the same T-shirts for Charlie and Laura. Later on you took them out to McDonald's to give me a break and yes, you did take them to see your other son. The next few pictures are of you and all your children. All the children I know about so far.

I go back to the thread. For a second it's as if there's a whole world out there mocking me. *How did you not know, Caroline? How could you have been so stupid?* But then it ebbs away and I realise I was right. This isn't just a bit of fun with another woman. This is seriously fucked up and it bolsters me. I was right. I was. Katy has posted another comment under the picture. 'Seems like Jack made a lot of promises he couldn't keep.'

I somehow manage to log into all the fake accounts and make

them like each other's comments. Then I post another Alicia picture. You and her kissing. '#cheatingbastard #allgirlstogether.'

In a strange way, I am starting to feel some camaraderie with your women, especially Katy. Closer to them and further away from you. After all, I suppose, I am one of them. You lied to us all. Katy posts again. It's a picture of you and Jamie. All smiles, a little boy who looks so like you. Our children are blonde like me. But Jamie is a mini-Jack. Katy is wondering how many more women there are. How many women you have lied to. She's obviously bitter and I'm starting to feel sorry for her and Jamie.

This is bigger than revenge. Yes, she knew that you were with me. She had my children at her home. I think about that day, when you brought Charlie and Laura home. When we all sat around the table later on and they were so quiet. I put it down to the fact that Daddy was home and they were behaving. None of the squabbling or poking each other, the kind of childhood behaviour that was normal for them when it was just me.

They were subdued. What had you told them? Had you told them not to tell Mummy? It all starts to fit together. Laura packing a backpack in her room. Then when she realised I had seen her, unpacking it quickly, pushing the clothes into a drawer and standing in front of it to hide it. To think that I was worried that she was going to run away because things were bad between us. Promising myself that I wouldn't criticise you any more because it was affecting the children.

You were going to take them to live with Katy. I go back to her profile and load more pictures. It writes its own story. You are there with the children. In her lounge, wearing slippers, with Jamie on your knee. At Jamie's birthday party, again with Charlie and Laura. Then, suddenly, no more Jack. Katy with Jamie. A worried expression and dark circles under her eyes. A forced smile because she doesn't know what's going on. Katy on nights out with her friends. Jamie's next birthday, no Jack. Katy's lost weight, had her hair cut. Katy with her new boyfriend. Katy and Jamie.

You abandoned her. Of course. My God. I feel sorry for her. She was the opposite side of the deceit, the other me. I can't help but think that it would have been easy for her, when you left her, to let me know what had happened, but I feel sorry for her. And I feel you slipping away, less of my Jack and more of someone I hardly knew.

Chapter Twenty-four

That's it. I can't take any more of this. You've got another child. With someone else. Neither of us knew the full story, the truth about each other. Something has snapped inside of me and I'm no longer hurting so much. With every revelation I'm a little bit stronger, more driven to get my children back.

Your mother is in custody and I'm entitled to access to my own children. I'm not going to let them go through another minute of suffering and this won't wait until Tuesday. I tell myself that it might count against me at the meeting but I can't take it. I can't. That injunction isn't worth the paper it's written on. It works in my favour, because it says that I can't go within 50 yards of you wherever you are. You and your bent fucking solicitor thought you were clever, didn't you, having it written up like that because you didn't know where you would be living after you were 'forced to leave the marital home'.

My solicitor had no choice but to agree to not approaching the marital home because I was still living there. She told me at the time that the solicitor's clause was pointless because I could claim that I had no idea that Jack was in a bar before I went in. Or in a town. Or a country. Or in this case, an address.

I'm not supposed to know where you live. It's been kept a big secret in case mad Caroline rolls up. That's where you'll have taken

Charlie and Laura. I just need to see that you're treating them properly, because I don't fucking trust you with them. Parading them in front of all these different women. They're probably confused. No wonder Laura wants her Mummy. The thought of it distances me further and I can't even picture you now.

I hurry out to the car, pull on the dark wig and throw the laptop onto the seat beside me. I open it at my Spotify cheating bastard playlist and select 'There You Go' by P!nk. That posh flat you're renting isn't far from here. While I'm driving, I get an uncomfortable sense that I perhaps shouldn't be doing this. That taking the children at this point isn't the best idea. That I should just check that they're OK and go through with the social services plan.

I'd do anything to be at home, insulated by my boxes, blocking the world out with vodka. But I'm not and you've got another child and Alicia's got my Grandma's ring. I pull over and remind myself that I opened Pandora's box. What did I expect? I knew what you were up to and now I'm facing it. I just didn't realise how bad it would be. There could be more to come. I stare into the night as I grip the steering wheel hard. I'm suddenly alone. I can't see the shape of what else could happen. What could be worse than this?

It's a remote location. I assemble my phone and its green screen light gives the inside of the car an eerie glow. I check your profile because that's the only way for me to see Alicia's thread. Three other women have commented. One, Janet Baines, is telling us that you took her on holiday then didn't return her call.

Another tells a very vivid story of you meeting for a second date, then saying you had to take a call and not returning, leaving her to pay the bill. The third, who I recognise vaguely from the list of one-night stands at the end of the journal, explains that you told her you were divorced, but, after seeing you a couple of times and you not inviting her to your place, she followed you and saw you with your wife.

It's incensing. My life has been on public fucking show. A steady procession of paranoid women waiting outside our home, watching me to see if we were still together. While I was watching to see if you were still with them.

I'm scrolling down the comments when my phone rings. It's DS Percy. I think about letting it go to answerphone but I decide that it would raise more suspicion, so I get out of the car and answer.

'Hello?'

I'm whispering into the darkness, the night pressing in on me.

'It's Lorraine Percy here. I just wanted a word about—'

'Oh, my signal might be bad. I'm just going for a drive. Blow the cobwebs away. Can't face sorting the house out just now.'

She pauses.

'It's about the holdall.' I let out a sigh of relief. For the first time in ages there's a tingle of anticipation in my tummy. I wait for her to carry on but she doesn't.

'Oh. Right. Have you arrested someone?'

'No. I just wanted to put your mind at rest. But there's something else.'

'OK. Is this to do with Peter Daubney? Should I be worried?'

I can hear her breathing. She's up against it, trying to work it out.

'It is and it isn't. We examined the holdall this morning. Forensics are having a look at it. It's thrown some light on the pictures that were posted on Facebook.'

I jump in. 'That's good, isn't it?'

'It is, but the problem is, we've questioned the person who had the holdall and they deny posting the pictures. And since we found it, more posts have been made.'

I smile to myself. She's going to have to tell me.

'I'm sorry, you've lost me. I don't see what this has got to do with me.'

'OK. The pictures were in the bag. The ones that were posted. The person who had the bag has accused you of planting it in their house. And your ex-husband has made another complaint about some Facebook posts since the bag was found.'

Come on, *Lorraine*, tell me that his mother has the bag. Listen to how ridiculous it all sounds.

'But that's impossible. I've never had any bag. Or pictures. None of this has anything to do with me. To be honest, I'm more concerned about those threatening messages and the photographs of me. I have my rights. They could be after me.'

'You do understand that I have to check, though, don't you?'

So far I've been as helpful as possible. I've been friendly and pliable and told her everything I know.

'I do, but as I said this morning, this has gone too far. I'm scared of going home. This could be anyone. God knows there are enough bitter women involved to make a bloody army of suspects. So why me?'

'You're the only one he has accused.'

'Of course I am. You've read the file. You know exactly what the deal is with me and Jack. He'd do anything to keep his glowing reputation. Usually at my cost. You must see that from our history.'

She pauses. I visualise her nodding into her phone.

'But that would give you a motive, wouldn't it?'

She's gone to a point beyond where she should have. She's telling me her game plan, so she can't believe it.

'No. That's the thing. He beat me in court. He had me in court and took my children. You've seen how I live. It's all I can do just to survive.'

It all screams that I'm the victim here, I'm the one who is being wrongly accused. Again. She's not stupid. She knows there is something wrong with all this. But she has to prove it, and she can't.

'Yeah, I know. Look. I don't want to do this on the phone. I'll pop round.'

Of course you don't. You want to see my reactions. My body language. Shit. I've just told her that I've gone for a drive but my own car is parked outside my house.

'Give me an hour. I need to go to the supermarket.'

'Oh, it's OK. I'll just wait outside till you get back.'

She ends the call. Shit. Shit. Shit. I jump in the car and reverse, screeching the tyres. I throw the vehicle around corners at speed and down, down, down towards town. When I'm a few streets away I call at a local shop and pick up some milk, then park up. I can see my house from here and her blue Yaris is parked up in my road. I hurry around the back of the trees and towards the shop.

Luckily, having been brought up round here, I know all the short cuts. I can't get around the back of the house without her seeing me, so I cut through a copper-birch-lined alleyway and come out at the end of my road. My heart is beating fast and I start to jog. As I pass her car, she jumps out.

'Caroline, you must have got back before me.'

'Just been for some milk.'

I fumble with my keys and try to put everything in order in my mind. My overnight bag in the hotel. Jamie. My grandmother's engagement ring. The Facebook #cheatingbastard #allgirlstogether thread. My hand is shaking and I can feel tears rising.

We go into the kitchen. She sits down opposite me and I can tell there is more. She gets out her little notebook.

'OK, so we still don't have a link between Peter Daubney and

Brian Patterson, the other fraud victim, apart from you, or an identity for the stalker. So we're working on that. But the other matter, well, it seems to have blown out of proportion. Your ex-husband has been down to the station with his solicitor demanding that you are arrested.'

Of course he has. I don't say anything. She looks at me and waits for a reaction.

'To complicate matters, the holdall was found at his mother's house.'

This time I gasp.

'You're kidding me! But why ...?'

'It was found this morning with some other things.'

'Right. So she was posting the pictures?'

She sighs. I study her face. She looks tired. Dark circles under her eyes. I wonder if she has kids and a husband. If she can possibly imagine what I've been through.

'That's the problem. We have no evidence it was her.'

'But she had the bag. When you thought I had the bag, you thought it was me posting the pictures. Have you charged her? And where are my children?'

She shakes her head. 'The thing is, she has no motive to post, well, pictures like that of her son. And she denies it. We would have to prove it. And there are other things. I'm afraid I can't tell you any more. It's more than my job's worth. But what I will say is that your ex-husband is gunning for you. He absolutely insists that you are behind this.'

She's warning me. She's telling me to be careful, without telling me. I'll take that. But I need to know something else.

'Have you got children?'

She reddens. She's actually wondering whether to tell me or not.

'Yeah, I have.'

'Then you'll understand why I need to know where my children are.'

'Yes. Yes. They're with his mother.'

I breathe out. So they're not with Jack and one of his lying girlfriends. Not playing happy families with Katy and Jamie.

'Thank you. I appreciate it. You know, they're all that really matters to me.'

She nods, but I see her looking at the bottle of milk. Checking it out, scoping where it came from.

'I'll get going, then. Give me a call if anything else occurs to you. I'll be in touch.'

Her eyes are on my shoes and my jumper, looking for clues as to where I have been. She has the journal now, so she has the key to all this. She suspects something. I need to act fast.

Chapter Twenty-five

I watch her as she walks down the drive. She stops beside my car and feels the bonnet. Then she walks towards her car and walks straight past it. I run downstairs and out of the kitchen door. As I duck through the back fence and up the alleyway I see her walking towards the shops.

Did they have CCTV? Shit. Shit. Shit. I still had the wig on when I went in. I follow her, keeping back. Outside the shop she looks around for cameras. There are none. She goes in and I stand around the side where I can just see her through a gap in the newspaper stand in the window.

She looks at the milk then speaks to the assistant. She raises her phone and shows her something and the assistant shakes her head. She looks around for CCTV and the assistant shakes her head again.

I run, run, run before she can see me and I'm back at home to see her take a last look at my house before she drives away. I wait twenty minutes – enough time for her to not be coming back but not enough time for her to send someone to watch the house. I'm shaky and upset. She's starting to believe them. She's starting to think it's me. It's just like before.

It's getting late now but I take the back roads up into the hills, then the dimly lit lanes. One thing in particular is playing on my mind. I saw your mother at the police station. They brought her in. She had the bag. So why haven't they charged her?

Some people lead a charmed life. They never get found out. For some people it takes a considerable effort to cover themselves, but others just charm their way out of it. She's like that. Melissa Atkinson. Missy, as everyone calls her.

She even looks like a Missy. A blonde bob, neutral clothing. Beige and navy. Chanel and Dior lines. Even though she's barely middle class and had to scrape enough money together to keep the house when her husband died, she was always considered 'posh'. Or 'snobby', as my friends called her.

But I've known her a long time. I know her secrets. I know how she would pay for a bottle of milk in the shop, the same late-night Costcutter's as I went to today, and take a loaf of bread on the way out. When she got caught she would claim that she was on her way back to the till to pay. If she'd been a regular run-ragged housewife, they would have called the police. I've seen it happen.

Because she was tidy and well-spoken it was difficult to resist her lies. She would explain to us that they couldn't have done anything because it's not a crime until you get outside the shop. She didn't pay for anything she didn't have to.

'Who can I use today?'

She would actually say it. Neighbours and friends would come around with shopping and cooked food that she never paid for. I grew to realise that she thrived on the awkwardness of situations that stopped anyone asking her for money. As a result, she could save her salary from the antiques shop she managed part-time and the family allowance and buy herself 'key items'.

These were mainly designer clothes that she would mix and match with charity-shop-sourced designer labels to give her an expensive aura. Jack seemed oblivious that it was wrong. That she was stealing and manipulating. He simply learned it and used it in his own life. I was too engrossed in him and my college work to realise how bad she actually was. How damaging the lies were, and how she believed her own hype.

It wasn't until my wedding day that I fully understood how destructive she was. I thought we were keeping her sweet because you were as desperate as I was for us to have our own lives. For us to be together.

I'd planned the day meticulously. We had a lot of friends – a very popular couple – and the reception numbers were brimming with hangers-on. Early on, she'd tried to muscle in on the planning, but gave in surprisingly easily, telling me she had other things she could be doing. I was relieved, because her ideas and my ideas did not match. Relieved but wary.

I thought she was being nice by offering to put down the deposit on a small semi-detached for us. We all went along to see it and I started to plan the curtains and the carpets. When I became busy with the wedding, she offered to take over the financial dealings with the house and I let her. I fucking let her.

I thought we would be going home. Home to our house. Missy had other ideas. I found out on my wedding day that the mortgage had 'fallen through'. I knew that look by now, a slight smirk to hide a lie. An amused expression, waiting for my response. Deep down I wasn't surprised. I wasn't surprised that she wanted you with her and I wasn't surprised when we left our wedding party and returned to her home and she had a room ready for us. Missy always got what she wanted and she wanted you. Then, when we had the kids, she wanted them. But not me.

So I learned from the best. Somewhere inside me I knew that everything I experienced, all Missy's little tricks, would come in handy one day. The problem was that until now I hadn't been able to deal with the accompanying feelings. I didn't think I had it in me to face it out. Not like her.

Now things are different. I knew back then and I know now that she doesn't hate me. She just doesn't care about me. Missy doesn't care about anyone except herself. Everything's a battle to her and for years I felt sorry for her. It must have been exhausting. Even when she took Charlie and Laura and I'd recovered from the initial shock, I knew she would look after them.

It would be a challenge for her. She would make absolutely sure that everyone knew she was the best grandmother ever. She would put everything she had into it and they would receive the best care, and her best attempt at love. She wanted them, but they were also a means to an end and I was confident that when they got older I would have my chance to love them again. It's what kept me going.

Now that time is here. If I can get it all to come together by Tuesday, to show that I am a good person, supporting other women, just fighting for my rights, then I have a real chance.

I drive a mile past the hotel and check Facebook on made-up Monica's laptop. While it's booting I assemble Frances's phone. I post some more photos to her Facebook. People are linking it to Monica's thread and tagging her. Five messages. I listen to the first one.

'Fran. I'm getting worried now. Why's the shop shut? Is it about that Facebook thing? Why did you post it? Where are you? Ring me back?'

Then: 'Hi. This is a message for Frances Burrows. Please could you call DS Percy at Greater Manchester Police. As soon as possible.'

I drop the phone in my panic to get the battery and SIM card out. My God. She's following it up. She's tracking the women and probably getting statements. They all think it's me. I jump out of the car and onto the soft moss at the side of the road. In the distance I see the moon reflected on a moorland pool. I run to the edge and hurl the phone and the battery into the water.

Think, Caroline, think. She's got the journal. Why wouldn't she investigate? This is why you took the phone in the first place, to find out. All she's going to find is evidence of lying and cheating. There's the little cricket and mouse incident with Frances, which I'm mortified about, but she's probably got a new phone by now and she'll get hold of her on that.

I never thought she was stupid. I knew she would get both sides of the story and I knew that this was where it would get tough, because he's so fucking plausible. Of course she has to look into what's in that journal. Some of those women will have complained as well. They'll have instinctively thought that it was me. So she's just ruling me out. She can't prove anything.

I walk back to the car, still mulling over DS Percy. She knows all this is connected somehow, and it's connected by me. So she's sticking by me. But how has it escalated? Why is Jack suddenly at the station again with his solicitor? I have to be careful. The only thing I can do now is carry on with my plan. It's the only way. Until I've been to the social services meeting. I'm too deep in now to do anything else, even though the only thing I really want to do is to hug my children.

I get back in my car and drive back to the layby. I open Monica's laptop and log into Facebook. I'm Alicia now and the thread has grown and grown. Lots more women are sharing their Jack stories and the whole thing has been shared. Other women who don't even know you are on the #cheatingbastard #allgirlstogether thread, sharing their stories about men who had sex with them and used them.

They're posting pictures of themselves and one of them has mentioned Twitter. I log into my Twitter account and type the #cheatingbastard keywords in and it's gone viral. It's trending. They've added a #Jacksthedaddy hashtag. Twitter has firmly divided itself into two camps – #teamJack and #teamCaro. I can see why you're so furious now. And I'm fucking delighted.

Chapter Twenty-six

#Jacksthedaddy. I couldn't have made that up myself. All I wanted was for people to realise what a cheating piece of shit you are, but this has exceeded all my expectations. Still, I know you, Jack. You'll already be planning to get your own back.

'I did it because Caroline didn't understand me' isn't going to wash with what appears to be a lynch mob gathering on social networking. 'She was no good in bed. That's why I marked them out of ten.' Nah. 'She was busy with the children and work.' Nope. Even, 'She was crazy and always accusing me of having affairs.' That definitely won't work.

The world's shrinking. Just you and your solicitor now. Sitting in his office, planning how you can stop me. There's no evidence it's me, so I wonder what the Director of Public Prosecutions will say? I haven't broken the injunction or the family access order. I haven't accused you of sending those photos like you thought I would, so you could have an alibi and I would look like a paranoid mess. As far as I'm concerned – and DS Percy is concerned, for that matter – all I know is what I've read on Facebook and Twitter.

I feel better now. Kind of supported. I know that studies have been done about empathy, and it always helps when someone else has suffered in the same way as you. I am starting to have a helicopter view of this now; I can look at it from the outside. The

Twitter storm is erupting, with men joining in to defend you. Real charmers, fellow #cheatingbastards and the kind of men who would let you get up before them so that you could make breakfast for them. Or fuck your sister. Which reminds me: Paula. Next but one in the queue. I Google her and try to find her on Facebook. I've reconciled myself that the other women were like me, duped, but Paula's different. She knew. I'll find her eventually.

I take a last look at Facebook. Someone has posted a blog article about the women in the journal. An analysis of everyone up to Katy Squires, with a little drawing of them at the side. She's drawn you as a good-looking but slimy wolf, preying on those poor girls. I thought I knew better. I thought that they were equally responsible. That they all knew you were married. But even as I think it, a question mark hangs over it. Did they know or were they duped, like Pam claims? I refresh the page and then check your profile.

There's a statement.

> As many of you know, Caroline and I divorced a year ago. At the time there was some fuss about my being unfaithful. Can I just assure my friends who have supported me, and Charlie and Laura, through this tough time, that what has happened over the last couple of days is a re-occurrence of Caroline's unfortunate mental illness. We wish her well but appeal to her to stop the damage that this is causing to lives.

That's it. I'm going to face you with this. You're the one who is mentally ill. You're a serial adulterer and a psychopath. Why didn't I just tell DS Percy that you're behind the photos? That you're trying to discredit me in a power struggle. Again, only my word for it. Anyway. Sod the injunction. I need to see you face to face. I can't carry on talking to you in my head. I need to tell you that I know for sure and so does everyone else.

As I drive up towards the posh flat up in the hills, I wonder at Jack's audacity. The odds are stacked against anyone believing him but he still has to stick the knife in and turn it. It's as if he can't come to terms with the fact that he's been found out.

I grip the steering wheel and my knuckles are white. I want him to look at me, right at me, now that we are equal. Now that I know everything. I want him to smirk at me now, look down his nose. Wave me away, be completely distracted because I don't matter. He won't be able to, because he knows me. He knows that he doesn't have the power over me that he used to have. It's fading. He's fading.

I pull up to the flats and there are several prestige cars parked outside. I make a bet with myself that his is the Aston Martin. He always fancied himself as a bit of a James Bond. I stop at the bottom of the driveway and park up behind some bushes. Even though I'm in Jane Smith's car and I'm disguised, you can't be too careful. There's no way of knowing how the layout is organised, so I have no choice but to go up to the main door and read the list.

Number 23 is a ground-floor apartment. According to a helpful leaflet in the entrance hall it's facing outwards on to a picturesque lake and a forest. How lovely. It also has a small raised balcony, which frames double sliding doors to the main living area.

I press the buzzer. I don't leave it long enough before I start to press it more urgently. I keep my finger on it and I'm just changing hands when a woman appears from the front flat.

'Can I help you?'

She's aggressive and annoyed and I check that I have been pressing Jack's buzzer and not hers. I just stare at her.

'You're pressing the doorbell to an empty flat.'

'It's not empty. Jack Atkinson lives there.'

She sighs.

'It's been empty for ages. Perhaps you've got the wrong building?'

I step backwards. The inlaid stone says Villa Place. The woman at United Utilities definitely said number 23.

'Oh, wait a minute. There was a bloke round here about two months ago. Had a look round with an estate agent, then came back a couple of days later. Tall, good-looking in a classic kind of—'

'Yes. That'll be him.'

She folds her arms and moves closer.

'Not seen him since, more's the pity.'

I walk away and she watches me as I turn at the bottom of the drive. I creep up behind the bushes and across the lawns at the back of the building. The flat with the balcony is in darkness but that doesn't mean anything. I know he travels a lot. Maybe that's why she hasn't seen him.

I have to sidle up to the nosy woman's window and I can see her eating toast and jam. I wait until she goes into the kitchen and then I run across the front of the window and climb up onto the balcony. The green velvet curtains are slightly parted and I peer through them, waiting for my eyes to adjust to the light.

She's right. It's empty. No furniture. I can see into the kitchen. No cooker or fridge. There's a mezzanine where the bed would go, but again, empty. The gas and electric are on – I can see a glow inside the boiler and plug socket switches show little red lights here and there. I'm about to walk away and admit defeat when I see a small bedroom window further up the apartment.

I tiptoe along and find a stone to stand on to see into the window. There's a small table and a single bed and, just behind the bed, I see the top of the tallest Samsonite suitcase. One of the four cases that were delivered to my house.

So he has been here. He's not living here. So where is he? I slide down the wall and sit on the cold stone pathway, picking away at the moss in the cracks. This just gets more and more confusing. Wherever he is, he can't have our children with him, because they are still at his mother's. Wherever he is he doesn't want to take his bags from where he's been before.

I should have looked in the bags. They're probably full of evidence. I've got enough and I need to push forward now. Make a plan. If I'm honest with myself I know where he will be. He'll be with a woman. He can't seem to manage without one, this stranger who I've been imagining is still my husband. Or two. He needs this place to bring his one-night stands to while he lives with someone else.

He was still seeing Louise Shaw towards the very end of our time together. I worked it out from the hairstyle on the photos. Just before we went to the very first marriage guidance, he changed his normally slicked-back curls to a tight crew cut. Neat, professional. I gasped inwardly when I saw him; I still lusted after him even though I hated him. It didn't really surprise me that other women wanted him because, to me, he was the perfect man.

On some of the pictures in the journal, the ones taken with Louise in a blue dress drinking cocktails, I noticed he had that haircut. I suddenly realise that I would have been desensitised by then. I'd looked at so many photos of him with other women that I kind of skimmed the ones at the end. But one thing's for sure. He's with Louise Shaw right now. She's there while he posts those insults about me.

It's getting cold and I don't want to be here all night. So I creep back round to the car and drive away. As I leave, I see that woman standing at the door of the flats. She's on her mobile.

I take the back lanes to the hotel. The car park is quiet, only two cars as well as mine, so I stay here and check the Facebook thread. More shares and more likes suggest that a lot of people know what a #cheatingbastard Jack is. I log onto Twitter and it's even better. #Jacksthedaddy is still trending and more women are sharing their stories.

I check his profile and a few people have liked his statement. From the looks of it, more people believe me now. More and more people are seeing him for exactly who he is. No doubt his bent fucking solicitor is monitoring the situation. What can he do, though? It's the truth. The whole truth and nothing but the truth.

Chapter Twenty-seven

I can't wait to have a proper look at Louise Shaw's profile. I find her easily. She's all tits and teeth, but when I look closer she's not smiling with her eyes. Hair extensions and false nails. A pouty set of botoxed lips and an expensive fake tan. Some recent pictures with a guy who could be her brother. There are lots of pictures of her partying, but also lots of pictures of her linking arms with friends. Solidarity.

Envy flashes through me. I've got Fiona but I suddenly glimpse how it could have been for me with more support. But wasn't I getting it now? I flick onto Twitter and #teamJack and #teamCaro are still battling it out. A few D-list celebs have got involved and someone from a reality show is making a rubbish argument for 'men being men'.

Back on Facebook and Louise's profile, I scan the background of the photographs, the ones in the city centre. All her friends are wearing suits, and when I look more closely I can see him in the background. Jack. Outside the courts. Hands in pockets. Quite far away in the distance. I can just make out Missy too. Bloody hell. She must have done something serious if Missy is there. But she's a liar too.

She's not the only mother who stands up for her son, but Missy is almost militant. It's as if she needs, at all costs, to believe that her boy is innocent of everything and that it's all the evil women who are corrupting him. And those two make such a wonderful team. She would say black was white if it meant not having to face the fact that her son is a lying bastard.

The shameful thing is that she must know. She must. It's as if something started and it's suddenly gained its own sordid momentum and she is carried away with it. She probably thinks it was loyalty, strength or defending her child. I've had much more time to think about it, though. Time on my own, holed up amongst my Amazon castle walls, time to think about this from all possible angles. It isn't strength. It's weakness.

Weakness. She's unable to face who Jack really is. A bit like I was, really. I know her. I've watched her watch him and it isn't with blindly adoring eyes. No. She knows what he's up to and it takes all her will not to say a word about it. But Missy is all about saving face. Pulling up the drawbridge and building defences to make it look like everything is normal.

I peer into the photograph, enlarging it. Jack's there with Missy in the distance, heads together, isolated from everyone else. She's smoking and he's wearing a suit. And a tie. What the fuck is going on here? What has Louise done? Whatever it is, he'll protect her. He'll hold her hand, soothe her, get his fucking solicitor to defend her.

I select a picture and post it. It's the one where she's in a model pose, her fake boobs almost in his face and he's looking directly at her over-made-up face. Naturally, they're in my bedroom, but I've come to expect that now. I see that she's a nail technician and has helpfully advertised her mobile number on Facebook – thanks for that. I dial it.

'Hi. This is Monica. From Facebook. I'd like to meet up with you to discuss it all. I know what you and Jack did. Could you call this number to arrange a convenient time and place?'

I sit in the car and wait. Not only is Jack a #cheatingbastard and a stalker. He's a liar. It's something else that I can prove now, but I'm not taking it for granted. People like him and Missy always get away with it. Wriggle their way out of things or just stay quiet. With her, it's usually fear as she lords it over everyone and makes them think that she is much, much better than them.

With Jack, it's smug silence mixed with shrugging. Big brown eyes making us all, even me at one point, believe that he is the unfortunate victim of a huge misunderstanding. Then when he's caught out, he just plays dumb. Outright denial is the next line of defence. No excuses, just a plain, 'I didn't do it.' Like when I saw him in Manchester. He just lied his way out of it. In the end, I almost believed him. Almost.

Eventually the old Samsung rings. I let it go to answerphone and, after a minute or so, I listen.

'Hi. This is Louise Shaw. It was a very bad line, but if you wanted to meet up to talk about things I can meet you in about half an hour. How about in Up Steps? I'll be by the bar.'

It's late but I drive down to town. I walk over to the church and sit on the wall near the Up Steps pub. I'm just in time to see Louise arrive with DS Percy. I duck behind the wall and wait. *Lorraine* leaves and Louise sits there with a Coke. She waits and waits and waits and, when I don't show, DS Percy comes back. It's been half an hour.

I watch as they walk to Louise's convertible and DS Percy to her own car. Louise will have to drive past me to get out, but DS Percy will reverse and go the other way to the station. If she doesn't, then I'll just have to think of something else.

But she does. Louise whizzes past and I follow some distance behind. She turns onto the bypass and I'm behind her. I keep close until she indicates right, then follow and drop back. She lives in Austerlands. She twists and turns off the Huddersfield Road and I turn my lights off. Eventually she turns into a cul-de-sac. I watch as she goes into a dormer bungalow and locks her car doors remotely.

As she does, she's greeted by strong arms. I can't see from here properly, but those arms enfold her and she throws her arms around his neck. It's obviously Jack. He hugs her and pulls her inside. I can only see the shadows behind the thin curtains, but she's explaining something. He holds her again and I wonder what she's going to say when she finds out that he's included her in his perfect ten, pictures and all?

I wait and wait, just to see if DS Percy turns up. She might send a car to watch the house. To make sure that Louise is safe. From me, though? It doesn't seem fair. All I want is the truth. All I want is for someone to finally say to me that all those things that Jack said about me aren't true. That they believe me. And for him to admit that he was a complete bastard. That he was a serial adulterer and that all the lies he told were to protect himself. He's in there and I want to ask him face to face. Then it's over.

It does concern me that DS Percy appears to be protecting Louise Shaw. I thought that she would understand when she saw the journal. That she'd know what I've been through. That I'm not the dangerous one. It's him who has been going around hurting people. Arranging people's lives through deceit to suit himself. *Lorraine* has bought into his lies and she's on his side now.

She clearly doesn't realise that he's led Louise along the garden path too. How could she? I go through it all again in my head, the photographs and the journal, DS Percy's suspicion weighed by her 'just doing my job here' stance. I'm risking everything now, confronting him. It's not fair, though. It's not fair that he gets to be happy with Louise Shaw, Missy gets the kids and I get nothing. So, now I'm strong enough, I'm going to try every avenue until I hit on the truth.

I breathe in sharply. For one second I let my mind wander to the final outcome of this. Not the bad ending, where I'm arrested and he gets away with it. The ending where I get my children back. I experimentally take it a step further because I thought I glimpsed my future with him still in it and, if that is so, I really am crazy and I'm heading for trouble.

It's so common, though. Women who have been abused finally escaping only to return a week later. They're fixers. They truly believe that they can change their man, that they have the magical qualities that will morph what has usually been a lifelong, if not generational, problem, into a fairy-tale relationship. He's the one. I'm the one. We're the one. Love conquers all. It's a delusion that is sadly perpetuated by society and peddled in every greeting card shop and love song.

So I think hard. Is this what I'm doing to myself? Am I hoping I'll get a second chance, even after everything? No. No. No. No I'm not. I want out. I want to get my kids back and I want him to know how I feel. How horrible it is to question your own motives, for fear you are so deeply manipulated that you're even duping yourself. That you're not listening because you're not real. You're just a figment of my tortured, manipulated imagination. 'You' are who I want you to be, but the real Jack, him, is someone else entirely.

I bet Louise Shaw doesn't know half of what he's been up to. But she's going to find out.

I'm fuming now, super-angry that I have to go to these lengths. I slam the car door behind me. This is the moment of reckoning, when I'll come face to face with Jack, he'll have no choice but to admit what he's done and let me see my own children. In my mind's eye I see Louise Shaw pouting at him. She's smiling up at him and holding his hand. She deserves to know all about him too.

I push the gate open and stride up to the door. There's a glass vestibule and I'm banging on the glass before I catch a glimpse of myself in it. I've still got the glasses and fancy-dress wig on. For a second I question myself. Is this like Frances or Pam? Is this what I said I wouldn't do? No. I'm confronting him to see my kids, not to get revenge. With my collar up I'm unrecognisable and I realise that's why Louise opens the door just as I was regretting knocking.

I barge in past her and she nearly falls over. She follows me, leaving the door open and hurries over to some guy standing in the corner.

'Where is he?' I hear my shrill, hysterical voice say. 'Where's Jack?'

She looks closely at me.

'Caroline? Is that you?'

The guy has his arm protectively around her shoulder. It's the bloke from the photographs who I thought was her brother or something. They didn't look romantically involved. I can't have got it this wrong. I can't have.

'Where is he?' I run through to the kitchen and back out again. Louise has her mobile phone in her hand and I snatch it off her. 'No. You're not doing that.'

They suddenly both look quite scared. They step backwards and I realise that I'm brandishing the phone like a weapon. I lower it.

'Sorry. Sorry. It's just that ... Look, I know what you did. You slept with my husband. While he was married to me.'

It's all coming out wrong. She stares at me. She tries to step forward but he restrains her. She shakes him off. She's right in my face.

'It's OK, Nick. I can handle this. You think you're the only one who's been hurt here, don't you? Poor fucking Caroline. I know all about you. All about how you harassed Jack's conquests. How you lost your kids because he walked all over you. How the police think it's all got to you and you're back to your old ways.' I can feel the spittle hit my face as she shouts. She's red in the face and then I see that she's pregnant. She's pointing a false talon with sparkly crystals dangling from it at me, right in my face. 'What about me, eh? What about the other ones?'

'You knew he was married to me. I've seen pictures of you inside my house.'

I didn't want to go down this road. But as I'm here it slips out. She steps back.

'Oh! Really? Well, you know, Caroline, shit happens. I met Jack. We had a relationship. It was fun.' I look at the guy. He shrugs. She continues. 'Nick knows everything. But you don't. You don't know the half of it.'

She sits down and I look at Nick. He nods and I sit down heavily on the sofa. How did I get this so fucking wrong?

'So I'm going to tell you, whether you like it or not, Caroline. I've seen all this stuff on Facebook and I expect you think it's all a bit of fun. But it's not fun for me because he had me arrested.'

I feel a shiver down my spine. It's a wake-up call.

'What? Who did?'

'Your precious Jack. He pushed me and pushed me, lied and slept with other women, and I didn't take it lying down. Oh no. I stood up for myself. But he was cold. Denied it. Drove me mad. Because, you see, he wasn't the first to do it to me. Some other scum ran off with my mate and lied. I thought Jack was different.'

Nick interrupts.

'Don't upset yourself, love. It's OK.'

She nods at him.

'I need to get this out. I'm sick of having to shut up. Make us a brew, sweetie, yeah?'

I look at her. Less make-up, fewer extensions. No tan. She carries on.

'So it went too far. I caught him in his car with this blonde bitch and dragged her out. He told me some fucked-up story about giving her a lift and she ran off. I punched him. I'm not proud of it, but he'd pushed me right to the limit. I lashed out. He called the police. I was charged with actual bodily harm.'

Bloody hell. I panic. *There but for the grace of God go I.* That could have been me and Pam.

'So to cut a very long story short, he abused me and got away with it, and I was punished for defending myself.'

We're both silent. It's all clicking into place, what a coward you are. *Like mother, like son.* Eventually I manage to speak.

'I'm sorry I came here. But you must realise—'

'How fucking mad you are? Yes. And so do the police. Some policewoman has read that fucking journal. She warned me you might come here. Said it had made you unbalanced. Join the fucking club.'

I turn to leave. This was a big mistake. But she grabs my arm.

'Not so fast. I haven't finished yet. The thing is, Caroline, we were all used. Sure, we knew he was married, but we all thought we could change him. And he let us think that. And now we're all caught up in your and Jack's little fuck-up. Whether we like it or not.'

She folds her arms and stands in front of me. My eyes stray to her stomach.

'Is that ...?'

'No, it isn't. I'm with Nick now. We're happy. We're getting married as soon as this nightmare is over. And a word of advice: if you ever come near me again, I'll have you locked up. I'm only not doing it now because I feel sorry for you. I know what could have happened and, just this once, I'll save you from that. But next time—'

'I'm not fucking mad.'

'I know. In fact, you're too clever for your own good. Him – Jack – he's not thinking about any of us. He doesn't give a shit. All Jack gives a shit about is Jack.' She shifts her position and leans on a chair. Her partner steadies her. 'You know what you need to do now? Let it go. Everyone else has. Especially Jack.'

I leave the phone on the table and walk out. Then I run to my car and screech out of the cul-de-sac and drive back to the hotel.

Chapter Twenty-eight

As I sit in the dark behind the hotel, my hands gripping the steering wheel, I wonder if it's worth it. I wonder if anything will actually change. If I've opened a can of worms. I hadn't really considered the effect he had on those women's lives. Are they as bad as him? Am I?

Of course Louise Shaw is angry now. Of course she hates him now. Like most of the others. All blazing eyes and pointing fingers, she's mad as hell because she's tied to him and his wrongdoing through a court case.

They think I'm stupid. They think I'm obsessed. They can't see how I sat there day after day, trying to make things right, then when the kids were gone, slipping into some kind of pit of injustice. They just got on with their lives. Because he let them. That's the difference. He didn't subject them to the lies that I couldn't prove and the slow destruction of my character to friends and family. Or did he? The doubt pushes its way in, making me wonder if I have seen the full picture here.

I know revenge is primal. It's a response emotion to anger. To injury. To humiliation. *An eye for an eye.* Or *an eye for an eye makes the whole world blind*? All those things I did. But I was damaged. It doesn't seem real because I don't have the visible scars. But revenge is a response to hurt and I was hurt. It strikes me that all of those women have their own revenge agenda and this could go on for ever. Not for me. I'm tired and sorry and wishing now that there was another way. But didn't Jack make any other way impossible? It's this or lose my kids for good. But it can't go on for ever. Once I've found Paula, it's over.

I have to carry on. I have to get through to Tuesday and go to social services. By then I will have all the evidence I need. Louise shocked me a bit, if I'm honest. I wasn't expecting her to lay into me, so I soothe myself with Facebook. The screen lights up the dark car interior with a soft glow and I see that someone has made an #allgirlstogether Facebook page which has over 800 likes. The thread started by fake Alicia has grown and has 403 comments. This story is writing itself and I close the lid and relax a little. Tomorrow is Saturday, and I can put the final phase of my plan into action.

It's late and I go inside the hotel to the bar. I almost order a large vodka, but then realise where that would take me and order a Diet Coke. I sip it as I perch on a bar stool in the corner. An elderly couple are sitting silently by the fire and there's a works do going on in an adjoining room muted by a pair of closed double doors. A guy is standing just outside the doors talking on his phone. He glances over and our eyes meet. In different circumstances I would have drunk myself stupid and tried to sleep with him and I'm quite proud of my moderation as I discount it.

I open my own laptop and log onto the 192.com website. I type in my sister's name. Paula Lord. And Manchester. Three records come up. One of them is a postcode for a flat in Chorlton. The other occupant was a P. Goldring. That bloke she was living with. Then I type in Jack Atkinson. Registered as living at Missy's. I try to shout in my head, Jack, Jack, Jack, but I can't picture him. I panic. He's really gone. I hold onto the edge of the bar. I feel like I'm falling,

falling, falling fast into a deep ravine. Alone. I really am alone now.

It feels strange. A sudden sense of freedom that comes from not being attached to Jack any more. Like there actually is a future and I can be part of it. Do something. I can see what's happened more clearly with this detachment.

I stare at my Diet Coke and long for the burn of alcohol in my throat. He must have been there when I put the bag in the house. He's been there all this time. That's why Missy wasn't arrested. Because he lives at the property where the bag was found. DS Percy wouldn't be able to arrest her because he would have dropped the charges and told them that he had made a terrible mistake.

How could I be so stupid? Then it strikes me. He's been hiding something. Hiding the fact that he's living at his mother's for some reason. He knows whatever it is, it's wrong. He knows people won't understand. He knows it will make him look even worse than he does already. Not just to his precious friends and colleagues. He's lied to the police and social services. And the lies are second nature, with no remorse whatsoever. Lie after lie. *Oh, what a tangled web we weave.* This is all suddenly looking better for me.

I turn away from the screen and the guy in the corner is looking straight at me. I half smile. An alarm bell goes off inside me and I realise that I'm scared of this. Scared that if I socialise with anyone it might end up like it did with Peter Daubney – with some sordid photos and minus a credit card. But then I remember that someone's sent those pictures. Jack. Part of this stupid fucking game he thinks he's playing with me. My mind involuntarily flickers to the image of him getting the photos printed, very old school, and writing on the back, I'M WATCHING YOU CAROLINE. Even though everything else is mad, this is downright creepy. He's living in the same house as my children and I know what he's capable of.

The guy's coming over. I try to turn away, but he's standing in front of me. Sober in a bar for a change, I realise that this is just a rerun of the 'business people killing time' scenario. Same shit, different hotel. Too late to deflect him now.

'Hi. Everything OK?'

I flash him a smile. He's blushing.

'Yeah, I just wondered if you wanted a little company?'

I giggle. I suppose it could be fun. Take my mind off going straight round to Jack's mother's house.

'OK. I'm Caroline. I'm just finishing up here.'

I close my laptop.

'Yeah. Right. I'm Lee. Drink?' Why fucking not? says my rapidly deteriorating integrity. But I manage to refuse. He orders a Diet Coke for me and half a lager for him.

'Have you eaten yet? They do a great steak here.'

For one incredulous minute I think he does just actually want the company. I find myself somehow looking directly into his eyes. He smiles and sips his drink.

'Ah. So what were you thinking?' He moves closer. 'What do you like?'

I've heard it all before. They always want you to do what their wives won't do any more. It's the thrill of the chase, not that I've been running very fast at all. I suddenly feel sad as I remember my previous encounters at the Premier Inn. They all love to play out whatever they've been wanking to on the internet. I've been a school teacher, the girl out of *Fifty fucking Shades*. I've been a nurse and a prostitute. I've had them take me outside and fuck me in public and behind bus shelters, 'like they did when they were young.'

Inevitably, they describe in detail what their wives are like. Usually it's the old 'my wife doesn't understand me' or 'she's too tired for sex'. 'She won't give me a blowjob' is popular too. Thankfully, I was mostly half pissed before they got a chance to launch into their sorry tales about why they are being unfaithful. That's the thing. They all believe that they are justified.

I'm wondering what Jack said. Did he tell them that I was tired? Did he mention the late nights and early mornings looking after his children? Caroline doesn't like that sort of thing. I picture Julie Carson in my mind's eye, giving him oral sex outside. Caroline would never do that. I can almost hear him saying it to them. He never gave me a chance. He never gave us a chance to develop a loving intimacy. To have fun. I was just quick, dutiful sex between business trips or, as I now realise, mistresses. But this is progress. I can see him from a distance. A stranger.

Lee tells me that he works for a charity. He's here on a works do blah blah blah ... I'm still thinking about Jack. Him and my slut sister. My anger is getting the better of me and I'm suddenly laughing too loud at something Lee said.

He's holding my hand and pulling me off my bar stool. I'm suddenly laughing with him as he chats about some guy in the other room doing an Elvis impersonation and he laughs too and pulls me towards the dining room. The elderly couple are tutting and getting their things together. The woman looks at me like I'm a cheap tart and I feel like slipping into the in-between, where I can finally get some peace. Some time away from it all. Instead, Lee passes me a menu.

'Bar food.' He looks delighted. Maybe this is just a weird way of getting me into bed. 'Live on my own, you see. Lucky if I can be bothered to make chips and beans. Or a pot noodle.' He looks away from the menu and right into my eyes. I feel something I have never felt before. 'What are you having?'

Chapter Twenty-nine

I wake up at two minutes past seven, alone. My head's not killing me and I don't feel sick. I'm not ravenously hungry from days of not eating because of the steak and chips I ate with Lee. That's what happens when you let some of the alcohol drain from your system. No hangover central today. It feels good. I do feel a little bit elated, though, and I laugh to myself about the #allgirlstogether and the #cheatingbastard hashtags.

The TV's still on low and I watch the news for a while. Last night somehow diffused my anger and now I feel lighter. This is no Premier Inn and I'm not sneaking out at the crack of dawn. I congratulate myself for making changes. It's probably the right time to draw a line under this now. Go back to work. Go and meet social services.

It had to come to an end at some point and I haven't lost. No. In many ways I've won, because everyone knows what a fucking cheating bastard Jack Atkinson is now. His infidelity has its own Facebook page. The journal is public knowledge and no one can prove that I'm involved. I don't think Louise Shaw will say anything. She just wants to get this over with and have her baby. Marry her boyfriend. Live happily ever after.

If she does, I'll just deny it. It's my word against hers. I won't be going looking for Jack again. He's not with any of these women.

He's discarded them, just like he did with me. The sense of freedom I felt yesterday heightens with this decision and I feel fresh. I'm even considering not bothering to find Paula.

I fish my own mobile out of my bag and switch it on under the duvet. I feel like I have the strength to face it all now. There are sixteen missed calls from DS Percy. I listen to them in order. The first few are just concerned, asking me to get in touch. The tone gets more urgent as they go on and the last message a whisper.

'Caroline. It's DS Percy. Lorraine. Look. You really need to get in touch. Your husband's gone public. Please contact me immediately.'

I look at the time of the message. Eight o'clock last night. Something catches my attention, a familiar voice. I stare at the TV screen. Jack's in the background. His mother's there too.

'... so we just want her home. She's not been well, you know, mentally. It's all come to a head with her ...'

Back to the reporter.

'Jack Atkinson, her estranged husband, claims that he has become the victim of a hoax, and he fears that his ex-wife is behind it.' The report cuts to a Twitter screen where the top two trending hashtags are #allgirlstogether #cheatingbastard. Then to Katy fucking Squires. The strip across the bottom of the screen reads 'ex-partner'.

'Yes, Jack and I had a relationship and we have a son together. I wouldn't blame his ex if she had done this; after all, people need to be responsible for their actions. I'm afraid that this is just a case of actions and consequences or, as I like to think of it, karma.'

I stare at her as she stares at the camera. I recognise her. The hard look in her eye. Concerned not only for herself but also for her son. Seeing the injustice, how he can just walk away and leave her and Jamie, and she is left to cope with everything. The screen cuts back to the reporter.

'Police refused to comment on this incident but confirmed that investigations continue.'

The breakfast TV team discuss cheating husbands with two relationship experts as pictures of Jack are flashed onto the screen. I can hear a woman with long dark hair telling them that it's no wonder I had disappeared and that this was the worst possible kind of psychological abuse. That she was surprised that Missy was still going with the 'mental health issues' angle when this was just hearsay.

I smile and remember Lee telling me that he's been single for a while now and that he just hasn't met the right person. I'm mentally assessing the effect all this will have at work. Then I remember that, actually, I haven't done anything wrong.

It's only just sinking in that my little campaign against Jack has gone viral. The eight o'clock news is on now and there's Missy again. The report's shorter this time and leaves out the bit about my mental health and focuses on the hashtags and Katy. She's being interviewed on her doorstep. I study her face on the screen and she's quite beautiful. But I look beyond her and onto the road, to the horizon. In the distance, I see the old church spire and the pylons on the skyline.

She lives opposite the old bridge. The car outside her house is red. I grab my bag, the wig and my jacket and run through the hotel. I drive the short way to the old bridge and check for the press. The red car is outside a charming stone-built townhouse. I park around the corner and wait for a moment. This morning I'd thought this was all over. Now I realise that it's only just begun.

Maybe Louise was right: I need to let it go. Get over it. But I saw that look in Katy's eye. The fear. Mistrust of everyone and everything. I recognise it. She's been through the same thing as me and I can help her.

I hurry around the corner and knock on the door of the house behind the red car. Katy opens it straight away and looks at me blankly.

'Are you wanting an interview? Only I've given an exclusive to—'

'It's me. Caroline.'

She steps back, tries to push the heavy door shut, but I shove my foot in it, and yelp when it crushes it.

'Look, I only want to talk to you. Can't we be civilised about this?' She's hesitant, looking into the house, she's obviously alone. 'I saw you on the news. I heard what you said.'

She opens the door slightly and I pull my foot out.

'Go away. I don't want anything to do with this. Or you. I've got a child and ...'

Go on say it. *And you're fucking mad.* I can see it on her face.

'Whatever he's told you, it's wrong. He did the same to me as he's doing to you. Lying. Come on, Katy, can't you see that?'

She looks uncertain now, backs away.

'The police are looking for you. You're not in trouble. That policewoman is worried about you. She said you were upset over some journal.'

I correct her.

'I'm upset because Jack's accusing me of stealing it. Somebody else has it and they've been posting the contents on Facebook. To be honest, it's crucified me.'

'And what do you want from me?'

'I don't know. I'm not entirely sure why I'm here. But all I know is that I think you've gone through the same as me. And I have no one else who knows what that's like.'

I listen for the sound of a small child. Jamie's clearly not here and I bet he's with him, playing happy fucking families. In the background to all this fuckery is me as a bad mother. When I tell people Jack has taken the children, their faces say: *Probably for the best*. But it isn't for the best. I'm not perfect, but I love my kids. I'm not using them as pawns in a power game the way Jack is. I genuinely want them back.

Katy stands back and I enter. Her house is beautiful and she gestures for me to sit down. There are pictures of Jamie everywhere.

'So. Your son looks a lot like Jack.'

She looks away. She's unsure. It's clear.

'Jack's his father. That's what you would expect.'

I nod.

'My children don't look like him. They look more like me. Without the wig, of course.'

I smile but she doesn't. She's debating whether to tell me that she knows. She knows Charlie and Laura. I mentally place a bet that she won't tell me. That she'll play her cards close to her chest.

'I know. But you know they've been here, don't you?' We stare at each other, unblinking. 'They must have told you.'

So that's what she thinks. She thinks I knew.

'Is that what he said? That I knew? I had no idea. None whatsoever. Well, I had an idea that he was seeing someone else. But he forced the children not to tell me. He made them.'

I see the shock on her face. She wasn't expecting this at all.

'How? I mean, what did he do?'

I shrug. 'I don't know. But they never uttered a word. When I asked where they had been, they just kept quiet. When I asked how they got jelly on their "My Daddy is a Scientist" T-shirts, they just stared at the floor.'

'Maybe they knew it was wrong. Jack's not like that.'

No. You don't want to believe he is. Because your son is with him right now.

'What was wrong? Telling me about your affair? That's not wrong, Katy. The fact that you were fucking my husband was wrong.'

I remember my episode with Louise and my promise to myself and shut up quickly. Katy's panic-stricken and I immediately regret being so horrible. She's close to tears.

'I didn't mean—'

'I'm sorry. I shouldn't have said that. But you know how it makes you ...' She nods. 'He made my children scared of their own mother, all because he didn't want to be found out.'

She wrings her hands and glances at a photo of Jamie. I look at her hands. Red raw. The house is immaculate. My God. He's doing the same to her as he did to me. A chill runs through me. I reckon she's just sitting here in her sterilised home waiting for him to turn up for inspection.

'He told me you knew. That you had an arrangement.'

I can't help it. I laugh. Really loud.

'Really? You really believed that? Fucking hell. Anyway. That's not what I'm here for. I want to help you. And you can help me. I wondered if you'd be interested in making a statement. Saying what Jack is like. I'm trying to get my kids back.'

She pales. Her eyes narrow.

'What do you mean, get your kids back?'

Oh my God. He never told her. He never told her what he's done.

'He took them away. Made people think I was bonkers. He had me thinking that I was dirty. The worst person in the world.' I focus on her hands. 'Had me scrubbing my house. He took them anyway. They've been living with his mother for the past year. That's what all this is about, love. It's not about you and all his other women.'

Sheer panic. She's beside herself now, on the edge of her seat.

'That's impossible. He told me he picks Jamie up when he picks your two up. So they can all be together. A family. He told me that you had met Jamie. That he liked you.'

I don't say anything. I let it sink in.

'Yeah. That's the sort of thing he would say. And God help you if you disagree with him. You'll end up like me. Sitting in a stranger's front room with a wig on because you're too scared to go home. Then there's the police. Been to see you, have they? Warned you I might turn up? So why did you let me in?' She doesn't have to answer. I know why she let me in. Because, like me, underneath all that calm, composed exterior, she is seething. She can't believe that Jack simply walked out and left her. She knows we have something in common. I lean forward. 'Between you and me, I think he's dangerous. Why do you think the police are so worried about me?' I put my hand on her arm. 'I can help you, Katy. He's doing the same to you as he did to me. And God knows how many others.'

But she jumps up and grabs her car keys from the table. I watch as she leaves the front door open and runs down the path. She jumps in the shiny red car and disappears to rescue her son.

Chapter Thirty

I know I'm right. Just the fact that she's left me, the crazy ex, in her house, proves it. I look around. This was the other home, then. Where he stayed while he told me he was abroad.

In the kitchen, the cupboard under the sink is packed to the brim with every kind of household cleaner you can think of. No cups or plates on the drainer. This is a show home and Katy is on the edge of her nerves.

With my new distance I know how he did it. With Katy, anyway. He wove a web of lies. He told her that I knew. Once I had the answers, I was going to post the pictures on the thread of shame and expose Katy. Her laptop is open on the table. I tap it. It comes to life and I see that she's logged into Facebook following Alicia's thread of #cheatingbastard comments. More than a thousand now.

I could easily log in as Alicia, place the blame on Katy, but I don't. She's as duped as me. I feel a pang of sorrow. No doubt, right at the beginning, she believed that he loved her. She believed that he was trapped in a loveless marriage where they were 'staying together for the kids'. She would have believed that he was just biding his time before he left.

Even when she had Jamie and Jack was living here (no doubt between 'business trips'), she still believed it would all be fine. I can see it in her, wondering what the fuck is going on. Wondering how he can drift in and out of her life and make her feel so bad, yet still want him.

She's like me. My science self kicks in and I wonder if there has been a study. I wonder if it's only women who have children with philanderers that can't get over them, that succumb to a certain brand of abuse.

I pick up a picture of Jamie. He's bigger now. I look closer. He does have a look of Charlie. Around the mouth. I tear up as I realise that he's Charlie and Laura's half-brother. I try to think about the future. If all this works out the way I want it to, Jamie and Katy will be in my life for ever. It suddenly strikes me that this is the right thing. Charlie and Laura deserve to know their brother. Poor little Jamie, none of this is his fault. And it wouldn't be too bad. Katy's nice. She didn't ask for this any more than I did.

But my work is done here – for now. I drive back to the hotel and pack my cases. It's time to go home. None of these women are going to the police. All of them have more to lose than they have to gain. The only person who is complaining here is Jack. And that's only because he's finally been caught out.

I leave a note for Lee behind the bar – *Nice meeting you, sorry I can't make dinner.* The barman discreetly hands me a piece of paper with a mobile phone number scribbled on it – *Call me, Lee.* I suddenly feel hot and my face glows red in the mirror opposite. I think it's a warm glow.

I check out under the watchful gaze of the elderly couple who nudge each other and whisper. I glance at the TV on the wall as the receptionist calculates my bill. I catch a glimpse of #allgirlstogether on the *This Morning* show. A muted Holly Willoughby talks to two women, one who is labelled as 'jilted' and the other as 'married to a cheater'.

I don't need to hear what they are saying as the Twitter feed scrolls up the page. They cut to an angry-looking man, palms up, presumably explaining why men cheat. He's labelled 'sex addict', and I snigger to myself. I sincerely hope that Jack is labelled a sex addict. I hope that everyone is following this now and they have seen the nine women that he has cheated with.

My bill is ready and before I leave I have one more thing to do. He's slept with other women in our bed. One of them was wearing my wedding dress. He had a secret baby. Proposed to another with a ring stolen from me. What could be lower than any of that?

I open made-up Monica's laptop and push in the flash drive with the journal on it. I scroll through the now familiar scenes of him with them until I come to the pictures of Paula. Somehow, even to me, now desensitised, it seems terrible. I don't really want to see but I have to.

The first pictures are from Janine and Freddy's wedding. We were both bridesmaids – Janine had six – and in these pictures Paula was doing her 'pussycat' look at the camera. When we were teenagers she would stand in her bra and knickers and practise her looks. Pouting, seductive looks that worried me. She was sleeping with her boyfriends when she was fourteen and she would regale me with details of what they got up to.

I told my mother, of course, but she just told me that Paula was on the pill. Did I want to go on the pill? Was I sleeping with Jack? When I told her that we were waiting a while she pulled her lips back and narrowed her eyes. That was part of the problem. Paula was outrageous and I was made to feel bad for doing the right thing.

Paula's pussycat look was designed specifically to give teenage boys a hard-on. She'd have her friends around on Friday nights when my mother was out and they would dance around in skimpy dresses practising their looks. I was supposed to be 'looking after' her. Babysitting. I had to come home from uni at weekends and struggled to keep up, studying while Jack sat beside me and his eyes followed Paula.

I blamed her. Her constant 'can I practise on Jack?' and 'Come on, Caroline, join in the fun'. Of course, Friday nights turned from nights in to nights out. I'd witness the 'getting ready' with her pouty friends and the ultra-short dresses. Then sometime after 2 a.m., she would arrive home loudly with a pissed-up man in tow.

Inevitably, I'd be making coffee or studying at the kitchen table when the hungover victim tried to make an escape. I'd nod and smile and lower my eyes and soon I became known as 'Paula's nice sister'.

Fast forward a few years and Jack's attraction to Paula became much more obvious. Karaoke night at the Red Lion consisted of him abandoning me for a sing-song with angel-voiced Paula, culminating in 'Hey Paula'. It was a great laugh to everyone, very funny, but I could almost see the sparks flicker between him and her. Every time he saw her he'd break into, 'Hey, hey Paula!'

I finally flipped one Christmas Eve when he danced with her almost all night. He told me I was paranoid. He told me that I was imagining it. She was my sister. What did I think he was?

Janine and Freddy's wedding is a surprise, though. Either that or I'd given up by then. I'd been fitted for my bridesmaid dress pre-baby, and although I'd regained my figure soon after having Charlie, my boobs were enormous and heavy with milk. The dress wasn't made for breastfeeding and in the end I gave up and decided to go home.

I fully expected Jack to stay. There was rarely any point in trying to get him to come home with me; on reflection it was always an opportunity for him to meet new women when I wasn't there. This night he came home. I can see why now. The pictures of Paula with the pussycat look are outside the church from a distance. Round the back. In the background I can see my father's grave and bile rises.

I upload the photographs of Paula as a new thread on Monica's Facebook. Straight away people are liking them and tagging them and sharing them and there's a direct message. It's a journalist from the *Sun* asking to meet Monica. Offering a substantial sum of money for her story.

I delete it. Now I've posted these final pictures I feel like I really am at the end of it. I've shown the world just how low he can go. Paula, ever-simpering and saintly, will be shown as she really is. A man-stealing bitch. There's still a slight niggle as to why she hasn't admitted it. Not that I've seen her since that wedding. She's disappeared off the face of the earth. Shame, probably. Can't face me. But she'll have to one day.

I Google her and there are no results. An old Facebook page with her smiling out, last updated five years ago. Where is she?

One thing's for sure, he won't be able to hide it now. The photographs already have over 100 likes. I check Alicia's thread and they've been copied onto there, with someone pointing out that 'that's her SISTER!' and 'You OK Caroline hun? We're here for you.' Fiona has sent me a message telling me to phone her if it all gets too much. I see now that she'd messaged me several times but I'd ignored her – I'd put that right when all this was over.

It's time to go home and face the music. My best reading of what's gone on with DS Percy is that she's concerned for my well-being, either because she's believed his 'mentally ill' line or because she wonders how much I can endure. I don't think I'm in trouble. She suspects I'm behind this but can't prove it. I think it through. I'm going to need a witness. I ask the barman for the note back and leave my phone number for Lee. I add two kisses and, *Ring me.*

Because I've felt perpetually that I'm in trouble for years I don't know if I'm a hero or a villain. I'm obviously the pioneer of the #allgirlstogether movement. I'm the vessel for the outpouring of #cheatingbastard behaviour from both women and men. What I'm not sure of is how the police will view this. I do know that they need a complaint in order to act, and the only one they have so far is from Jack.

I log off and switch on my own phone. Back to the real world. As soon as I switch it on it flashes with messages. I can deal with this later.

Chapter Thirty-one

My mind races all the way. I could take this further. I could go on TV and really let everyone know what I've gone through. Everything that is happening now is a public record of me fighting back against what Jack put me through. All the more reason to maintain a dignified silence.

It isn't illegal to make a fake Facebook account. It isn't illegal to post pictures on the internet. Just like it isn't illegal to break someone's heart. It isn't illegal to ask someone why they slept with your husband. I didn't hurt anyone at The Tea Cosy. Not physically. I bitterly regret that, though. The rest is revenge. I wonder if that's how it will work.

Or, like everything else in my life so far, I'll somehow be punished for someone else's mistakes? It doesn't matter now. I started from a losing position and that was the problem. If it all goes to shit now I haven't lost anything.

Will the police be waiting for me? Will they have believed him? As I turn the corner I see a red car parked up across my drive. As the driver sees me, they pull across and let me in. I turn up the drive and park behind the skip. It's Katy.

She looks angry and I feel sorry she has to go through this. I wonder what happened when she went for Jamie, what he said to her. I half expect her to fly at me, call me a liar. Instead, she stands right in front of me. Her eyes are sad but there are no tears. Her face is set in a harsh stare. She says just one word.

'Sorry.'

It's what I need to hear. I just needed to know that somewhere in all this someone had considered my feelings. That they hadn't just disregarded me. A wave of relief washes over me and I hug her. She hesitantly hugs me back. Katy takes the key from me and opens the front door. The door scrapes a pile of mail into a bigger pile of mail. I'd almost forgotten what happened before with Pam. The mess.

Katy looks around in wonder.

'Fucking hell. Fucking hell. What happened here?'

I put the kettle on.

'Things haven't been so good. Then ... one of his women came here.'

I show her the bedroom. She already knows which door it is, a tiny detail that isn't lost on me. She stands and stares.

'Bloody hell.'

I know what she's thinking. *There but for the grace of God go I.* Her turn this time. *This is what could happen to me.* We go back downstairs. I make tea. The milk I bought at the corner shop is still fresh.

'So what did he say?'

I can't help it. I still need to know. I need to know what words came out of his lying fucking mouth, even if it's second hand.

'Well, I went to get Jamie. He just thought I was early at first, then obviously he saw the look on my face. He ushered me into the hallway ...'

'His mother's house?'

'Yes. She was in the kitchen with your two.'

My two. My children. I envy anyone who has seen them more recently than me and I almost hate her, but remind myself that this isn't her fault.

'So what did he say?'

'He asked me what was wrong. I told him I'd seen everything on the internet and I didn't think Jamie should be there at the moment. There were reporters outside. He said that he'd fight me for custody if I stopped him seeing Jamie.'

I look at her. She's terrified.

'What else did he say?' Her pupils are small and she pales. She doesn't know whether to trust me. I reach out and touch her hand.

'He said that ... that ... I would lose Jamie because I couldn't look after him. That I had no chance. He had custody of his other children and this would go the same way.'

'Did he, now? Well, it won't. I'll help you, Katy. He's done this once, he won't do it again. And he doesn't have fucking custody. Everyone knows what he is now. Where is Jamie? You didn't ...?'

'No. He's at my mother's. I had to come here and tell you I was sorry. Not just that. I want to help. I want to help you to ...'

I get up and hug her. We can help each other. Through the distrust and jealousy and hurt we can help each other. The house stinks and it's like some kind of fucked-up charity shop, but it's home again and somehow Katy is sitting here and she's sorry.

'We'll sort something out. I need to tell you what's happened.'

I don't tell her about the journal. I tell her the DS Percy version – another witness to what I said. She listens and sips her hot, sweet tea.

'So it was his mother all along? I thought you said she hated you?'

'Yes. But she's a mother at the end of the day.'

The lies spew out and I can't stop them. I'm careful to not let her know that I've seen the journal, only the bits on Facebook. I suddenly feel bad about Missy. I did all those things when I was mixed up and weak. She took my kids away.

Yet I can't get away from it. *She's a mother at the end of the day*. I remember Jack telling me that she wasn't well liked within the family. I realise now that he isolated me from his relatives, but he did talk about them. He told me that Missy had two sisters, both 'worse than her' – his words.

There had been an incident where they had found out what she was really like – self-centred, grasping, greedy – and there had been a suggestion that she didn't pay the attention she should to Jack. A bad mother, they called her. He told me that was the only time he ever saw her cry. It must be why she saw my kids – and now Jamie too – as a second chance.

So Missy knows that feeling of persecution. She knows what it's like to be deemed a bad mother. Yet she still did it to me. I've often wondered if that was when it started? That all paths from there led to that afternoon in the meeting room where she took my children.

Katy's talking, telling me all about what he has done to her, but all I can think about is whether it really is love that makes the world go round, or revenge. I push it to the back of my mind and give Katy's plight the witness it deserves, the witness I never had. Right on cue, my phone rings: DS Percy. I wait for three rings.

'Hello?'

I can hear her exhale.

'Caroline. Where are you?'

'At home. I told you I was going away for a few days to clear my head. I've been staying at a hotel on the tops.'

Too soon? Too needy? Too much information?

'I'm going to come round. There have been some developments.

You've obviously seen the media reports.'

'Not really. I've been off the radar. Stress. But feel free to come round.'

I'm obviously not in deep trouble. I am, however, going to get a quick catch-up on what's happened on Jack's side. Between Lorraine and Katy I'm getting a pretty good picture of just how pissed off he is.

Katy is telling me that just before Jamie was born Jack went on a month-long trip 'with work'. That she bought him a ring, a band with a tiny diamond in it. When he returned, two days before she went into labour with Jamie, the ring was gone. He told her that he had lost it scuba diving.

She tells me that she has followed the Facebook thread carefully and had never realised about all the other women. When the pictures of Jack and Louise were posted, she enlarged them as much as she could and he was wearing that ring. She tells me that she never suspected.

Katy is crying and I feel tears well up too. She truly believed that, as the other woman, she was the one he had risked everything for, and sacrificed everything for. She had never imagined that there was a chain of other women. She was horrified, sick for days. He came to pick Jamie up and acted like nothing had happened. Telling her that she looked rough, that the house was a mess. What was that smell? That Jamie came back in completely new clothes, the old ones in a black bin bag. Missy was going to throw them out but ...

I knew it. I've practically done a public service. All those women will be looking at the clues, trying to work out where they fit in this sordid jigsaw puzzle. But Katy's sobbing. I hold her and tell her that we'll sort it out and that he won't hurt her now.

Katy's just telling me how he still liked to sleep with her and, afterwards, as he got dressed, joked that she was an eight out of ten this time, try harder next time. Except it didn't seem like a joke. I ask her if he ever hurt her. She said he didn't, but her eyes betrayed her. She said it was playing, like in *Fifty Shades*.

She told me that he did all this when Jamie was there, but he fitted a lock to his bedroom door so that when you were having 'Daddy time with Mummy' Jamie would stay in his room. That she could hear him crying. That she'd asked Jack to stop, but every time she asked things got worse. He made her feel like shit. He 'suggested' that Jamie should come to stay for 'two weeks or a month'. That Missy was his Nana and he loved her.

So she carried on sleeping with him. She got pregnant again and told him, but he simply opened his wallet and gave her 500 pounds to 'get rid of it'. Then, when she did, he resumed sleeping with her. And she was only doing it because she thought he would come back in the end and that they would be a family, like he promised. That she knew how stupid that sounded now, but then, in her tired, hormonal, confused state, it seemed real.

I listen attentively, because these are the things that I have never wanted to say, I've never had the strength. These are the things that happened to me too. Private things between me and him, so horrible that I couldn't articulate them and now, when I think about them, even to me they don't seem real. But I have the strength now. For me and Katy.

When she's finished she's breathless. Neither of us cries. I simply say, 'He did that to me too.'

I know we'll be friends for life now. What I didn't know was that DS Percy was standing behind me.

Chapter Thirty-two

She's been listening since Katy began to tell me that Jack carried on sleeping with her. I heard fucking Rover but I didn't realise we'd left the door open. She's here with another policewoman and she coughs gently. Katy jumps.

'Sorry. We didn't mean to scare you.'

Katy stands up quickly, but I am calm.

'Come in. Have a seat. What can I do for you now?' I can hear the sharpness in my voice from Katy vocalising my deepest hurt, and I try to swallow it down. She's staring at Katy. 'This is Katy Squires.'

Katy extends her hand.

'We spoke on the phone. You told me to ...'

DS Percy sits down in front of me. She looks very tired. Her nails are bitten to the quick.

'Yes. Yet here you are.'

I interject.

'We're here for each other now.'

I wonder how much they heard before we saw them.

DS Percy sighs.

'OK. This is DC Lincoln. We've been following up the Premier Inn robberies.'

Katy's eyes widen.

'What's this got to do with you?'

I shrug.

'Nothing. Except I slept with them before they were robbed. So I'm the link. So how can I help you? Did we miss something?'

DS Percy gets out her little notebook.

'Two things. This and your ex-husband. But I'll come to that in a minute. I just wanted you to know that we've arrested someone for those photographs of you.'

I hold my breath. Both DS Percy and DC Lincoln study me intensely. At first I think it's a trap and they're waiting for my reaction. Then I realise that they're waiting for me to say something.

'Oh. Thank goodness. You've got him, then.' It's over. It's finally over. Thank goodness. DS Percy has managed to solve the case herself and I didn't need to jeopardise myself after all. She visibly relaxes.

'Yeah. We arrested the perpetrator outside your house and he admitted it straight away. It turns out that someone was paying him to follow you.' It's not fucking over. They haven't arrested Jack. They've got the wrong person. I can feel the colour drain from my face. I can see DC Lincoln looking around at the Amazon boxes and the days' old food. There are pieces of crime scene tape left from the search and the remnants of ripped-up boxes. DS Percy continues. 'I have to warn you that he had some more photographs of you with him. Rather compromising ones. Some of them from a while ago. This guy had been following you for a long time. We also found a stolen watch from one of the rooms.'

I quickly gather my thoughts. This is wrong. A ghost of a pissed-up memory permeates reality and filters into the possibility that I could have been wrong about Jack setting this up. Auto-suggestion isn't that rare in criminal cases.

I was so sure. But it gives me some leeway.

'Right. Only I heard something the other night. That's why I went to the hotel. I was scared. Someone creeping around. The dog barking.'

Katy strengthens my case, hands over her mouth.

'Oh my God. After everything Jack has done to you, and now this.'

DS Percy nods. She's agreeing with Katy. Sympathising. Thank goodness. I might be on the way back to myself but I'm not in the clear yet.

'The thing is, he might get bail. It might be better if you find somewhere to stay. Just until we know for sure. And we'll be looking into who put him up to this.'

Katy jumps in.

'You must stay with me, Caroline. You must.'

DS Percy is taking it all in. She knows what has happened. She's read the journal. She's listened to Jack moaning on, telling her how I'm persecuting all the women in his little book. How I'm mentally unstable. Yet here I am with one of them, best friends. She's offering to let me stay at her house where she lives with Jack's child.

'Oh, I don't know; I don't want to impose ...'

Katy shakes her head.

'I absolutely insist. All girls together, and all that.'

I see DS Percy's expression change. No doubt she's sick and tired of #allgirlstogether and #cheatingbastard.

'About that. As you can imagine, Mr Atkinson has made further complaints. He's claiming that he is being harassed. His solicitor is in the process of issuing an injunction against any libellous or defamatory statements from social networking.'

I stare at her. It's unbelievable that he would go to those lengths when it's clear that he is guilty. The evidence is right there, all over the internet, yet he is still trying to defend himself. I suppress laughter. I imagine his bent fucking solicitor's face when he tells him he wants to prosecute everyone who has insulted him. Everyone who has commented on those posts. I imagine him scrolling through the social networking, pages and pages of it.

My natural thought process leads me to what is really at the nub of this matter. What he is suggesting does sound ludicrous, but is it more ludicrous than serial adultery and the cruelty Katy and I have endured? I focus in and realise that what he really wants to do is stop whoever is doing this. Stop them exposing him in public. Stop them. In fact, stop me. It still comes down to him and me, even now?

I know him. And he knows me. He's worried about his reputation. Naturally. But now it's all out there he hasn't stopped. He knows that I will never give up and I know that he will never give up, but neither of us can sustain this for ever. Now it's escalated out of our control, it's a natural impasse. He's not stupid. Far from it. He knows when he's onto a loser. What he is proposing now – mass injunctions – will cost him everything.

Why, when there's nothing more to tell? When the world knows everything? Because there's something else, isn't there? Something that wasn't in the journal. Something that we must be very close to discovering if it makes him so nervous.

'It's nothing to do with me. I've been at the back of beyond with a … friend. You can check. I have his number …'

'He's absolutely adamant that you are posting the pictures.'

I take what she thinks is the bait.

'But wasn't it Missy? Isn't that what you said?'

'Some more have been posted. Of your sister. And a video of another woman.' I've never been good at acting. But I summon up the horror I felt when I first saw Paula's pussycat face pouting at Jack. Katy puts her arm around me.

'He slept with my sister?' I rush over to my own laptop, which has been dormant since I was last here. I make a show of switching it on and logging onto Facebook with my password. I load the history. 'Here. You can look. I haven't even been on Facebook.' We all sit there in front of the laptop in silence. I push it as far as I can. 'So where is it, then? Where is it?'

DS Percy leans forward and finds Monica's profile. All the photographs load, with Paula's at the bottom. It's a complete triumph. He's there, in all his #cheatingbastard glory. Katy is horrified.

'Oh my God. I'd only seen the other page. The one with the hashtags. I hadn't seen this. Bloody hell.' She looks more closely. 'Are there any of me?'

I want to tell her that I spared her because she came clean, but I don't. I let DS Percy scroll up and down through the women. She's seen the journal so she knows exactly what he recorded about Katy. While she scrolls and Katy and DC Lincoln watch mesmerised, I wonder who this stalker guy is.

From time to time something happens that makes me wonder if I really am mad. If he was right and I'm just deluded. Like when he left. I was sure that it was just a blip. That he would call me and tell me that he was sorry and that it had all been a mistake. When he didn't, I knew that I had seriously misjudged what was going on. That I was completely wrong.

Now I realise that I was more wrong than I thought I was. He left me long before we officially split. I'm fairly sure that we were still together when we married, but even that is hazy now. I can't be sure that he wasn't seeing someone for the whole of our relationship.

He left me almost as soon as we got together. We probably never even made it past the three-month honeymoon period – he was ogling Paula Pussycat well before that. Even before Christine fucking Dearden and the Chanel incident, he was distracted. I told myself that it was OK to look but not to touch. That all men look at women, but he had chosen me. I suppose he had really. Chosen me to be his mug.

Every blip in the matrix, every suspicion, every little slip or unusual receipt was met with stony-faced silence. If pursued, an indignant statement would follow. *Don't you trust me? What's this about? What's wrong, Caroline?* I'd been living in a container where he projected exactly what he wanted me to see on all four sides. I was trapped. I suppose there had been hints from our friends. Lowered eyes, shaking heads, sad looks, all before they dropped out of our lives. But I was so committed that someone would have had to hit me over the head with it.

So what am I not seeing now? The journal is exhausted, the pictures are published, Jack's reputation is in tatters. None of this can possibly have escaped the attention of most women. It's been on the national news. It's time to give up, but he's not giving up. I just have no idea what else there could be?

But that's how manipulation makes us. It makes us doubt ourselves. Or grow too sure of ourselves. I was completely sure that he was living with Louise Shaw. What else have I been wrong about?

Chapter Thirty-three

DS Percy is chomping at the bit. She's fuming. Katy is obviously shocked and DC Lincoln doesn't know what to make of it all. I have to remember that, as far as they are concerned, I haven't seen the journal. I still have the flash drive of pictures in my pocket and it feels dangerous. I decide to ramp it up.

'Wouldn't it be better to just arrest me, then? You keep telling me that Jack is making complaints against me. So wouldn't that clear things up?'

She sighs. I can tell that it's been a very long week for her.

'We don't have any evidence. Look, Caroline, this has got completely out of hand. When it was just a domestic issue, with the missing holdall, it was bad enough. But now it's much bigger. And public. It's all going to come out in the end, so if you know anything about this, now is the time to tell me. I could understand why you would have kept that bag. And the book.'

I wrap my fingers around the flash drive. It would be so easy to tell her. *Let it go.* I could plead diminished responsibility and probably get away with it. Everyone would be on my side now they know what he is like. But I wouldn't get the children back. I wouldn't be able to meet social services on Tuesday and at least put my case to them. I've made some good choices since all that business, stopped myself acting on impulse. I can only get stronger now.

'It's nothing to do with me. I can't actually believe that you know what I've gone through and you can still accuse me.'

She sighs again. She looks at her empty coffee cup.

'I'm not accusing you. I might as well be honest with you. I know that you have gone through a lot. I've seen it all in black and white. And I heard what Katy said before, which, by the way, would add to the harassment charges I urged you to bring and you still could. But you don't come out of this snow-white either. If it carries on I won't be able to keep this case and the Premier Inn robbery case separate.'

My stomach snarls up into a knot.

'What? You mean that he's allowed to do whatever he wants, but I'm not allowed to have a bit of fun?'

She nods.

'No. We can all see that your ex-husband's bit of fun hasn't gone down well at all. But this guy who has been stalking you – his name is Allan Parrott. Do you know him too, Caroline? He's got a comprehensive record of what you've been up to over the past year or so. You know, the men. Once that gets out you're not going to be the woman scorned. You're going to be the woman who picked up married men in Premier Inns.'

Her mouth curls in disgust and DC Lincoln shakes her head.

'That's not how it was. I was ...'

'Yeah. Course. But that's what everyone says. Everyone's got their reasons, haven't they? So those pictures on the screen could just as well have been you with those men. I'm just trying to diffuse this before that happens.'

Fuck. Fuck fuck fuck. She isn't trying to fucking diffuse it. She's trying to make me panic. What she hasn't bargained for is the fact that I'm used to this. I'm used to people giving me misinformation, pointing out what the consequences of things are to me like I'm a fucking child. I'm used to it because Jack did it all the time. But not any more. No. And I would like to avoid what was me in a very bad state becoming tabloid fodder. Unfortunately I can't admit to what I haven't done.

It's stalemate. She's shown her hand. She hasn't got anything on me, just a load of suspicion and a testimony from my ex.

'OK, have it your way. But when this breaks it's going to get ugly. And, if Allan Parrot gets bail, dangerous. So I'm just doing my job and advising you to get out of here now.'

They leave and Katy sits in stunned silence. I throw all the excess packaging and piles of dirty plates into the skip. We tidy up the best we can. Katy's looking around with a *this could have been me in a year* look. I pack up my laptop and push the remaining clothes in the tumble dryer into a holdall. When we've finished I find Katy in the lounge, staring at the family picture still on the wall.

'You know, it all looks so normal on the outside, doesn't it? But we've both got ourselves into a right situation. What the hell is the story with the stalker?'

I sit down heavily on a huge pile of newspapers.

'I was getting pissed all the time. I probably can't remember most of it. I certainly don't know who Allan Parrot is. And this lot. Again. Pissed. Late-night ordering on Amazon Prime.'

She shakes her head.

'We could never have known, could we? When I went out with Jack, I just thought people were basically good. It never occurred to me that he would lie. But you were here with your children waiting for him. And that Louise. She was at the other end.'

'He had her arrested, you know.'

'Yeah, I know. He told me. It was a warning without actually saying it. Warning me that if I tried anything that's how I would end up. There must be something wrong with him. Compulsive liar or something.'

That's what I used to believe. Compulsive liar. I scoured psychological case studies to find a condition where someone lied constantly about where they had been and what they had done. Where they believed their own hype. It's a symptom of lots of psychological pathology. I guess he got so caught up in the endless lies that he could never have put it right.

Now I believe that he didn't want to. Katy is an earlier version of me and, just like Louise Shaw said, people must be wondering why she doesn't let it go. To someone on the outside it looks like we are holding on in the hope of reconciliation, but in reality Jack is forcing us not to let go, because we have invested so much in keeping him that we might let go of ourselves.

I did let go of myself. I became out of control and put myself in danger. I slept with people I didn't know. I could have caught an STD or been killed. It just seemed like pissed-up fun mixed with danger. Now I realise that I was fraternising with people who are transient and searching for danger themselves. Misfits. Hanging about in bars night after night, sleeping with each other on a fucked-up circuit of middle-aged hell.

I literally had no idea that Allan Parrott, whoever he is, was following me around. Taking photographs. A shiver runs through my body. What if he's been tracking me over the past week? What if he has photographs of me going into Frances's tea shop, taking her phone? It's too late for guilt now. It's Sunday tomorrow and I only have to make it to Tuesday to present my case to social services.

If I lay low at Katy's I might be able to avoid all this fucking mess being linked to my pissed-up promiscuity and Jack's perfect ten. The last place anyone would look for me is Jack's babymother's house.

We go upstairs. Katy helps me to pull the slashed mattress outside and into the skip. We gather up the remnants of my wedding dress and the twisted tiaras and push them into a bin bag. The last rites of my wedding day finally laid to rest. Eventually, the bedroom is tidy again and all that remains is the chipped wood of the doors and the bare bed base and the scrawling on the wall.

We go downstairs and get ready to leave. I look around, unsure when I will be back here. I promise myself that if it goes well on Tuesday and I am allowed to see Charlie and Laura, I will spend every last penny sorting this place out.

We leave and Katy drives away. I'm just about to open my car door when my neighbour appears. She's got her arm raised in a fist salute and she high-fives me.

'All girls together, yeah?'

I nod at her.

'So you saw it, then?'

'I bloody saw it all right. Your hubby. A right one, isn't he? I can hardly believe it. But then again, he was in and out of there with those women. Taking photos, though—'

'Yes. Yes. Look, I have to—'

'Right, but I came out to tell you that the papers have been round here, asking all sorts of questions. Course, we didn't spill, but just to let you know that if they offer us money we might have to tell them about him.'

'Him?'

'Your ex. And all his women. You know. Thing is, the mortgage, and all that ...'

I hug her. I'm suddenly doing a lot of hugging.

'Do it. Tell them. It's the truth. I'll be away for a bit. Tell them that as well. That I had to leave my own home because of all of this.'

She's chewing her acrylic nails now.

'And shall I mention the kiddies? I saw him, you know. Taking them. I saw him and they were crying.'

I brighten up a little. She's the obvious witness. She's had a ringside seat.

'You just do what you have to. But not so much about me.' I whisper in her ear, make her my confidante: 'I'm going to try to get them back.'

She winks at me and crashes my knuckle.

'Stay strong, sister.'

She salutes and I can't help but notice that she's wearing a #teamCaro rubber bracelet. But what just happened? I feel like it's all been turned around on me again. It's made me feel like I need to take even more action. How could I have known that some crazy fucking guy was following me around? No doubt at some point I'll be called in for questioning and I'll see a picture of him and everything he has seen me do will be laid bare.

DS Percy is right. This is going to look bad for me. I've accused Jack of cheating on me and then gone off, got pissed and slept with random men. I didn't mean it. I love my kids. That would never have happened if they were here with me. Never. Nor the drinking. But that's the official story and it doesn't put me in the good light I need it to for Tuesday.

Back to me now. I'm no longer made-up Monica or the woman in the wig. No imaginary husband to lay all my anger and frustration on. I'm Caroline Atkinson. In three days' time I'll be sitting in front of social services fighting for my children. I need to lay low now. No more drama. Jack can wait. I'll deal with him after I've made my case for the kids.

My neighbour's checking her phone, scrolling through photos

she's taken and muttering that she knows it's here somewhere. She intermittently shows me Jack and a woman outside my house and I wonder if I can get her to send those pictures to me. Then she points her talon up the road.

'Oh. Here's one of the reporters. Round here earlier asking where you are.'

I spin around and see a long blonde ponytail emerge from a BMW. It's swinging as the woman stomps towards me. Not so much Paula Pussycat as Pissed-off Paula.

Chapter Thirty-four

We lock eyes as she passes me and I follow her up the path. She pushes the front door open and it slams against the wall, making a small amount of paint drop onto the floor, which, if it were possible, makes me angrier.

Like most people who come into my home, she momentarily stares around. I haven't seen my sister for years. Not since Mum and Dad moved to Canada just after that fucking wedding. I'm a little bit shocked that she's lost the little-girl innocent look she prized so highly. It's been replaced with a high-maintenance sheen that I know only comes with many trips to the beautician.

But she's still Paula. Her eyes are narrow and accusing, like the time she mistakenly thought I had taken her chocolate bar or her pocket money. She stands in my kitchen, hands on hips.

'What the fuck is this?'

Her eyes sweep the boxes and the dirty pots. She walks around and examines the piles of boxes and newspapers. I feel a little bit self-conscious as my feet stick to the dirty tiles when I try to move, making a sucking sound.

'You've got a nerve coming here. What do you want?'

She lifts her phone.

'Why did you do this?'

It's the Facebook pictures of her. Above it are the damning photos of Jack and Alicia. I try to remain calm but my voice comes out louder than I intended, as a scream.

'Because you slept with Jack. You slept with my husband. You're one of them.' As an afterthought I add a denial. 'And I didn't post it. Someone's ...'

She slumps down onto the kitchen bench.

'Don't do that, Caz. Don't. Everyone knows it's you. So let's bypass that bit.' She smooths her hair, which is a clear sign that she is under stress.

'Why are you even here? After Mum and Dad moved I left messages but you didn't answer. But you turn up now, when the shit hits the fucking fan? Typical. Save your own arse.'

She takes out a gold lighter and a cigarette case. She carefully extracts one and offers it to me, which only highlights that she doesn't even know me. She's got the skin of a smoker now I look closer. Little lines around her eyes and mouth. Crinkly skin just waiting for the depth of wrinkles.

'Actually, I came here to help you.'

'Fuck off. You? Help me?'

'Well, it looks like you need it. All this? You can—'

'Send it back. Get it moved, donate it to charity on eBay? Yes. I know. But I've had other things on my mind.'

'That Jack. That fucking Jack. And for the record, I never slept with him.'

I stare at her. Paula isn't, or wasn't, the most truthful person, but I was one of the only people who could tell when she was lying. I'm confused. Why would she be in the journal then?

'OK, your name is on a list of people Jack has slept with. Marked out of ten. And there are pictures of you.'

She's nodding vigorously between drags on her cigarette.

'Yes, I know. But I didn't sleep with him. He's a fucking stalker, Caz. How do you think he met those girls? Chance meetings? He's not all that, you know. Fucking hell. Do you think they were all just waiting around half-clothed for him to come along and fuck them?'

How does she know? What does she mean? I have a horrible feeling that Paula is going to reveal something I don't want to know.

'He's a predator. He's clever. Making women feel that they're special and interesting. And yes, he did try it on with me. But do you know what? I'm your fucking sister and I didn't.' She's crying. Paula's crying. 'God, I know we never speak since Mum and Dad moved, but that's how it is. But if you're in trouble, I'm there. Like you would be for me.'

I want to believe her, but there are so many questions. So much is swirling in my mind. I pluck one of them mid-thought.

'So why the pictures? Why did he put you with ... them?'

She wipes her nose on her expensive jersey top and she's suddenly the little girl I grew up with.

'He's a liar, Caz. You know that. Wishful thinking? I don't know. But the fact that you're even questioning that shows you're still fucking invested in him.'

It's like a revelation. She's right. Paula's right. I've taken that journal as the truth, but he *is* a liar.

'Everyone else is the liar, but not your precious Jack? Even now you know, you still think his word is gospel.' She puts her hand on my arm. 'He wanted to fuck me. He followed me and took pictures. Propositioned me. Sent me flowers. Gifts. But I never even kissed him. Yet he includes me in his harem. What does that tell you, Caz?'

I think hard.

'How do I know that's true?'

She pulls up her sleeve. She's got a tattoo with the date of the wedding on it. *Paula and Pat. For ever.*

'I met my partner that evening. I didn't want Jack. Not then. Not ever. I met the person I was going to spend my life with.'

I remember the wedding pictures. I didn't see her with anyone. Just a group of bridesmaids, giggling and drinking champagne. I suppose it could have been after I'd gone home, but I'm still not sure. But I'm grabbing at another query. The million-dollar one. The question that has driven me through this. Made me pursue Jack's women. I could have understood anything but this. I savour the words.

'Oh. So why didn't you tell me? Why, Paula?'

Why didn't she tell me? Why didn't any of them tell me? If someone had just told me, if I'd had confirmation, even anonymously, it might never have come to this. Paula shakes her head.

'I don't fucking know. I suppose I didn't want to get involved. I've had my own shit to deal with. Worried that you'd side with him and not believe me, which incidentally you would have. And you knew what he was like.' She points at me. 'Don't try to deny it. You fucking knew.'

I did. I was sneaking around, trying to find out what he was up to almost from the beginning. She stubs out her cigarette on the same saucer Pam used and glances around again.

'So, what time do you pick them up? I can come with you.'

'I don't pick them up. He took them. He took my babies.'

My God. She doesn't know. I wait for her to say 'well I'm not surprised, look at the state of this place' or, like other people have said 'oh, to give you a break until you are feeling better'. But she doesn't. We sit in silence for a few minutes. Paula is processing it all. Finally she speaks.

'This is a mess. All the Facebook shit and the stuff on the telly. You need to do damage limitation here. Let me help you.'

It's the first time since all this started last year that anyone has directly offered to help me. I'm unsure because it's Paula. But what have I got to lose?

'How? How can you help? And what makes you such an expert?'

'I've done it loads. Usually the other way round, you know, for my mates who've got caught shagging someone's husband. Or wife.' It's tense as she normalises what has become my life. 'Just think of me as a kind of clean-up service, you know, like in those gangster films when they come and move the body.' She smiles a little and so do I. 'So you need to tell me everything. Then go somewhere safe.'

'Safe? This isn't a film, Paula.'

'I know. But you need to get out of here. Just until it dies down. Which it will, you know.'

'Yeah. I was just on my way to stay with Katy for a couple of days.'

Paula's eyebrows shoot up her forehead.

'Not Katy ...?'

'Yep. She's lovely. Obviously I hated her at first, but she's just the same as me. Gullible.'

Paula drags her chair over and sits next to me. She links arms with me and she smells like vanilla.

'You're not gullible. You're a strong person. A professional. But you know what, Caz, you've been abused. He's a bastard. Fucking selfish. He's made you think you are less than you are. And that those other girls are responsible.' She pauses and rests her head on my shoulder. 'And with us. Well. That's how abusers work, isn't it? Isolate their victim.'

I nod.

'It's my own fault, though. Like you said, I knew. But I was trying to keep my family together.'

She laughs.

'Yeah. Vicious circle. But it's not your fault. Nobody tells you because they think you already know. Divide and rule. That's what he did to us, you know. I felt bad because he was coming on to me. So I couldn't be around you and the kids. So I just left it. The thing you're not seeing is that all those women you've posted pictures of are in the same boat. Isolated. They believed a bullshitter.'

It's a little too far for my imagination to stretch.

'But they knew he was married.'

'Yeah. But they also knew he was leaving you. And by the time they discovered he wasn't it was too late; he'd trapped them. You know, Caz, this is only one person's fault. Jack. It's Jack's fault.'

I know she's right. I know she is. But I hated those women. Even so, that's no reason to ruin their lives. What have I done?

'The thing is, I've done more than post pictures.'

I tell Paula everything I've done and she listens intently. I tell her about Christine Dearden, Frances's shop and how I only just stopped myself from taking revenge on Pam. I tell her about the Premier Inn men and the photographs, leaving out the stolen credit cards and being careful not to mention the journal. When I've finished, she shakes her head.

'So what happens now?'

It's suddenly very clear to me.

'I need a fresh start. But first I have to finish this. I can't go back and I can't move forward without my children. You know, I was talking to him in my head. He literally drove me mad. But since I saw my kids in that house, he's gone, Paula. I can't feel him any more.'

'What about his mother?'

She grimaces as she says it. Paula never liked Missy.

'She's got the kids. She's backed him all the way. But he hasn't got custody. I need to hold it all down until Tuesday, then I have a chance to have my say at social services. Laura's been asking for me.'

She finally smiles.

'Right then, I'm going support you. I want to make it up to you. I'm not the bitch I was, Caz. I've had a bad time, but let's get this sorted out first, then we'll have a good old chat. Yeah? Tell you what, if the shit really hits the fan and it all comes out about what you've done, I'll be your alibi. You were with me, right?'

'I can't, Paula. I've done those things, not you. I don't want to drag you into it.'

She smiles.

'I'm your sister. Family.' She does a Marlon Brando impression and we both laugh. 'It's the least I can do after my appalling behaviour as a teenager.'

She pulls a Paula Pussycat face, which looks silly now she's a grown-up. I think about what has happened. What I feel bad about. And how that makes me not a psychopath.

'There is one thing you can do. You could go up to The Tea Cosy and see how Frances is doing. I wanted to close her down but that was fucking horrible of me.'

She nods.

'I will. And I'll phone you. Just leave the pictures for now. Not much you can do about that anyway, but if you're going to get your kids back none of this can be linked to you. Just don't lose the fucking plot.'

She hugs me and I wonder what would have happened if I hadn't posted that photo of her on Facebook. Would she still be here?

Will she really back me up? We'll see, won't we? No time for that now, I need to leave.

She promises to call me later and hurries to her car. My phone makes a beep, signalling more activity on social networking and I have a sinking feeling in my stomach. Paula was right. I can't believe I'm thinking it, but Paula was right. I blamed anyone except Jack. It had to be someone else's fault. Despite my psychological training, I became so conditioned that I couldn't possibly have blamed Mr Perfect. Coupled with my insatiable drive to fix everything, to make it all right, I lost sight of what was real and what wasn't.

Those poor women. I'm their worst nightmare. The ex coming back to haunt them via his estranged wife. It could happen to me. Any of those men from the Premier Inn – to their wives I am the other woman. What have I done?

My psychological training kicks in now and I focus on the conditioning. Unfuck myself. Like Pam said. Extinction of learned behaviour. The revenge I felt towards Jack's women was provoked by his perceived presence in my life. Now he's fading and so is my hate, replaced with an equal measure of determination. I need to keep away from him. If I have any chance of unfucking myself I need to stay away from him – even thinking about him. It's going to be difficult, and, as with any conditioned response, it may be reinforced temporarily, but I will do this. I will.

For now, though, all I can do is lie low and hope that Paula's damage limitation will work.

Chapter Thirty-five

Ten minutes later I'm sitting in Katy's lounge. Her house is warm and comfortable and Jamie is running around. He's a mini Jack, which is very painful for me at first. He keeps bringing his toys to me and looking at me with those perfect dark eyes that are my ex-husband's. But it's not his fault. I pull him onto my lap and give him a big cuddle and I miss my own children.

I spend the rest of the day helping Katy and playing with Jamie. I'm Aunty Caz and we've already got a rapport. Katy cooks pasta and then, at eight, I run a bath and try to relax. It's impossible. Despite my guilt, I'm fuming about DS Percy's take on my night-time activities. And at Jack, for not knowing *when it's time to turn the page*, like Tori Amos says. For not knowing when he's beaten.

Katy shows me to the guest bedroom and I lie in the pristine bed under a feather quilt on soft pillows. In between sleep and wakefulness I wonder if, if I had my time again, I'd do anything differently. I can't imagine a time before Jack and I were married when I would have realised what he was like enough to call it off. I suppose I thought I could change him. That when we were married he would be mine.

If we hadn't married I would never have met our children. Yet, deep down, I know this romanticised kind of excuse-making is only me trying to explain to myself why I was stupid enough to fall for his manipulation. I believed that love trumped everything and that he loved me. I do regret it. I do regret ever meeting him. I can't change the past, but I can make the future better.

As I drift off in the early hours I feel a sudden burst of optimism as I realise that Charlie and Laura and Jamie will, after all, have a future together, not with Jack but with me and Katy as friends.

Katy wakes me at eight. She knocks on the door and brings in a cup of tea, which I drink in bed. I switch on the TV and there's a woman on *Breakfast Time* talking about infidelity and its effect on children. I quickly flick it off. Kids are resilient and, it turns out, so am I. I get dressed and go downstairs.

Katy is still very quiet, and I know that her internal dialogue has taken over, just as it did with me. Sunday is the day Jack used to pick up Charlie and Laura, and is no doubt the day he usually gets Jamie. I was so busy rehearsing what I would say to him, and how I would fit everything in to meet his demands, that I could go days without talking to anyone. My office door, which used to be open, was firmly shut. I'd make lists and tick them off in work time. I had a special calendar on my phone, on which I marked off all the aspects of his life that he told me about when he dropped the kids off – just in case I needed to take them into account.

He demanded that he was the centre of everything, and now the same thing is going on here. Katy sits down and I broach the subject.

'Want to talk about it?'

She half smiles, but it's flat.

'Is it that obvious?'

I'm so used to hating everyone, the dubious mistrust that Jack lulled me into, that I'm finding it hard to say what I need to. But I have to. I bite the bullet.

'Yeah, it is. Look, Katy, things aren't easy for either of us. We both need some time to process this. But I can help you. Or even just be here for you. I wanted revenge, but, you know, it's in the past. For me. But if you don't want to ...'

She picks Jamie up and he begins to fall asleep on her lap. She waits until he's dropped off then lies the cute little man down beside her on the sofa.

'I told him he couldn't see Jamie until further notice. I'm worried what he's going to do now.'

'What can he do? He's not really in a position to do anything. He's threatening to sue everyone on Twitter. What can he do?'

She looks surprised.

'But I feel like I'm in danger. Like he's holding all the cards.'

That's how I felt. I remember yesterday's revelation, Paula telling me I was still invested, and give Katy the benefit of it.

'Of course you do. That's how he's trained you. It's classical conditioning. He's got you believing that he's right and rewarding you with things that he should be doing as a matter of fucking course.' I look at Jamie. 'Sorry. Sorry about the language. I can't help it. I'm just ... just ... angry.'

She pauses and I think she's going to close up, but she doesn't.

'So, that guy – the one who was arrested for the pictures. Who is he?'

It has to come out sometime and while she's asking me about this she's not asking about Jack's exes and what I've done to them.

'Some guy who's been following me.'

I don't add that I think Jack sent him. I'm saving that one. She whistles low.

'Bloody hell. What are the odds?'

I consider her throw-away comment. Quite high, actually. At the high, or low, point of my out-of-control drinking I slept with quite

a few men. That could be ten men. Then there were the majority
I didn't sleep with but just used to validate myself. I suddenly feel
very sad. What happened to the Caroline who respected herself?
Who would avoid flirting like the plague? But out of those men, the
chances of meeting someone who had, say, borderline personality
disorder, is pretty high.

'Yeah, I suppose. But I was out of control. That's not the real me.'

She nods and sips her coffee.

'I know. Jack talked a lot about you.'

'Did he? How strange.'

'Yeah. He talked about all his exes. He was quite cruel, really.'
She's wringing her chapped hands now and staring at them. I see
a tear fall. 'He marked them all out of ten. You were a ten. There
was only one other ten. I was an eight. It really upset me.'

I hold in my temper. It's difficult but I need to keep calm.
Something inside me ignites.

'So what else did he say about me?'

'Just that you and he were over and that you'd told him that you
wouldn't sleep with him any more.' She hesitates and I can see she's
suffering. Then she lets me into the real state of her psyche. 'So …
were you still sleeping with him? I mean, were you still together?'

I want to shake her and I want to hug her at the same time. She
still hasn't realised fully what's going on. Instead, I answer her gently.

'Yes, we were still together. We were still sleeping together. He
was still living with me.'

'But …'

'I know. He was living here. He was telling us both that he
was on business trips. And after he left me, he was telling that to
Louise Shaw.'

She's staring at me incredulously.

'The whole time?'

Her bottom lip is shaking and I want to lean over and hug her, but I remember that she knew all about me. That's she's been in my house. Fed my children. I push my own conflicting feelings away and I do it anyway. I've been warming to her and Jamie. He's a little love and, although I've resisted it, I have to admit he's so much like Charlie and Laura. I finally acknowledge that Katy and Jamie are in my future, a permanent fixture.

'Yes. The whole time. What did he tell you when he brought you to my house? That it was all a set-up? That it was over long ago? Because it wasn't. He lied and he lied fucking good. But I knew, really, somewhere inside, that he wasn't really there. That part of him was always somewhere else. And you do too, if you're honest with yourself.'

We sit in silence, me beside her now. Her eyes scan the surfaces as she mentally counts the cleaning processes she has to go through, then she remembers that she told him not to come.

'Do you think he'll still come for Jamie?'

'It wouldn't surprise me. But don't worry, I'll keep out of the way. It won't go down too well if I'm here.'

I worry for a second that him coming here will invoke the injunction so near to Tuesday. But I know him. He won't come. He'll be too busy covering his tracks.

'No, no. It doesn't matter now. I'm not letting Jamie go. If he calls the police, let him. As well as everything you've said, there's the stuff on the TV. I've sent my solicitor an email and he said to tell Jack to contact him. Not to get involved.'

I look at her. She's trying to dredge up strength, do what's right for Jamie.

'I'll help you. We can do this together.'

After lunch we sit at the kitchen table and look at the Facebook and Twitter messages. There are thousands of them now. All from people who have been lied to, cheated on and exposed for the #cheatingbastards they really are. Yes, I'll be friends with Katy; she's a lovely, warm woman who's been taken in. That's all. She never meant to hurt me. If I keep telling myself that I will believe it eventually, instead of the conditioned playing off against each other. Because this is the truth, not Jack's truth.

The time passes when he would have turned up and he's a no-show. Katy is nervous and Jamie is asking where Daddy is. Isn't he coming today? When she says no, he asks if he can phone him. Then he tells Katy very earnestly that he was going to have dinner with Charlie and Laura and they'll get his pudding. That Charlie wants to play football with him.

My heart is breaking. All these children, blissfully unaware of their father's failings. Not understanding why Mummy is so sad. All I can do is make this right again for them as best I can.

I panic as I realise that all this is public knowledge and for ever. Will my children see it? Will my parents? I quickly Google my own name to see if I've been implicated in the Peter Daubney case yet.

I haven't. But it's news – the Premier Inn robberies, anyway. I read about Allan Parrott, a loner who has previous convictions for stalking. How the common link between Brian Patterson and Peter Daubney is 'a woman they both knew'. Thankfully, it doesn't say 'ex-wife of the man at the centre of the #allgirlstogether #cheatingbastard viral'.

I can't help but look up what's being reported about Jack. I search his name and there are various appeals for privacy from his solicitor and a denial that he had anything to do with it. Another ex has obviously sold her story to a tabloid and she's posing in an animal-print bikini. The incredible thing is that, save some references to Jack Atkinson's wife, I haven't been named.

Katy sits beside me. Jamie's gone off to his gran's in case Jack turns up and there's any unpleasantness. At least Katy's got her mum on her side. She looks tired but I can't resist.

'So he marked us all out of ten, did he?'

'Yeah. It was as if he wanted to make me suffer. He always told me how you were 'the best he ever had'. He told me that after Laura was born you went off sex. That's why he turned to other women. He used to go through them and describe them. It was awful. It made me feel like I had to try harder. To be honest, if I hadn't got pregnant I would have ended it. But he begged me not to. And you know the rest.'

I feel a strange elation that I am a ten. But Katy said that there was another ten. My rational self knows it's all bollocks but it's gnawing at me. Who is the other fucking ten? I go through the journal, scanning my memory for another ten out of fucking perfect ten. The flash drive is hot in my hand but I daren't look at it. Not here. It doesn't make sense, unless this has affected me so deeply that it's still some kind of validation. She continues.

'I suppose I got used to it. The only thing that bothered me was that he kept going on about this particular woman. It was as if he … I don't know … loved her. All the others he just laughed at. But her … I could tell she was different.'

I'm inexplicably seething again, but I push it down. *Don't rise to it, Caroline. Be strong.*

'Loved her?'

'Yeah. He kind of worshipped her. Always saying how pretty she was, what a good heart she had. How he met her ages ago and he kept going back to her. The rest he called sluts and tramps. But his eyes changed when he talked about her. He gave her a—'

She doesn't finish because there's a loud knock on the door. We both jump up and Katy runs to the window. My heart thumps in my chest.

'Is it him? Is it Jack?'

Is it? Will we finally meet face to face? After all this time?

She opens the door slowly, but it isn't Jack. It's a plain-clothes detective and two uniformed policemen.

Chapter Thirty-six

He's gunning for me. I can tell. He's staring at me and his head isn't tilted to one side in a sympathetic stance like DS Percy. Katy invites them in, but they don't move.

'DI John Ball.' He flashes his ID. 'I'd like you to come down to the station, Caroline. Just to answer some questions.'

I swallow hard. This isn't all friendly like before. He's deadly serious.

'Am I under arrest?'

'No. Just some questions. At this point.'

'What's this about? I haven't done anything wrong.'

I think I see the mouth of one of the accompanying policemen twitch. He's probably heard all this before.

'Let's just go to the station, shall we?'

I grab my jacket and my car keys. But he shakes his head.

'No. You can come with us.'

They're in a police car. DS Percy's little car is nowhere to be seen. We get in, him in the front and me in the back with one of the policemen. No one makes conversation on the way there. He's checking his phone and texting the whole way.

When we get there, he takes me through the custody entrance and into a small room. I can see the coffee machine at the end of the corridor.

'Can I grab a coffee?'

He doesn't look at me.

'Won't take long. You can get one then.'

We go in the room and I expect us to be joined by someone else, but he shuts the door. He doesn't switch on the recorder and he doesn't ask me to sit down. Instead, he leans on his hands on the table.

'Right, I'm giving you one chance here. Where's Emma?' I start to open my mouth to protest but he carries on. 'No one's seen her since yesterday and she's been reported missing.'

I shake my head.

'Emma who?'

He moves closer to me. His teeth are gritted. The door opens and DS Percy comes in and stands behind him. She speaks now.

'It really would be for the best if you told me everything. Right now. This is serious enough as it is, but I need to know where Emma is.'

I sit down, lean back and fold my arms.

'Why don't you ask Jack? This is his business, not mine. Ask Jack about Emma, whoever she is. Because I'm fed up of having all this blamed on me.'

Fuck. Fuck. Fuck fuck fuck. Emma Parsons. I hadn't even got to her. I had a quick look but I couldn't find a Facebook profile. But Jack knew she was next in the journal.

I'm shaking now, but I have to hold it together.

'I thought this would be about the Peter Daubney case. Don't you want to interview me about that?'

She shakes her head.

'No. We've got your statement. You need to get a solicitor. They'll handle that side of things. But this, Caroline ... I know it's you. I know it. And in some ways I don't blame you for what you've done. But if you've hurt her—'

'I haven't hurt anyone. I'm the injured party here. I'm the one who's been hurt.'

'So you thought you'd get revenge. OK. But just tell me what happened with Emma.'

I think. It would be so easy to admit everything. To tell her what I did to all these women. As if it isn't obvious. And how I regret it now. But I don't know anything about Emma Parsons. Then something inside me shifts. Is this his finale? How I'm going to be damned for ever?

'I want to make a phone call. I want to call my solicitor. Am I under arrest?'

DI Ball opens the door and it bangs against the wall.

'Be my guest. I'll be here waiting.'

I walk up the corridor and I'm already dialling. I hear the ringing at the other end and then Katy's voice.

'Hello?'

I've got a one-track mind. My vision has narrowed to a tiny red dot and I spit out the words.

'Who was the other ten?'

She's silent.

'Caroline?'

'It's me, Katy. Yes, Caroline.'

'Why are you shouting? What on earth is wrong?'

'Who was the other ten?' She pauses. I'm losing it. The room is spinning and people at either side of me are in curved vision. 'Who was the other fucking ten? Was it Emma? Was it?'

I realise that I'm screaming and my voice is echoing around the vast 1970's entrance hall.

'Yes. Someone called Emma. Yes. He gave her a ten. Why? What's going on?'

I can't breathe. He gave her an eight in the journal. Why would he lie, even to himself? I can't comprehend it. Then I remember what Paula said. Of course he'd fucking lie. His whole life is a lie. But what has she got that I haven't? No. No. Don't get drawn back in. Something has clearly happened to her and I think about how I can reasonably deal with this. It feels like the walls are closing in.

Think, Caroline. If you admit everything now, that's the end of any contact with the kids. Jack will be right. I'll be crazy. If I don't say anything, there's a woman missing and they think it's me. Oh my God. Has he planned this?

Then there's her own actions to think about. She was the one. Like Katy said. He loved her. Kept going back to her. She knew all along about me.

Knowing what I know now, I expect he told her that it was all but over between us. Still, who did she say she was to Charlie and Laura? Daddy's friend? Bullshit. I want a cigarette even though I don't smoke. Both #cheatingbastards, Jack and Emma. They're in it together, still. She isn't a regretful ex, like Paula said. I should have known.

I push the coins into the coffee machine with shaking hands and wait for the clunk of the cup. Everything is amplified and my vision is extra sharp. Fear can do that to you. I take the steaming cup and get another one for *Lorraine* and DI Ball. I hurry back down the corridor and open the door.

'Can't get hold of him. But I got this for you.'

They're staring at me. Arms folded. DI Ball speaks.

'So?'

'Like I said, I don't know where she is.'

'OK, have it your way.' DS Percy gets up and opens the door. 'You're free to leave. But don't blame me when we're arresting you. You've had your chance.'

I look at my coffee, steaming in front of me. DS Percy's not looking at me. She's staring at the floor, livid.

'You know I just want my kids back, don't you?'

She nods ever so slightly and pulls the door to.

'I do. That day when I told you about your daughter, I felt sorry for you. I thought you'd got the rough end of the bargain. Involved in the Peter Daubney thing with the photos, and that. But this. A woman missing. An innocent woman. I'm trying to help you here, but you've got to help me.'

Is she trying to help me? Or is she trying to get me to admit it so she can arrest me? I just don't know. *Lorraine* has softened a little.

'Look. You can still save yourself. Nothing bad will happen. You'd be charged and then bailed. It's a crime of passion and you'd probably get community service.'

It's tempting. But then I would look weak. I'd never be able to address my issues again. And I'd never get to see my kids. And I'd always be as scared as I am now. And there's the small matter that this is probably another way that Jack is trying to get at me. Make me accuse him, then Emma magically appears. Frame me so I look mad. No. It isn't going to happen like this. DS Percy opens the door again.

'OK, have it your way. But you're getting yourself into trouble, Caroline. More trouble than before.'

I hurry out of the station and onto the front concourse. I'm still seeing red but I manage to call myself a cab. I scrabble around in my handbag and finally find my house keys. I watch as the town turns to the suburbs and the tidy town houses dot the edges of the avenues.

My mind is clouded by the realisation that Emma is the one. Emma is the one Jack loves. I'm fighting this backslide but the realisation that even though she was a ten he still cheated on her as well rains down on me and I feel slightly better. I try to remember what she looks like from the journal. She seemed familiar, like I had met her before. Young. Blonde. Bubbly, perhaps. Is that what he wanted in a woman? I realise I'm crying in the taxi and the driver is looking at me in the rear-view mirror.

'You all right, love?'

I nod.

'Yeah. Just had a nasty shock.'

'Oh. Police not very tactful, are they? Don't spare no feelings.'

We turn into the street before my house and I get out there.

Chapter Thirty-seven

I rush into the house and switch on my laptop. Emma. I have to find out about Emma. Find out what game Jack is playing. I've slipped up a little here, taken my eye off the ball. All this with Katy has mellowed me a little. Made me think I was on the winning straight.

But he's gone a step further. He's framed me. Found a way to make it look like I've gone much, much too far. Harmed Emma Parsons. I push the flash drive home and open the PDFs right at the end. The first one is a picture of a blonde girl, young, wearing a fur coat. Then there are three more of Jack and her, taken in a booth. Both laughing. They look really happy. There are more but I need to find out about Emma.

I can hardly wait to see if Emma Parson's has a Facebook profile. I search Facebook for her but all the Emma Parsons are not her. So I look at Jack's profile and go straight to his friends list. He knows lots of Emmas, so I type 'Parsons'. Nothing. I type Emma and scroll down the list of women called Emma. I don't have to scroll very far until I find her. Emma Atkinson. He fucking married her. He married her.

I kind of know what she looks like from the pictures, but when her profile picture appears it looks familiar. I wonder who it reminds me of and then I realise. Me. She looks just like me. Long blonde hair. Tall and slim. She even dresses like me. Or like I did. Jeans and plain T-shirts. Short jackets.

I look at her biography. I don't believe it. She's a psychologist. She trained at the same university as me. The one I work at. She's a couple of years younger than me, but you'd never know it. I'm just beginning to think she's a carbon fucking copy of me.

I flick back through her photos and there are the standard ones of Jack and her. Holding hands. Drinking champagne. On holiday. In our bedroom. It still hurts me. He took all of them there. It must have been the danger of getting caught. I suddenly realise that I'm desensitised. I'm so used to it now that I'm searching for something worse than my grandma's engagement ring. A baby. My wedding dress. How much worse could it get?

There are a series of photographs at a rally. Jack with his arms around Emma's waist. Her with a placard that I can't read. These are the pictures in the journal. I push the flash drive into the laptop and scroll through the journal. Emma. Nine out of ten. Lies. He told Katy she was a ten. I magnify the second picture and read the placard.

I LOVE FEMINISM.

What is it about some women?

I check again and Emma Parsons did the same training course as me. She trained as a research psychologist. Instead of working at a university, she set up on her own as a coach. So I know that she would have had the same grounding in feminism as me.

She would have learned all about the way women are marginalised and seduced by misogyny. She would have studied Simone de Beauvoir and understood that feminism means choice. At first she would have been puzzled by that – how could that be right? How could you choose anything?

Then she would have realised that you can't. That the choice only applies to things outside the trap of patriarchy. I always used to think of it in terms of high heels. I could be independent, have my own income, but if I spend it on high heels to look good for men, then that's not feminist choice. It's conformity.

These days I prefer to think of it in terms of husbands. Other people's husbands. If you're a feminist and you tell everybody and go to rallies, then sleep with someone else's husband, then that's not choice. It's not feminism. It's fucking someone else's husband.

So in many ways this is the worst of all. She's one of us. Someone who is trained. The other women probably didn't realise they were being used. They were just his puppets. But Emma is a real traitor. I Google her and, sure enough, she's written papers on feminism. She's lectured on it. She has deep knowledge about the camaraderie of feminism and even rallies other women to the cause, when all the time she's poaching their husbands.

I look at the pictures again. She's got an 'I love feminism' T-shirt on. When I look more closely, so does Jack. So fucking false. He wound himself around the lives of the women he had affairs with, took them to the places they were interested in. All so he could get them into bed.

This is beyond the pale and my blood is boiling. I Google Emma again but I can't find any of her other social networking, any clues to where she is. She'll be wary, in any case, warned by everyone. No doubt DS Percy would have called her and told her that whoever was posting on Facebook would be after her next. I finally see that she is working in Central Manchester. Her coaching practice takes place in a small office in the trendy Northern Quarter and there's a picture of her recently, thinner and blonder than before.

I start to make an appointment for tomorrow morning from

a fake email address but then I remember that she's missing and that I'm not chasing his women any more. I see that she parks in the multi-storey. She's got a convertible and it's decorated with eyelashes on the headlamps and lipstick on the bumper.

I scroll through the rest of the photographs. Jack and Emma in our bedroom. Jack and Emma in her bedroom. At the zoo. With some of our friends. Of course. They all fucking knew really, didn't they? I was a fool. We could have been out to dinner or at a barbeque with them the week after this. If anyone was in any doubt they certainly aren't now.

Part of the disadvantage I have is that I can't even imagine what is going on with DS Percy. She appears to believe me, but then she starts to check up on me. She would have been round to see Jack now. Has he convinced her I'm insane just like he convinced everyone else? Have he and Emma planned this, to get rid of me once and for all – Emma reappearing and telling them that Caroline kidnapped her? *Lorraine* will have got in touch with all those women, asked them if they had any contact with me.

I know Jack. He'll have tried to win her round. He'll have talked about me like I was mentally ill, tried to distract her from the journal. Anything to discredit me and to make himself look good. I don't see any way that he could explain it away. And *Lorraine* is so strait-laced that she would be aghast at the contents.

I scroll and scroll, there are a lot of pictures of Jack and Emma. They were stuck on top of each other in the journal and I remember I had to separate them carefully before scanning them. Some of them are graphic and some of them are blurred. I'm used to it now, the sight of him with someone else. It used to be my worst nightmare; I couldn't imagine what I would do if I ever caught him.

Tap, tap, tap through the pictures and then stop. There she

is, in my wedding dress. Except it's not my wedding dress. It's a different wedding dress and she's in a beautifully dressed room with a bouquet of daisies. Jack's there too with two people I don't know. I don't recognise the room or the outside where someone has taken a photo of a photographer taking a photograph of the wedding party.

The wedding party. It's just dawning on me. The fucking wedding party. This is his wedding to Emma. I study the photographs and it's difficult to judge if we were still together then. We definitely were earlier in this relationship. Even so, it took a year for the divorce to come through and, according to the pictures, they met in early spring and this was the summer.

The next pictures in the series are Jack at the airport with Emma. A Just Married sticker is plastered on her case. That would have been around the time you left to work abroad. I go back to Facebook and scroll down Emma Atkinson's profile. She's posted a life event. *Married. 21 August.*

I rush upstairs and get the decree absolute out of my document case. Dated 30 September the same year. He married her while we were still married. This is it. This is really it. Proof.

This is what I've been waiting for. Legal proof that he thinks he is above the law. He really is a psychopath. And I'm not. There is so much I can do with this, but first I need to find Emma. She's just a pawn in Jack's little game, potentially in danger, and I need to find her.

Chapter Thirty-eight

I don't know where to start. There are two possibilities: that Jack and Emma are trying to blame this on me or that he has done something to her. Either way, I'm holding all the cards now. I pick up my mobile and find his number. I'm suddenly scared and hot. Even speaking to him will be difficult.

And what I have to tell him is the ultimate revenge, but also painful. He cared so little about me that he just went ahead and married someone else before we were even finally divorced. But it will save Emma, stop him doing whatever he's doing to her. I have butterflies in my tummy and I wait a while, scanning the kitchen for alcohol. Then the phone suddenly rings in my hand and scares me to death.

It's an unknown number and I ready myself for someone flogging house insurance or asking me if I've had an accident in the last two years. Instead, it's Emma.

'Caroline, it's Emma. Emma Atkinson.'

'Where are you, Emma? Only the police—'

She's loud and angry.

'Fuck the police. Turn around. I'm in your back garden.'

She is. I see the glow of her mobile phone against the copper birch leaves and her pale face, solemn. Rover is barking loudly and trying to dig through the fence but she doesn't notice. She is sitting beside the hole and the contents are spread around her. Oh my God. How the fuck has she found out about that? Fuck. Fuck, fuck, fuck. I open the back door and go outside and she stands up. She's holding the credit cards, fanned out in her hand. Beside her is a large pile of photographs, the top one shows me in a hotel with a random male. I move towards her.

'I don't understand ...'

She steps back.

'Oh yes, you do fucking understand. I'm your worst nightmare, Caroline. I've put up with this, the fucking photographs on Facebook, the Twitter hashtags, #teamfuckingCaro. But this is going too far now.'

I sit down on the grass.

'Yeah. Well. At least you know what he's like now.'

She shakes her head.

'He's not, though. Not to me.'

I can't help but laugh. Poor deluded Emma.

'Really? You're special, are you? Only it looks like his behaviour is really getting to you.'

She is fuming.

'No. It's your behaviour that's getting to me. You're the fucking crazy ex. You posted the pictures. You stirred all this up. Now you're going to seal my fate.'

Seal her fate? What the fuck does she mean? I haven't done anything to Emma.

'Oh, right. Is this something else Jack has made up about me? What I'm going to do? How mad I am?'

'No. The way this is going, he's going to get custody of your children.' She steps closer to me now and I can see her properly. She's my double. That's why she looks so familiar. 'The thing is, Caroline,

I don't want your brats. I want Jack. I want to move away from his crazy fucking mother and your kids. We've got an apartment, beautiful it is, but it's not big enough for your kids as well.' Of course. Villa Place. 'I want us to have a life and you're stopping us by ... all this. He was planning to get legal custody of them.'

It sinks in through the hurt and the pain very slowly. Pushing through the shell that's formed around me over the past year, thick and thorny. We stare at each other and, for once, I'm at a loss for words. She doesn't want Charlie and Laura. Emma's not on a mission to discredit me. She's not the enemy. I am. I'm her enemy. She's on her own mission on an entirely separate trajectory. She's got a mad look in her eye that I recognise. I used to have it 100 per cent of the time when I was chasing Jack's exes around. Emma jumps up dramatically.

'So, unless you've got a better idea, I'm going to have to tell the police about all this.' She points at the contents of the hole and the photographs. 'That's where I've been. I had to get the photos out of Allan's flat when he was arrested. Private investigator. Got too greedy, he did. Obviously I couldn't tell Jack, so he reported it because he thought it was your doing. So it conveniently looked like I was missing. But this has to stop.'

I can't believe it. It was her, not Jack. It was her who nearly got me arrested.

'So you've had me fucking followed?'

'Yeah, I was building a case. I was going to blackmail you with it. Make you leave Jack alone. Make you take the kids back. Then all this happened with the journal and—'

I intervene.

'So you don't mind about the contents of the journal? That he's marked everyone out of ten? Taken pictures? Doesn't that disturb you a bit? You know, as a feminist?'

I can't resist. The sarcastic note in my voice pisses her off even more.

'He's explained it all. It was just a photography project. Art. Anyway, that's rich coming from you. You've systematically hunted down Jack's exes and done ... stuff.'

I shake my head.

'I'm just defending myself. Looking after what's mine. Most of them even apologised one way or another. Come on, Emma, you must have heard of retribution? That was my reason. But it's over now because I've realised that actually it wasn't their fault. It was his. He did it. And it wasn't fucking art. That's just another lie. What about you?'

She stares at me.

'You have to wade through the mud to find the gold.'

I laugh loudly.

'Jesus Christ. You don't believe that, really, do you?'

But she does. Like me, she's conditioned. Here we are, two educated women, both experts in the nuances of the human condition, standing in a muddy back garden arguing over a man.

'Look, I just want to be with my husband.'

It's like an echo from the depths of my marriage. *I just want to be with my husband.* As if that excuses everything.

'So what's that got to do with me? Be my guest. I don't want him. Please, take him.'

'Well, I want you to take those pictures down. It's the past.' I knew it. She is upset about them. 'And I want the children to live with you. I encouraged Laura to go to her teacher. She cried for you every night. I told her to ask to see you.' My temper flares at her manipulation of my daughter and frankly I can't see how Jack will agree to this, but I hear her out. 'So if you agree to this and promise to stop fucking with my life, I won't tell the police about what you've done.'

She thinks. There's more.

'Oh yes. That fucking simpering Katy. Obviously Jack's going to want to see his kids at some point, so I want it all coordinated so it's all on one day every two weeks or so.'

She's staring straight at me expectantly.

'So how do you suggest I get the kids? You know exactly what's happened. You know how he's painted me. It's not that easy.'

She smiles.

'Not my problem. You'll find a way. But you have to tell me now. You have to tell me now.' She's kicking the stolen stuff into the hole and she gets her phone out. She throws the photographs into the hole, reaches into her pocket and brings out a Zippo lighter. 'Come on, Caroline. My finger's on the last nine.'

She flicks the lighter and I see her phone light up with three nines. She's fucking crazy. But haven't I been here with Frances? Pam? Christine Dearden? What choice have I got? If I agree and she burns the photos she's got less evidence, but I'm not naïve enough to think she hasn't got digital copies. She appears to be as capable as I am, if not more. If I don't find a way to get the kids back, I'm in real trouble. What fucking choice have I got?

'OK. We've got the family review on Tuesday; I'll do it. I'll take down the Facebook accounts but I can't do anything about the Twitter or anything people have shared. Yeah?'

She stares at me. Her blonde hair is wild and snakes down her shoulders, her eyes are blazing.

'You loved him once. You know why I'm doing this.'

I nod. Yes I do. But I also know how it ends up with men like Jack.

It's not about the woman they are with, it's about them. Nothing anyone else can do will change them. There are certain things in life that you can't tell someone. They have to experience it. One of them is that your children are capable of everything you are – a lesson Missy has yet to acknowledge. Another is that you can't change someone. They have to acknowledge that they need to change, be willing to change and do the work themselves. Anything else is manipulation and facilitating. Emma takes her finger off the nine button and drops the lighter into the hole.

The flames shoot high and there is a small explosion – probably the Chanel No 5. She jumps away and closer to me and I can see she's crying. I go to hug her, but she pushes me away.

'Fuck off. Just fuck off.'

God, I know what place she is in. Untouchable. Brittle. Isolated. I also know that there's not much I can do at this point to help her. She'll go back to him and try to please him and she will until he finds someone different. The hole burns itself out and I go back into the house. Emma watches me, her face a little bit dirty from the smoke.

'I'll let you out the front.'

She follows me through the house, staring at the boxes. *This is how you'll end up*, I want to tell her, but I don't waste my breath. She marches to the front door, still stroppy.

'If you don't get those kids away from me, I'll go to the police. I've got photos of you going into that woman's shop in Uppermill. Lots of you leathered in Premier Inns with various blokes. And I'll post them on the internet and the university intranet and see how you like it.'

I just stare at her. She walks away and I close the door. Oh God. How am I going to pull this off? One thing's for sure, if I don't I'll lose my job *and* my children.

I sit down heavily and look at Twitter. #teamCaro is trending again, and someone is arguing that feminism is in its sixth phase. A couple of teenage boys are baiting an academic who is trying to argue that posting the pictures on Facebook is postmodern communication. It's out of control and has exceeded what I could have ever imagined, but now I need to curb it.

I put the kettle on and pour some water down the hole onto the glowing embers of my past misdemeanours. I feel strangely cleansed and suddenly optimistic. The one thing Emma didn't mention was her marriage. How he married her while he was still married to me. I hurry back into the house and grab the decree absolute. This is my way to get my children back.

This really is it.

Chapter Thirty-nine

I switch on the TV. I watch a nature programme and sip a cup of tea and then, at the end of the news, I turn the volume up for the local news report. I need to keep calm and not let my mind race to the meeting. I'm just dropping off to sleep when there's a knock on the door. I peer out from behind the curtains. It's Paula. I let her in and she stands in the hallway in front of me.

'Come and sit down.'

I push a box off the couch but she stays standing. Something's not right. She gets her phone out and shows me a picture. It's The Tea Cosy. Busy, and Frances is behind the counter.

'Never shut.' She's sullen and sulky. 'I had a brew and one of the old dears told me it was just an infestation. Got the pest control in and it was all over in a day.'

I breathe a sigh of relief. I'm genuinely pleased I didn't cause any real damage. I look more closely at the picture and Frances is smiling. But Paula is still standing in my lounge looking uncomfortable. She finally speaks.

'There's something I didn't tell you.'

I fucking knew it. I get up and face her. I fucking knew she was lying. But she's swiping the photos on her phone, one after another. She stops and holds it up in front of me. It's her and a woman with long black hair. She's got a tattoo on her arm, the same as Paula's. She's showing it off to the camera.

'This is Patti. This is why I kept away.' Her eyes fill with tears and she shakes her head. 'It's been hard for me. I had to move away. My mates didn't understand. I've moved in with Patti. I didn't know how you'd feel about it.'

I look at her. Patti. One of the bridesmaids.

'So you're ...?'

'Gay. Yes. You can say it out loud, you know.'

'My God. Is that all this is? I thought you were going to say that you had slept with Jack after all. God, Paula, as long as you are happy, I'm happy.'

A tear rolls down her cheek and drops onto a small pile of boxes at her feet.

'I wasn't sure how you'd react. It all looked so perfect, your life, and I was scared of telling you in case you didn't understand. But it turned out that you were struggling just as much as me.' She sits down heavily. 'We could have helped each other.'

I take her hand.

'We can now.'

I make something to eat and, later on, when it's properly dark, I push made-up Monica's laptop, saved from burning in the hole by my obsession with Facebook, in my bag and we head for the trams. I feel a little bit sad that this will be my last time as Monica. I log on and it's incredible. The #allgirlstogether thread is so long now that it's impossible to read it all. I switch on my mobile and there's a call from a TV researcher asking if I would consider giving my point of view.

A couple of days ago I would have done, but not now. Even if

Emma goes back on her word, it's the end. It is. I delete the message and go back to the Facebook thread. I hover over the delete button, but change my mind. I'll deactivate the accounts instead. That way it will always be there. Just in case.

I go to made-up Monica's account and scroll through it. I'm listening to my cheating bastard playlist with Paula, an earphone each like we did when we were kids, and 'DOA' by the Foo Fighters comes on – definitely in my top ten. I silently acknowledge *High Fidelity* and this difference in my state of mind since I read the journal. My anti-*High Fidelity* resolve, revenge rather than making peace. I know now it's not that simple. The pictures still make me wince, but I'm used to it now. It's been reported to Facebook for nudity and they've sent an email telling me to remove a particular image, the one where Jack is fucking Pam in our room.

We ride round and round on the tram, getting off to buy a new ticket every now and again. I don't want to get into trouble. I wonder what Emma must really think of all this. How she must feel when she sees Jack with these women? Knowing Emma and knowing him, she'll think that she has changed him. She'll believe that she's different, that she's the one who has made him settle down.

We all think that. No doubt everyone in the journal thought that until the next one came along. I snigger and shake my head because for all his protestations that I didn't, I know Jack. He was trying too hard. He still is. Making himself believe that Emma was the one. That he didn't want to blow it with her. That he would do anything. Maybe he really does believe that himself, that each woman is the one – until he gets bored and finds an excuse why she's not.

When the tram reaches full circle, we get off at the park and sit on a bench at the station. I deactivate made-up Monica's profile and give the laptop to Paula, who changes the passwords to something I don't know. I switch off the laptop; it's nearly out of battery anyway. I won't be using it again.

When I get home I go to put everything in the hole, forgetting that it's a smouldering pit now. Paula takes it all from me and I have to trust her. I have to trust someone again. I wonder what Emma will have told the police and how she has persuaded Allan Parrott not to tell them it was her behind the photos. I conclude that it's none of my business and I've got enough to think about.

I must have fallen asleep on the settee because when I wake up it's a dull Monday morning and Paula's gone, back to Patti. I make coffee and my phone rings. It's Katy.

'Hi. You OK?'

I feel a bit bad that I need to convince her to let Jack see Jamie, but I'm glad she's phoned.

'Yeah. How are you? Feeling any better?'

There's a pause. She's crying.

'Not really. Did you see that they found that Emma? She was locked in a shed or something. Do you think it was him?'

'No. Wasn't it a woman?' I make it up as I go along as usual. Careful, Caroline. Not too many details. 'Look, I'll be over to get my car and my stuff in a minute. Now they've got that guy, I might as well stay at home. But thanks for the room.'

She brightens.

'Yes. Come over.'

Twenty minutes later I'm sitting in her front room with a cup of tea.

'So what did the police want?'

She's biting her nails, constantly worried.

'Oh, they thought I'd done something to Emma. Can you believe it?'

Katy tuts.

'God, you're the last person to do that after what you've had to go through with all that Facebook stuff.'

I want to tell her the truth and promise myself that from now on, after this is over, I won't lie to her.

'Yeah. Anyway, Emma's OK and that's all that matters. I've got other things on my mind. I've got a meeting with social services tomorrow. I'm going for full custody and letting Jack have visitation rights.'

She pales.

'So you're letting him see them – if you win? I thought you said he was dangerous?'

God. I have to do this, but I feel bad. If I know Jack, and with Emma's influence, though, it won't be him looking after Jamie, it'll be Missy.

'No. I know Jack is a bastard, but he's their dad.'

'I thought you said—'

'Yeah. Well. He's a prick, that's for sure. But no matter what's happened between us, the kids need him, so I'm letting him see them. As long as I don't have to see him. It's me he's the danger to, not Charlie and Laura.'

She looks confused.

'So have I done the wrong thing? You know, stopping him from seeing Jamie?'

I sigh.

'Only you know that, Katy. Maybe you could get him to pick him up from your mum's so you don't have to see him?'

I know how she's feeling right now: surprised because she knows that she was hooked on his little visits, the thread that she dangled on; reluctant, even now, to let that go. It's like Stockholm Syndrome. Dependency. *Love is the drug*. Except it isn't love.

'I suppose so.'

I help her out.

'Jamie'll be able to spend time with ...' It sticks in my throat with the emotion it holds but I manage to get it out. 'His brother and sister. You won't know what to do with your time, but we could have a little exes club, couldn't we?'

She smiles at this. I look at the photograph of Jamie, Charlie and Laura with Jack and Katy that she still keeps on her mantelpiece. Still pretending they are one big happy family. I smile back. Those children will still be together and in my heart I know that's the first priority. And me and Katy. I'm slightly giddy as I realise that his 'divide and rule' has crumbled. She's engaged now and chatting away.

'Oh, did you see that all that stuff about Jack has been deleted off Facebook? I expect the police have done it.'

I nod sagely.

'Yes. We'll just have to go back to stalking him on his own page now, won't we?'

Her expression changes. She looks like I've just exposed a big secret.

'I ... I ...'

'God, Katy, relax. We all do it, you know. That's partly why he leaves it public. Because he knows we will. It's all part of his little game.'

As I say it, I remember my conversation about the future with Jack's wife. She agreed to my terms and I've agreed to hers – and by default to Jack's. No more game-play for us. I feel free. And my work here is done. I leave her with a hug and assure her that it will all be OK. I promise to phone her when he has the kids and I will. For once I'm not faking. I actually want to. It feels good.

I'm home. Home. Suddenly it feels like home. I go into the lounge and clear a space on the sofa. The room smells musty, the stink of old newsprint and cardboard. It's a big job but I take some of the newspapers outside and put them in the skip. Then I take all the takeaway menus from the hallway and the unopened junk mail and chuck that in as well.

The empty boxes, the piles of Thomson Locals I shoved behind the kitchen door – all in the skip. By the time I'm finished, the hallway is almost clear. I keep one of the Thomson Locals and find the number for a charity shop. It rings and rings, and then I remember Lee.

I find his number and my stomach has a knot in it as the call rings out. I know by doing this I am starting something. I know. It rings, and somewhere inside me a feeling of distrust comes. My mother's voice saying, 'They're all the same.' Are they? Are they all the same? They can't be. There has to be something else for me. Somebody else. It's still ringing and this feels like a huge risk. But I can take it slowly, take it slow. Then I recognise the chink of light breaking through. Hope. It's hope.

It turns out to be a shop number and he's not there. I explain the situation and they say that they'll be around later to pick 'the things up'. I'm giggling and telling them that they might need a few trips and they thank me and wonder if I'd be interested in a charity auction.

I find a box in the kitchen that has a Dyson vac in it and get it out. It's a long time since I've used a vacuum cleaner. Or seen more than a couple of inches of carpet in here. It feels kind of good.

I polish the mirror and the door panels and I've made a start. I polish up the banister and before I know it I'm standing outside Charlie's bedroom. I know in my heart that I have to go in and assess what I need to do to make it right before they come here. But I suddenly can't move my arms. It's a heavy feeling, a dread that comes with facing your worst fear.

The terror at going into my son's bedroom is overwhelming. It brings into focus the chance that all this might be too optimistic; that it might not work out, no matter how promising it seems. After all, I can't tell them Jack is a bigamist, because I would have to explain how I found out.

I have to take the chance. I have to let go of the past and hope that fucking Emma is worth so much to him and that she keeps her word. I stand there and run it over in my mind: what could go wrong and, if it did, what would happen. Then I turn the handle and go in.

It's dusty and smells of damp. There's a patch on the ceiling just under where the cold water tank would be. I make a mental note to get a plumber in. I sit on the bed and pick up Barney, Charlie's teddy. I don't expect he'll be wanting him now, or all the Lego. I expect he's into computers.

I feel a pang of panic as I realise that I don't know my own children. I leave the room as it is for now and check Laura's. As I open the door, the butterflies I suspended from the ceiling years ago flap their wings and dust dislodges and makes me cough. Her tiny bed has a princess headboard and canopy. I need to order a new bed for her. And one for me.

This is it. It's all coming right at last. I'm planning, organising.

Waiting for my children to come home. I've made a real start on sorting out my life. I leave their bedroom doors open to air the rooms and I get out my laptop and go to Amazon Prime. Instead of drunken ordering, I've got a purpose. I order 200 strong bin liners and an assortment of cleaning materials.

I look around at the piles and piles of Amazon boxes, monuments to my lost years. It's an imposing task but I need to do it. I need to get rid of everything. Start again. A new life. I can feel that tomorrow is going to be a good day.

Chapter Forty

I wake up crying. I've had one of those dreams when you believe that you have murdered someone. I was searching the whole house for loose floorboards and felt like someone was coming to get me. I'd finally settled on the notion that I'd buried someone in the cupboard under the floorboards. I was sitting in the hallway just waiting for the police to arrive.

I sit up in bed and realise it was just a dream. Just a dream. Of course, everything that has happened has had an effect on me. Why wouldn't it? This is my subconscious trying to sort it through. It isn't real.

No time for lying in bed analysing my psyche today. I check my phone and there's a text from Lee telling me he'll be round at nine. The meeting's at two so I need to be in town by one. I desperately need to go into work. I can fit it all in. I can. This is what life's going to be like now. Full-time busy. It's exciting.

Just as Lee turns up in a large van, the postman appears.

'Thought you'd finished with all this.'

He hands me an Amazon box and stands there waiting for me to say something.

'I have. This is just bin bags and the rest is going. As soon as possible.'

He shakes his head and peers around me into the house.

'Bloody hell. Big job.'

Lee appears. In the light of day, away from the bright hotel lights, he's about forty and he's wearing jeans, hands in pockets and a bobble hat. Long brown hair. He assesses the situation quickly.

'I'll be sorting this lot out. She's donating it to charity.'

I suddenly wish I'd had a shower and put on some make-up.

'Right. Shall we make a start?'

We walk up the path and he's looking at me.

'Aren't you that woman whose husband ...?'

'Yes. Yes I am.'

He stops.

'Yeah. I saw that. Terrible. I'm sorry.'

I laugh inappropriately. It's the nerves.

'It's not your fault. Don't be sorry. Anyway, it's sorted now.'

But he persists.

'But I *am* sorry. I'm apologising on behalf of decent men everywhere. We're not all like that.' He looks serious and I know that my face shows my mortification. But he starts to laugh. He touches my shoulder. Then he looks horrified. 'No. No. We're really not. That made it look like I was joking. God. This isn't going well. I really shouldn't be around people.'

I smile.

'I know what you meant. Thanks. But it's sorted. I just need to get rid of all this. It's been ... well, a long year.'

We go inside and I'm embarrassed. He's looking around in awe.

'Jesus Christ, this is the worst I've ever seen.'

He's right. He shouldn't be around people. He goes from room to room, writing on his hand in black biro. Then up his arm. Eventually he sits on the bottom stair and looks up at me.

'OK, two options: either I can just cart this all away and store it and sell it in our various shops – proceeds go to cancer charities – or we can have a charity auction and the proceeds can be split between different charities.'

I stare at him. His eyes are … beautiful.

'I hadn't thought about it. I thought you would take care of it.'

'Yeah, we do. But if you had a preference … Look, it's going to have to go into storage anyway, so how about I take it and you decide later. Within a week, if possible.'

'Yes, that would be good. Do you do this for a job?'

'Yep. Minimum wage. I just get paid for thirty hours a week and donate the rest.'

I have to go. I want to stay here with Lee and my stuff, but I need to call in at work.

'Look, if I give you a key, do you think you can get this done in a morning? I'm willing to pay.'

He gets up and looks around again.

'I can get it done in a day. It'll need two of us but no need to pay. It's our jobs. OK to put any crap in the skip?'

It kicks in. My fear. The fear of having nothing, being in an empty house creeps up and batters me over the head. I'm looking at the skip and looking at the stuff and the tears come. I'm suddenly sobbing and Lee holds me to his chest and pats me lightly on the back.

'It's OK,' he says. It's soothing. 'I've seen it before. People having a big clear-out and they don't want to part with it. It's part of them.' He holds me in front of him, hands on my arms. 'But, you know, it's just stuff. If you're not strong enough today, we can do it another day.'

I wipe my eyes and shake my head.

'No. It has to be today. It's good of you to do it so quickly.'

He laughs again.

'To be honest, we don't get an opportunity like this very often. The local domestic violence unit would love some of this stuff. Always looking for white goods.'

I repeat his words.

'Domestic violence.'

After everything I've been through it's a relief for someone to just say it. It's like I've been avoiding it for so long and now it's out in the open. Lee takes my statement as a question, and I suppose it is, really.

'Well. Yes. Isn't that what's been going on here? It's not just physical violence, you know. Silence can be violence.' He smiles and nudges me. 'See what I did there? Seriously, though, I've got some numbers if you need them.'

I hadn't thought of myself like that. Not as a victim. More of a survivor. A fighter. For justice. But I guess whatever happens now that's how a lot of people will see me. A victim. So I can only be either mad or a victim. Which one made me do all this? Insanity or survival?

It doesn't feel like that. Just as I realised when Jack took the kids, life goes on whether you like it or not. And I don't want to be a victim. I want a life. Even admitting that feels like a risk, but I'm testing myself. Am I up for it? Yes. Yes.

I take a good look around. It's mainly boxes of different sizes with mounds of newspaper and prints of academic papers between them.

'OK, just throw all the papers in the skip.'

He thinks. 'Or I can get the recycling guy to come round.'

I need to go.

'Great. Whatever you can do by tonight would be great. Here's the key. I just need to get ready, then I have to go out. Give me a call if you need to check on anything.'

He takes the key and stands in the front garden talking on his phone. I take a shower and dress, then watch him for a moment as I collect my things. Suddenly he's captivating.

He waves as I go to the car. In twenty minutes I'm in the staffroom at the university surrounded by my colleagues. Eileen represents.

'My God, Caroline. We heard what happened over Jack. You were right all along. We just want to tell you that you have our full support. And that lovely policewoman who was here yesterday told us about that man who has been following you. She was very thorough. Wanted all the footage of you in the university going back months. He must have been following you for ages.'

My blood boils. In one way this couldn't have worked out better. I knew that some of my colleagues thought I was completely off my rocker. 'Why would they take her kids otherwise, and all those boxes …?' I heard Candice Potter from Art Therapy say one day. Oh yes. Several of them thought I was mad. Now they're all having a rethink.

But bloody DS Percy's been nosing around here. Finding out about me. I have a horrible suspicion that this isn't over yet for her. But all she's going to find is Emma Atkinson. With a brown envelope. Not my problem.

'I know. I never even suspected. I've been very lucky.'

I nearly laugh, because lucky is not what I have been. I should never have had to go through this, and I still think it's Jack's fault. He can be as nice as he wants at the meeting – I know it's only because there's something in it for him. But I'll take it where I can because if I don't go through with this today then he could get the children full-time and I'll be back to square one.

Eileen takes me to her office and we discuss what will happen with the big psychopath project. I've been given the lead and it's all down to me to plan it out. It's what I've wanted for a long time. I lean forward and indicate that I'm taking Eileen into my confidence.

'Of course, with all that's happened over the past week, things have changed at home.' She's leaning in too, eager for the gossip. 'I've got a meeting with social services this afternoon. I might be getting the children back part-time.'

She clasps her hands in front of her and offers me a doughnut. I glimpse a #teamCaro rubber band around her arm.

'Oh Caroline, that's wonderful.'

'Yes, it really is. So I might need a couple of days to sort things out, then everything will be back to normal.'

She looks pleased. The clock ticks on and I need to get to town.

'Great. I'll start it all on Monday, then. I honestly can't wait.'

I can't. I've got the perfect subject in mind to model my thinking on.

I'm out of the university and back in my car. I sit outside for a minute, still fuming about DS Percy. I get out my phone and call her, but it goes to answerphone. I wait a couple of minutes to see if she rings me back but she doesn't.

Why was she here? She's got what she wants. She's got Peter Daubney's thief and Emma is safe and hasn't spilled the beans. If she had, I'd have been arrested by now. I've deleted the Facebook profiles so Jack will have to drop the charges. I expect she was looking for evidence against my stalker, but something deep inside tells me that isn't the case. She knows it's him, she told me. She's got evidence.

As I drive towards town I can't help but think about Lee and my house and it gradually emptying into the big van. I don't even know what's in those boxes. I don't know what I ordered from Amazon when I was pissed. I feel a little bit ashamed – of that and of all the men I slept with and robbed. The in-between has a lot to answer for. But Jack made me go there. It was the only place that I could retreat to. Bad things happened there, but in one way I was safe. It was somewhere that I didn't have to think about what he did to me, or why.

That's the big question, isn't it? Why? Why requires a deeper analysis of his reasons. He wasn't happy. He hadn't found the right woman. He wanted to keep his kids. They aren't reasons. He could have asked me for a divorce. I would have been angry to start with, but in the end I would have agreed. The kids wouldn't have been damaged and he could still have gone on his fucking quest to find 'the one'.

It's pathetic, but I have to acquiesce. It grates against my soul and makes me wonder why even more. I'm doing it for my children. I have to agree to Jack and fucking Emma bringing them up jointly with me. I could go for full custody, but he'll still be able to see them. He can't spill about his bigamous marriage because it works both ways, like that fucking injunction he took out against me.

I sorely want to use it against him, make it public, but I need to keep it just between us. It will be our secret, and one that I can use every time he starts his old tricks again. Tough shit if someone else notices; after all, none of this is really secret; it's all there if anyone cares to put it together, all on public record. I just had to do a bit of digging to find out. He's as implicated as me. All I have to do now is face him with it.

I go over the scenario in my head on the way to the meeting, over and over again, and before I know it I'm standing at the checkout at Morrisons with a litre of vodka.

Chapter Forty-one

I pay for it and hurry outside. Morrisons backs onto a canal and I duck around the side and into an alcove. I open the bottle and hold it in front of me. I could have a small sip, just to ease my nerves before the meeting. Just a small sip.

I anticipate the softness that I will dissolve into if I have more than a small sip. I raise the glass to my lips. It's cold and this is just like an automatic action. Classical conditioning. I've conditioned myself to self-medicate. I know this already but it's not stopping me.

A couple walk past with their dog and stare at me, standing there in a business suit with the bottle. Will it always be like this now? Has life levelled itself into a terrible baseline where I will always have to find a way to ease the pain? Where I will be a perpetual victim? Is there no way out for me?

I screw the top back on the bottle and place it carefully in the corner of the alcove. Then I think again and pour it into the canal and drop the bottle into a waste bin as I hurry back to the car. The assistant who served me is smoking a cigarette outside Morrisons and she looks amazed as I pass her.

I'm back in the car. It's one-thirty and I'm behind schedule. I have to do this, even if it ends in disaster, which is what I guess I am scared of. I drive into town and park up. I'm not going into the social services building until I absolutely have to. I check my phone again to see if DS Percy has called me back. Nothing at all. On the bright side, there's nothing from Lee either, so he hasn't run into any problems.

At quarter to one I see Jack's bent fucking solicitor arrive and go in. Maybe Jack's not coming after all. Maybe it's a trap. This was just supposed to be a chat, not a meeting. Panic. Panic. Panic. I watch as he waits in the doorway, talking on his mobile and looking at his watch.

Ten to one. I guess I should go in. Just as I open the car door I spot Jack walking across the park opposite. Hands in chino pockets, he hasn't bothered to dress for the occasion. He looks casual and relaxed. I still feel an attraction, even after everything that he did. What the fuck is that? How can it happen? I expect it's hardwired – we're attracted in the first place through the urge to reproduce, it's only afterwards that the emotional bonds that bind us are set.

I wait until he goes in and then walk with wobbly legs across to the building. I hurry my step and soon I'm right behind him. It slips out.

'Jack.'

He stops dead in his tracks. He turns slowly. I'm shocked to see grey at his temples, but kind of hope that I'm the cause of it.

'Caroline.'

It sounds smooth and carefree, but I see his face set into a *this is going to be interesting* expression.

'I wondered if we could have a chat before we go in?'

I'm suddenly fucking terrified and angry at the same time. Everything in the journal, his perfect ten and his little hobby photography avalanches over me and I can fully understand why Louise Shaw went for him. But violence is never necessary. Never.

You can hurt people without it, but that's wrong too, as I now know to my cost. He rocks back on his heels and stares at the sky.

'I've nothing to say to you.'

He half turns but I put my hand on his arm.

'I think you have. You see, I worked something out.' I take our decree absolute out of my pocket. He's still smirking. 'What date did you marry Emma?'

It's hardly perceptible but his face slightly crumples.

'October. Why?'

Nice try. Only what I expected.

'I don't think you did. But if you're sure—'

He grabs me and pulls me into an alcove.

'Don't you think you've done enough, Caro? Honestly? I'm a fucking laughing stock. All over the fucking internet. Why would you do that?'

I can't believe what I'm hearing. He feels sorry for himself.

'You marked us out of ten. You took photographs. You were married to me at the time. That's fucking why, Jack. You convinced everyone I was mad and took everything I love. But it's backfired because then I had nothing to lose. You're a fucking monster, Jack.'

He stares at me. Then he leans forward and puts his hands on my shoulders, his mouth near my ear. I feel my skin bristle, a muscle memory of the intimacy we once shared.

'Look, there's no need for all this. We can work something out ...'

He's coming on to me. It really is unbelievable, but I play along. I whisper back.

'Yes, we can. I want my children back. Living with me. I want them back. And if you don't agree, the pictures and more go back up and I'll report you to the police for bigamy. Which, if I'm not mistaken, your current wife has no idea about?'

He steps back. Blinking into the sunlight. Thinking if there's a way round it.

'Suit yourself. But my mother won't like it.'

'I don't give a fuck about your mother. I won't let her bully me any more. You call her off too.'

He nods. I don't trust him. It can't be this easy. He's walking away as if we've just discussed the weather. I wait until he's gone in and then I follow.

Once inside I'm guided to a corridor where he's sitting with his solicitor, whispering behind his hand. He doesn't look at me but he laughs and the solicitor grins at me and I fear the worst. Just as I get within speaking distance the door opposite opens and a small woman with a manila file comes out.

'Mr and Mrs Atkinson? Come. Have a seat.'

We file in and the room is small. Jack still doesn't look at me, but his fucking bent solicitor stares at me. I stare back. We're so close that I can see Jack's designer stubble is two days old and I can smell his aftershave. His nails are perfectly clipped and I compare them with mine, the edges torn with worry.

The woman begins, 'Right. I'm Mrs Porter. I represent the family court. We're here today to discuss the welfare of your children, Charlie and Laura. As you both know, Laura has spoken to a teacher and asked if she can see Mrs Atkinson. We put this to you, Mr Atkinson, and there was a refusal on the grounds of your ex-wife's mental health. We've checked her medical records with her permission and there are no mental health issues.'

The solicitor sorts some papers and I try to catch Jack's eye. Mrs Porter carries on.

'Since then I understand that there has been a retraction of the refusal and a suggestion that the family situation be reconsidered.'

Yes. Yes. His solicitor speaks now.

'Mr Atkinson has requested that living arrangements be revised. He is happy that the children live with Mrs Atkinson and that this will be in the interests of the children. He would like it to be placed on the record that he has the utmost interests of his children at heart and it is this that has brought him to this decision. He will be happy to have visitation rights with Charlie and Laura under the following conditions.'

He clears his throat and takes a sip of water. Jack's staring at the table. Something is wrong here.

'That Mrs Atkinson agree that while the children of the family are with Mr Atkinson and his partner, they will stay at 6 Gimble Lane for visitation until Mr Atkinson informs the family court of any change of address or different arrangements, and that Mrs Atkinson agrees to make no further objection to this arrangement.'

With his mum. With Missy. Something tells me that Emma has already laid the foundations for this. I wait for him to go on. Mrs Porter and the solicitor look at me, but Jack doesn't. Mrs Porter speaks.

'Mrs Atkinson? Do you agree to this?'

Is that it? Is that all he wants? He's not going to go over what we discussed? I suppose not. It wouldn't make him look too good, would it?

'Yes. Yes, I agree. I just want my children back. What will the arrangements be? I mean, when does this begin? When will I have them?'

The solicitor finds another piece of paper, which, from a distance, looks hurriedly written out in longhand.

'These are the suggestions. Pending your approval.' I can't believe it. I'm being given options. 'The arrangement will begin immediately. My client suggests that every other weekend would be a good arrangement, with Friday, Saturday, Sunday constituting the visitation period and Tuesday, Wednesday, Thursday the mirroring period every other week.'

That will suit Emma. She's been dying to get rid of them so she can have Jack to herself. I bet she's doing cartwheels. He continues.

'Mr Atkinson would be happy to collect and drop off the children at Mrs Atkinson's property. There is a concern that Mrs Atkinson does not confront Mr Atkinson's partner and this will save any unnecessary upset for the children. There was also a concern about the dilapidated state of the property—'

'No. I want Mrs Emma Atkinson to bring and collect the children. Under the circumstances. I am an adult and I can act like one. I have no issue with Mrs Emma Atkinson. And, by the way, I'm Dr Atkinson. Not Mrs.' They're all watching me carefully. 'The house will be fine by Friday. I'm having it deep cleaned. And that's all fine with me. But I'll be meeting the children at the door. I'd appreciate it if Mrs Atkinson left them at the door.'

I can hear my voice, calm and even. My hands on the table, palms down. I didn't need the vodka after all. I look up and he's looking at me now. I smile a little and he nods a little, then it's over.

Mrs Porter looks over a document prepared by his bent solicitor. In advance. I didn't even need to confront him like I did. He was already defeated. When she is satisfied, we both sign it.

'So. Can I trust you to make the rest of the arrangements between yourselves? I hope that we don't have to see you back here again. This is about the children, you know. What's best for them. Don't let them down.'

Jack gets up and leaves, his solicitor in tow. I want to chase after him, thank him, even though he's giving me something that is mine already. I rise from my chair, elated, but Mrs Porter blocks my way.

'Have you got a minute? Only I have a few concerns.' I sit back down. I knew there had to be a problem. She sits and looks at the papers. 'OK. Two things. We had an anonymous report about the state of your home. Someone sent in a photograph and it seems that there are some, er, space issues.'

I smile politely. I can hold this down.

'Yes. I've been through a terrible time. Losing my children. I don't want to go into blame, seeing as we have a good outcome, but the year hasn't been good for me. You must understand that?' She nods. 'I can confirm that my home will be restored to its normal state by Friday. It's underway as we speak. I can give you a number to call?' She smiles.

'I'm assigning you a social worker, Mrs ... Dr Atkinson. She'll call on you on Thursday afternoon and check the premises. She'll be available for Charlie and Laura to talk to should they have any concerns about any of the arrangements. So. The second issue.'

She leans closer to me.

'This is an unusual case. With the disclosures on social networking, including your sister and other women.' Bloody hell. They're having a go at him now. 'I'm sure the children will need some help coming to terms with all that has happened. But what about you? How do you feel about it?'

Careful, Caroline. Careful. Don't blow it now.

'I'm fine. I just want to see my children. Honestly, Jack can do what he wants. And for the record, the claims about my sister were untrue.'

She pauses and looks upwards.

'Yes. I know. She called our office. Look, how can I put this? I've been following the antics of your ex-husband. In fact, I don't know a woman who hasn't. Someone would have had to go to some considerable effort to get this information and post it online. I just want some assurance that this isn't going to continue.'

I lock eyes with her. She pulls up her sleeve slightly and I see a #teamCaro rubber bracelet. She's sat in this room with the full knowledge about what Jack has done. I consider my words carefully.

'It seems to have stopped now.'

She smiles tightly.

'Yes. I'll be monitoring it closely. Here in social services we take a dim view of such things. Whatever the rights and wrongs of the situation, from now on it's straight down the line. I've looked at the full picture, Caroline. You've got no record. This is the first time either of you have come to our attention. You're an intelligent woman. But those children need stability. If I get a whiff of anything like this in the future, I'll have you both back in here and put your children in care. Understand?'

She looks at the CCTV camera above us and I nod.

'As far as my behaviour is concerned, it will be exemplary. I've just received a promotion at work and I'll be focusing on Charlie and Laura. You won't have any problems from me.'

'Good. Here's a copy of what you have agreed to.'

She reads through some papers and then closes the file. She slides across a transcript of what Laura said to her teacher and her eyes tell me not to say a word. I read it and tears prick my eyes. It starts with some minor complaining about one of her friends and ends with, 'I just miss my mummy.'

I stare at the precious words. I always knew it. I always knew that she wouldn't forget me. I eventually slide the paper back.

'I understand.'

She rises and it's my signal to leave. She walks me along the corridor and I wonder for a moment if it's just a strategy to allow Jack to leave without me having a go. But as we get to the doorway she pulls me to one side.

'I just wanted to say, nice work.'

'I'm sorry?'

'The Facebook posts. Honestly, off the record, any one of us could have done that in the same situation. But he really is a #cheatingbastard of the highest rank. You're well rid of him. Nice work, marine.'

She salutes, turns and walks down the corridor.

Chapter Forty-two

I'm going to see my children. I'm going to see them. This is real. They're coming back.

I sit on the wall outside social services and assess if anything else can possibly go wrong. I don't think it can. I'm just going to move forward now and accept what has happened. Mrs Porter's right, I am well rid of Jack. He looked wounded in there. As if someone had taken away his favourite toy. But I don't care now.

I can't face going home yet so I go back to work and spend the rest of the afternoon on damage limitation. I Google myself and the Peter Daubney case and resist the temptation to make another file of evidence that I will take home, throw on the floor and never look at again.

I check Twitter and the #cheatingbastard hashtag is still going strong. It's assumed a life of its own, with thousands of spurned lovers using it as a therapeutic tool to spill their emotional guts all over social networking. The Facebook threads have disappeared so I make a start on my Facebook messages on my own account and I push on the cheating bastard playlist for the last time. Lucinda Williams rasps 'Changed the Locks', and I smile to myself. Yes. Yes. I've unfucked myself. Well and truly unfucked.

Plenty of people apologising for doubting me. Some mutual friends telling me they always knew. A few angry messages and about twenty-five messages from men wanting to take me out.

I've been named in the stalker reports, but the focus is on Peter Daubney and Brian Patterson and they have been given tabloid inches. No one seems to have made the connection between the Caroline Atkinson in this case and Jack Atkinson's wife in the media explosion that followed. Mainly because I have not once been referred to by name. Poor Jack's wife. That's who I was. The victim. But something inside tells me I'm not a victim now. It's a strange feeling, but I feel like I've survived.

I save all the links in a document and bury it in a folder on my external hard drive. I'll keep monitoring it and adding to it just in case anything crops up.

I turn my computer off. I have to get home. I put my earphones in and select the cheating bastard playlist and Kelly Clarkson is telling me that *since you've been gone I can breathe for the first time*. I've been putting it off, wondering what the house will be like with all that space for my thoughts to gather in when I am alone. Lee will have left by now and all my stuff will have gone.

But he hasn't gone. As I pull up in front of the house, the large van is still there. The skip is piled high with crap and my next-door neighbour is standing looking at it and talking on her phone. She waves at me and goes inside.

Lee appears and stands on my lawn. He's holding a cup of steaming tea and he smiles at me.

'Two trips it took. But all booked in and catalogued now. Just have a look in there and make sure there's nothing you want.' He points at the skip. 'And I did a bit of a clean-up. Wasn't too bad, really, under all that.'

I look in the skip. It's just papers. Just stuff. None of it matters. I step inside the hallway and the first thing I notice is the echo.

The house sounds completely different. I go through to the lounge and feel the carpet beneath my feet. It's still marked in blocks from the boxes.

'That'll fade.'

Lee's standing behind me, hands on waist.

'I can't thank you enough. Honestly, there was no need ...'

'I wanted to. This is such a lovely place, needs looking after. It's been a pleasure.'

The kitchen looks brilliant. He's cleaned the table and washed the tiles. The walls have stripes of grease where the cooking has seeped between the piles of white goods. But overall it's brilliant. I open the fridge and it's empty.

'I threw it all out. Start again. Best bet.'

I turn to him.

'Can I pay you for this? You shouldn't have to—'

'No. No. I insist. All the donations will make a lot of money. You must have spent thousands.'

I nod. I have spent thousands. I had nothing better to do. He brings out some boxes.

'I found these. I didn't throw anything away that looked personal.'

The kettle's on and he's making me tea. I open the lids of the boxes and they're family photographs. Pictures of Jack and me. Then us and the kids. I look at them with my new knowledge and see that on some of them he looks strained. Distracted. Interested in the kids but not in me.

Did I know? Did I know all this and desperately try to keep him? Was it all part of a super-competitive game where I couldn't bear to lose? I go through the pictures. I think I read a paper somewhere that said family photographs are usually 60 per cent landscapes to contextualise them. I throw away all the landscapes. These photographs don't need a context because they don't represent reality.

I watch as Lee washes up.

'Sugar?'

I shake my head.

'No. Thank you. Did you do all this yourself?'

'No. I called two people to help, but they went about fourish. I thought I'd better wait until you got back to make sure it was still fine. You could have sold some of that stuff, you know – eBay.'

I laugh.

'Yeah, but that would mean effort. I just needed to get rid. It's been difficult.'

He nods and sips his tea.

'All right now, though?'

He looks like he really cares. He's looking directly at me. Maybe he's just worried. He's seen the inside of my home, which reflects the inside of my head. Maybe I'm over-analysing.

'On the way.'

There's a long silence and he's finished his tea. He stands up and sits down.

'Right. Right, then. Look. After the other night at the hotel ... I can come back and paint that cupboard if you want. I was going to ... but I'm not big on going out.'

I stare at him. He's asking me out. He's asking me out and he knows who I am. He's seen that I'm some mad hoarding lady and he still likes me. It feels dangerous. Risky. He somehow senses it.

'It's just a date. Don't worry.'

I nod. I want to trust him. I do. I want to. The notion that this is what brave means washes over my consciousness. Doing something you are scared of. But if I don't, I'm a victim. Jack's victim.

'Er. OK. Not this weekend, though. I'm getting to see my kids.'

His eyes betray him. He's been in those rooms and he knows that they haven't been used for a long, long time.

'That's brilliant. Really brilliant. So what about Tuesday? Next week?'

He's nice. Unassuming. And attractive. It's been a long time since I found anyone attractive. Obsession has no space for attraction.

'Yes. I'd like that. But can I just ask ...'

He moves a little closer.

'All this.' He looks around to the empty space he's made in my life. 'All that stuff. No one's perfect. You've been through a bad time. You're not the only one, you know. You don't get to our age unscathed. And anyway, you haven't seen my gaff yet!' He smiles and blushes a little. 'I like you. Just want to spend some time around you. That's all. Take a chance.'

He's staring at the floor, embarrassed. So he's been hurt as well. Take a chance or be alone. I nod.

He's gone and I'm alone with my tea. It's suddenly very quiet and I look around. The house is beautiful. I go up to my bedroom and it's the only room left that reminds me of what happened. The door is damaged and the mattress is missing. I switch on the light and immediately hundreds of seed pearls glitter through the pile of the carpet. I reach up to the back of the wardrobe, to behind where I kept my wedding dress, and I pull down a box.

I open it and take out the pressed buttonhole flowers and the ring boxes. Underneath are all the wedding cards, and the standard Valentine's cards he sent me. *To my wife.* Inside. *From Jack.* No romance. No mystery. No fun. Yes. That was it. No fun. It was all very functional. Going through the motions. I'd kept all these things. All the letters from him when we were actually in love.

Every concert ticket. Pictures of us together.

What did he keep? Nothing. Instead, he kept a perfect ten record of things he enjoyed. I enjoyed him, he enjoyed them. I take the box downstairs and throw it in the skip. No point keeping it now it doesn't mean anything. I'll always have the memories, but if this is going to be over it really has to be.

It's seven o'clock and it's going dark. I stand outside for a while and look over to the park. I need to get rid of that car somehow, but that can wait for another day. It's well hidden. It should be OK. I go into the lounge again and sit on the sofa. I switch on the TV. It's odd.

Lee's nice. He's straightened all the pictures and wiped the fireplace over. I take the family portrait from the wall behind me and rest it on the sofa. It's a shame, because it's a beautiful portrait. But it can't stay. Things have changed and I need renewal. It's left a huge pale mark in the disgustingly dirty wallpaper and I resolve to get it decorated. I wonder if Lee does decorating?

I go into the kitchen and open the cupboards one by one. There are still some small boxes but they will wait until another day.

Chapter Forty-three

On Thursday the social worker comes round and looks at the house in all its newly cleaned glory. It feels opulent and new, even though I've lived here for a long time. I've splashed out and bought a tablet each for the children and I show her their rooms.

My tummy still feels a little bit fluttery when I go in there, like it's not going to happen, but she assures me that it's all set for tomorrow and that Emma will drop them off in the morning. I've told Eileen the good news and she has spread the word. Fiona texts me to tell me that she'll be round over the weekend and a couple of school friends have invited me to a night out, a kind of reunion, which I suspect they have hastily arranged to get the gossip.

When the social worker leaves, I take a screenshot of Emma's life event on Facebook and the scan of our decree absolute and I put them together in a folder on my phone. I'm going to print them out on Monday and keep them safe if Jack tries to change anything. It's sad. Sad that it's come to this, but it's my life now and I'm going to make sure I'm ready to defend myself in the future. I set about shovelling some soil into the hole and I'm about halfway done when I hear the doorbell. I answer, all dirty hands and grubby clothes, and it's Lee.

'Hi. I saw your car and I wondered if you needed ...'

'Yeah. Come in.'

We sit at the table while the kettle boils and he tells me about how he's just organising a charity ball and would I like to go with him?

'Is it a date?'

I hear my voice, slightly worried.

'Yeah, it is. You see, I talked to my mate about you and he advised against the cupboard painting. Said I should take you out, treat you like a lady. So ...'

I touch his hand gently and he doesn't draw it away like Jack would.

'Cupboard painting is just fine. But yes, I'll go to the ball with you.'

We both laugh and the tea is ready. We drink and chat about nothing and he says he has to go to work. There's a moment at the front door and we kiss. It feels good and for the first time in more than a decade I smile inside.

I lie awake most of Thursday night; why is it that you can't sleep when you most need to? What if they can't remember me? What if they don't like me and want to go back to Jack? And what would Emma do then? I conclude that it's all a matter of time, time's a great healer, and poor Emma's going to have bigger things to think about when Jack gets bored with her.

On Friday morning at exactly nine o'clock I see a shadow in the glass behind the front door. I peep through the front window, fully expecting Emma to be there alone, having changed her mind or something. But it's DS Percy. I let her in. She looks around.

'You've been busy.'

I nod.

'Yes. I'm getting my kids back ...'

'Yes. Yes. I know. I just wanted to come round and kind of close the case.' She looks tired and angry. Not her usual self at all. 'The thing is, Caroline, I know all this was you. I know you kept the bag and it was obvious it was you posting the pictures.' God. I'd forgotten about the bag. She shifts in her seat. 'I could have charged you, you know. Perverting the course of justice. Theft. I believe in things coming out in the wash, though. And you'll still be called as a witness in the Premier Inn case. But as it is, it looks like this is all over and it's the last time I'll need to call round here.'

It's more of a question than a statement. But she's wrong. It isn't all over. As long as we're involved with each other in the slightest way it will never be over for Jack and me. I'll always be wary of him and he of me. He's got bigger problems now because Emma is more like me than I really care to admit and more than a match for his manipulations. I expect he'll be distracted by her for some time.

But there will always be the parents' evenings and the weddings of our children and the christenings of their children where we will both be reminded of what a cheating bastard he is and how I made him pay. A fragment of him will always be embedded in my heart like a shard of sharp glass, prodding me painfully at certain moments when I will have no choice but to remember.

It will be worse for Jack. Never knowing if I will flip and spill the truth. I'll be like a fly buzzing around his head, one that he can never quite swat. Nothing he can do can ever manipulate those mismatching dates – they are wrong for ever. And he'll suffer for ever because of it. Good. But I'll never act on my feelings again. I owe that to my children. If I've learned one thing from all this, it's that they're the loves of my life.

She reaches into her bag and places an envelope on the table. She looks straight at me now.

'I heard what Katy said to you. About the abuse. And that you had suffered too. I asked our domestic abuse liaison officer for some information.' I stare at the buff envelope. It's the first time anyone has acknowledged the depth of what happened to me. Saw it as more than *let it go* or *get over it*. More than a break-up. 'You don't have to, but it's there if you ever want to take it further. But as I said, it's the last time I'll need to come round.'

'Yes. The last time. Thank you. Thank you for all you have done. And for this.'

I take the envelope. She waits for more, as if I am somehow going to offer a full confession. Then she goes and drives away in her little blue car.

Hours pass slowly and at the allotted time I sit by the window, waiting, waiting, waiting for a car to arrive with my precious cargo. I still don't fully believe it will until I see a blonde head in a black BMW stop outside. I rush to the door and see two small figures getting out with backpacks. Emma is leaning into the boot of the car and pulling out the four large brown Samsonites that arrived here to begin this. She pulls them up the drive, two at a time. Her face is set in a false smile.

'Come on, kids. Home!'

They rush towards me and I drop to my knees and hug them. Emma watches, arms folded. She turns and walks away.

Charlie takes my face in his hands.

'I told you we'd come back, Mummy. I told you.'

The tears flow and a huge wave of relief rides over the part of me that has fought for this moment with every fibre of my being. We go inside and they run up to their rooms, squealing with delight at the new tablets and bouncing on their beds. Laura shouts downstairs.

'Mummy. Mummy. Can I have a drink?'

It suddenly all feels normal, as if nothing ever happened and Jack has just disappeared. But the still-simmering anxiety I feel inside assures me that nothing is normal and he is still there in the background. Or is he?

I feel my phone buzz in my pocket and it's a text from Lee: 'What colour do you want that cupboard painting?'

It's already more choice than Jack ever gave me and I think he and Emma deserve each other. It's not perfect, but it's a start to the rest of my life.

Chapter Forty-four

Three months later

It's Laura's birthday and we're having a party. Since they came home, the kids have been telling me about Daddy and Aunty Emma and how they used to go away for weekends and leave them with Nana and Jamie.

Laura took my hand one day and said that she loved me very much, but she missed Elijah, Nana's cat. I searched deep inside my soul that day, looking carefully for a reaction. Something that would make me act on the emotions that this conjured up for me. There is nothing. You see, part of my problem now is guilt. A terrible sinking feeling when I recall what I did. The hate I felt for those women.

One of the bitchier members of staff tried to engage me in the staffroom with talk about mixing business with pleasure. I knew where it was leading and I was right.

'The thing is, Caroline, I don't understand why you would go to such lengths. Social experiment, yah.' She touched her chin in faux consideration. 'I just don't see why you were so upset. This kind of thing happens every day. And, you know, the effects ...'

I knew what she meant. She meant the effect on my children. I've seen the looks, even when it was all ongoing, the questioning glances. *No wonder she lost her children. Look at her. She doesn't deserve to have them back.*

I even thought it myself. My mission for revenge was so intense, I was so engaged with Jack, or who I thought he was, that I thought of almost nothing else. But it was always a means to an end. Of course I went the wrong fucking way about it. Of course I did.

In the final analysis, I was damaged. I endured a life of mind games, abuse and isolation, until I had to find a safe place, somewhere inside me, somewhere to hide. The in-between. And to get there I took the alcohol route. I was literally falling apart. The lies Jack spun – and he was very convincing – meant that people abandoned me.

By the time Jack's suitcases arrived the cracks were already wide, but I never completely fell apart. My love for my children was the glue that held me together. And hope. Hope for a future with them in it. As that future slipped away, all sense and reason fell through the cracks and I adopted an 'if you can't beat them, join them' mentality. *Fight fire with fire*. I shudder as I realise that I almost became the feckless piece of shit that he is.

But I didn't. No matter how angry I was, how much hate-filled revenge I planned, and carried out, I always had remorse. I hid in the in-between from myself, because that wasn't me. Isn't me. I do deserve to have my children back. Even though I'm damaged, I deserve a second chance. And I'll prove it.

I carefully place the cake I have baked in the middle of the table. Paula and Patti arrive, and I hug them both. Paula's been my rock, my sounding board. She's so happy with Patti and a million miles away from the insecure teenager she was.

Katy arrives with Jamie and he runs off to play in the garden. Lee's out there supervising; he's filled in the hole and grassed it over. I feel a bit funny every time he looks at me and, when the kids aren't looking, I kiss him. And he kisses me back. He's only stayed over once, when Charlie and Laura went to stay with Jack and Emma for the night. He brought a plant with him and put it on my kitchen windowsill. They came back telling me that 'Daddy's house is nice but he's going away on business and Aunty Emma will be there alone for a while so we can't go again until he comes back'.

I know what 'going away on business' is and I momentarily felt sorry for Emma; I know she'll be smiling bravely and ironing his collars and checking his phone. But I feel nothing for Jack. No hate. Certainly no love. Just a welcome distance.

It turns out Lee is excellent at decorating and, as I watched his long strokes cover the scrapes from the flying tiara and the lipstick on my bedroom wall, I felt the sadness drain from me, replaced with something soft and mellow.

He stayed that night, but told me that he wouldn't stay while the children were here. Not at first. He didn't want them to be confused. I appreciated that more than anything, because it meant that he was thinking about all of us and not just himself.

Katy sits at the table with us and there we are, #allgirlstogether. But we're not a bunch of miraculously repaired women whose lives are suddenly wonderful. No. Patti reaches into her bag. She's rock chick on the outside, but softly spoken. She works in graphic design and she's made me a poster. She holds it up.

'DON'T ENGAGE.'

Paula laughs loudly.

'See, Caz, that's what I was on about. If you feel the pull towards a fake profile or hunting down an ex, just look at this.'

She stands it up on top of the fridge. Katy laughs too.

'Can you make me one? I might need a reminder as well.'

It's not funny, but laughter is a coping strategy. Like stoicism. I open a bottle of wine and pour them a glass each, but I have lemonade. For the time being. We silently acknowledge broken lives and I vow that I'll do everything I can to make my children's lives the best they can be.

I've only known Lee three months, but I've talked to him about my regret. I told him everything: all my feelings, all about the Premier Inn men. All about how Jack treated me. He didn't say much, but his advice was to put as much right as I could without giving in. I can tell we are going to get on.

I look out over the garden now. Jamie is chasing Laura, and Charlie is tying up a net to some goalposts. Jamie's going to stay over tonight while Katy goes out with friends. A five-year-old little girl, Faith, runs up to Lee shouting 'Daddy' and I'm reminded that all our lives are intermingled with each other's, and none of them are perfect. But they are, with care, love and understanding, manageable.

Lee comes into the house and puts an arm casually around my shoulder. We look over to the shape huddled in a blanket on a deckchair.

'That was nice of you. Really nice. You're a good person.'

He kisses me lightly.

'Do you want to take her a cup of tea, seeing as she won't come in and sit with us?'

He pours a cup and I watch as he goes outside and hands it to Missy. She glances sideways at me and I swear I see the beginnings of a smile. Or maybe I imagined it. I haven't forgiven her fully, but it's not about me, is it? The children asked if Nana could come over for the party and I didn't hesitate. She's been a huge part of their lives for the past year and they love her. So it's only right.

I mull over what would happen if they wanted Daddy to come over. While I feel nothing for him, I haven't forgiven him. I don't think I ever will.

But I will forgive myself.

Acknowledgements

I'd like to thank everyone at Corvus Atlantic Books, particularly my editor Sara O'Keeffe for her amazing insight and Susannah Hamilton for her guidance. Thank you all for believing in me and Caroline. The whole team is so wonderful and an absolute pleasure to work with, I am so lucky.

None of this would have been possible without my friend and agent Judith Murray, who saw Caroline for who she really is and helped me to shape *Perfect Ten* in the early drafts. Thank you for all the advice, the encouragement and the apricot soufflé – you have changed my life. Thank you to everyone at Green and Heaton for your warm welcome.

Thank you so much to the Refuge and Women's Aid, the domestic violence charities. I already understood domestic violence through my work, but my further research for this book uncovered dedicated professionals who struggle daily with communicating the complexity of abuse. To those people, thank you for making a difference.

I simply cannot list all the fellow writers who have helped me over the years as the list would be too long. But thank you all for examples of persistence and success. In particular, big love to Anstey Spraggan, who has relentlessly listened to me almost every day since we met at a book launch ten years ago. I'm also grateful to my friends Bridget Davison and Lindsay Bowes for early readings of the finished manuscript and their comments. Also to Elinor Davies, who was enthusiastic about Caroline's story and listened endlessly.

Massive thanks to my family. To my mum. Whilst she entered the world of dementia and we waited in the memory clinic, we amused ourselves with 'woman number 9' and tried to imagine all the revenge scenarios that a someone could have been in. You are there, mum, in those pages – this is for you.

To my children, Michelle, Victoria and Toby, thank you for your love and encouragement to have the confidence to write. To my brothers who are a constant in an ever-changing world. To my grandchildren, Evan, Leah, Lincoln and Phoenix – you are amazing.

I could not have achieved any of this without my partner, Eric Bourdiec. Eternal thanks for your advice on 'reining in the crazy', your support, your love and your cups of tea.